The Hill

By

Bill Halamandaris

Forward

Much of what follows is true.

I wish that were not the case, but it is what it is.

Hearts were broken. People died. Elections were won and lost. Investigators were hired and fired and resurrected to fight another day.

Crooks were caught. Some, including the Governor, went to jail. Some got away.

Rocco was real. So were Max, The Snake, StaffAss, Tiny Tony, Christoff, Fine, Broadbent, and the rest.

Some will say this is not possible. Others will see themselves here and swear they were there.

Where you sit determines what you see. There is truth enough to support either persuasion.

Such is the nature of "The Hill."

Chapter One

The telephone called me out of a deep sleep. It made a cruelly insistent sound. It was distant at first, then fiercely compelling – like a police siren pulling me from a peaceful place into the present.

I waited, hoping it would stop. While I waited, I wished something unpleasant would happen to whoever would call me at this time of night. Then I wished I had connected the answering machine I was given for my birthday. It was in the closet with the others given to me by the people who keep leaving messages on my cell phone telling me to turn it on.

When I couldn't stand it any more, I reached for the phone.

"Can I speak with Leanne," someone said.

"Just a minute," I replied.

I put my hand over the receiver and waited a moment. It was another wrong number - the third that week. At least this time the caller had responded. The others had simply hung up at the sound of my voice. I wondered if it was my imagination or if the number of wrong numbers and disconnects had, in fact, increased since I returned to work on The Hill.

"Who's calling?" I asked.

"TJ."

The clock on the nightstand said 3:10 - less than two hours before the alarm was set to go off, three hours before I had to head to the airport.

"Just a moment," I said.

I dropped the receiver 6 inches from my face.

"It's TJ," I said to no one in particular.

I counted ten and brought the receiver back.

"She said to tell you she is busy. She'll have to call you back."

I returned the phone to its cradle and tried to get back to sleep. After tossing and turning for an hour, I gave up and headed for the shower. I consoled myself by trying to imagine the conversation my conversation with TJ would inspire.

A knot forming in the pit of my stomach tempered my satisfaction. If they weren't coming after me, I knew they would be soon.

Chapter Two

At 10:00 AM on Friday, the 12th of September, I was in Miami, looking for Michael Thomas Scarpace - known to his friends, his enemies, and the authorities as "Rocco." A former New York street-cop, Rocco was said to be doing odd jobs for the mob in his retirement. He was one of the loose ends left dangling the last time I left The Hill.

When I returned, I made finding Rocco my first priority. For three months, Rocco had found a reason he couldn't talk. He had a spinal separation, a split disc, and then rheumatoid arthritis. When Rocco said he couldn't travel, we asked him to appear at the Federal building in Miami for a deposition. On the 9th of September, the day before the scheduled deposition, the Committee received a letter saying Rocco could not appear. It was signed Artero Sartella, M.D.

Dr. Sartella said Rocco had been hospitalized. He was in great pain and would have to be placed in traction. He would be totally immobile for at least three weeks. He could not speak. He could not have visitors. He would not even be able to nod his head "yes" or "no" in response to questions.

Sartella said in all probability Rocco would require surgery to repair damaged discs in his spinal column. He would also need surgery for an enlarged prostate which would complicate things further and make testifying even more difficult. In all probability, Rocco would be unavailable for some time.

A scan of the Florida Medical Directory told me Sartella was a physician in good standing. Curiously, he was listed as a cardiologist. From the Doctor's report, the heart seemed to be about the only part of Rocco's body in good condition.

Even if you are not given to flights of fancy, there is something about the word "Mafia" that gives you pause, raising deep-seated concerns and unpleasant possibilities. I found myself feeling strange - slightly paranoid, and slightly silly for feeling so paranoid. It's hard to remember the last time anyone took out a Senate investigator. Still, when you think about it you find yourself doing peculiar things - like checking the rear view mirror as you drive, looking over your shoulder as you walk, and inspecting whoever sits down next you closely enough to make them uncomfortable. You also feel a need to be cute.

Instead of picking up the phone, calling the doctor's office, and asking a simple direct question, I skimmed the phone book at the airport until I found a florist with a name I could remember. Then I called the hospital.

"This is Dave Kelly with Bayside Florist," I said to the switchboard operator, wondering as I did why I always pick on the Irish when I want to hide my identity. "We have some flowers for Mr. Scarpace. Can you give me a room number?"

"Just a minute," the operator said.

I heard some papers rattle. Then there was a long pause. I couldn't help thinking a six-six, two hundred and seventy pound patient shouldn't be that hard to find – particularly one in traction.

Finally, I heard a vague conversation in the distance – "Well, what do I tell him?" I couldn't hear the response, but a moment later she was back on line.

"Hello, sir? He is in 714."

The address said the hospital was somewhere in North Miami. The map from Budget didn't go that far. I could have used a GPS, but I don't react well to being told what to do – particularly by a machine. Instead, I drove to the area where the hospital was supposed to be and started asking questions. Everyone seemed to have heard of it, but no one knew exactly where it was. After and hour and a half, I stumbled on it.

The hospital had three entrances. A large canvas banner hung over a public entrance with a circular driveway. The banner said, "grand opening" in letters small enough and faded enough to suggest the opening wasn't all that recent and probably not all that grand. A concrete ramp led to the emergency entrance and a parking garage on the north side. The service entrance was in the back.

The problem with being cute is that once you start it is hard to stop. It was too late for me to walk in the front door like everyone else. Instead, I decided to try to catch them at lunch. At a quarter after twelve, I walked in the service entrance, found an elevator, and hit the button for the seventh floor.

As I hoped, the halls were empty. Even numbers ran to the right, odd numbers to the left. I walked down the right side until I found 714 and looked inside. The man I sought would be in his forties, strapped to a bed, and in great pain. The man I found was closer to my age and appeared to be about as healthy. He was fiddling with the TV, flipping through the channels.

He said his name was Thompson. He had never heard of Scarpace.

...

Esperanza Torres was cutting a piece of cantaloupe she had brought for lunch when Alexander approached. Her first thought was that who ever he had come to visit would get a lot of attention that afternoon.

He could have been anything, but the cut and quality of his jacket said something professional. His size and the way he moved suggested something physical. He wore a tan suit over a black T-shirt. The boots looked like Luchese.

"Can I help you?" she said, giving him her best smile.

"I'm looking for Mr. Scarpace."

His voice was deep and warm.

"Who?"

She stopped what she was doing, stood straight, and looked directly at him, arching her back as she did and stretching her uniform a little tighter than it needed to be. She knew she had a good figure. It wouldn't hurt if he noticed.

"Mr. Scarpace," he said. "I was told he would be in 714."

She saw a suggestion of a smile. Maybe he liked what he saw.

"He was released this morning," she said and offered him a piece of melon.

He accepted her offer. "How is he feeling?"

"He's all right," she said with a wave of her hand. "He's in and out of here all the time."

She offered him another piece of melon. Again, he accepted. His eyes were more intense now. She returned his gaze and felt the base of her spine tingle.

"How long was he here?"

"I don't know exactly. Not long. He's never here very long."

"Is he here often?"

"He has been here three or four times in the last few months," she said, smiling again, trying to decide how much more to say. The only thing she knew for sure was that she didn't want him to leave.

"He has a bad back. He comes in every now and then and we put him in traction for a while."

"Sounds painful."

"Can't be that bad," she said.

She had never liked Scarpace. It was hard not to let it show.

"He goes out for dinner every night he is here."

"Maybe he doesn't like hospital food."

She nodded.

"He likes Mario's. I've seen him there."

"Is it nearby?"

"A few miles."

Esperanza had been looking for an opening. Now she had one.

"I can show you if you like."

"You are helpful."

His tone was playful.

"What can I say," she said, dropping her eyes. "It's my nature."

She extended her right hand as she spoke, looking back and up at him. Her nails were the color of blood beginning to oxidize.

"Esperanza."

She turned her palm up as he took her hand, showing her wrist and inner arm. Her fingers enveloped his, deliberately holding on a little longer than necessary.

"Nick Alexander," he said. "My friends call me Nick."

"Happy hour starts at five, Nick," she said; and then after a short suggestive pause, "Care to join me?"

Chapter Three

I took the elevator down to the lobby. A card table had been set up near the public entrance. A wiry, dark-haired man with the face of a ferret sat behind it. A stenciled cardboard sign on the table said: "Reception."

Most of the help desks in Florida are staffed with seniors looking for part-time jobs or volunteer opportunities. This one was some distance from retirement and not inclined to be helpful. I handed him a card and asked to see the administrator.

Ferret-face looked at the card carefully: Gold Seal of the United States left corner. Nicholas Alexander, Director, Permanent Subcommittee for Oversight and Investigations, United States Senate, Washington, DC, 20510, centered. Phone number bottom left. Email bottom right. Heavy, linen stock.

If the ferret was impressed, he didn't show it. He tossed the card in a box on his desk and motioned toward a girl in a cubicle on the left side of the lobby.

The girl looked like she could have come as part of the design package along with the ferns, lamps, and potted plants. Twenty something. Bleached blonde. Plastic smile. Pneumatic body.

I walked over, identified myself again, and asked to see the administrator. I spent the next ten minutes watching her try to get a phone call through to the administrator's office. It proved to be more difficult than I would have thought possible.

It was the noon hour, she explained, and his secretary was probably out to lunch. While I waited, I saw the man behind the card table leave. Another, this one taller, older, and fifty pounds heavier, replaced him.

With that, I decided it might be better if I tried to find the administrator's office on my own. The girl tried to dissuade me, but I told her not to worry. I would just follow the signs.

As I entered the administrator's suite, another girl came hurrying out of the back office. She looked enough like the one I had just left to make me do a double take.

"Come right in," she said. "He is expecting you."

He was a small nervous man. His hair - what there was of it - was bottle black. He wore it in a comb-over that started just above his left ear. His desk plate said his name was Frank Lantos.

There were watercolors of birds on the wall behind him, windows to the left. The blinds were drawn tight enough to shut out the light, keeping any real birds and anything else that might pass by out of sight. A plaque pasted to the wall on the right side of his desk said the hospital was owned and operated by Total Health Care, a New York Corporation. Another said the facility was accredited by JCHA.

Lantos came around the desk, extending a small, wet

hand. He motioned to a chair and then retreated, putting his desk between us. We danced around each other for a while, exchanging pleasantries. We compared the weather in DC with the weather in Miami. Lantos admired my card. I admired his desk. We were getting along fine until I asked him where Scarpace was.

"I don't know," Lantos said.

Only 10 percent of the information we get from people comes from what they say. Forty percent comes from how they say it – tone, speed, inflections and other vocal patterns. The rest is body language. I knew Lantos was lying. His eyes narrowed and looked away.

"How long has he been gone?"

"I don't know."

He spoke with a heavy accent. Cuban, I guessed.

"When did you find out he was gone."

"Just now. I just now find it out."

"How long was he here?"

"I don't know."

"Why was he admitted?"

"I can't tell you."

Sometimes the best thing you can say is nothing. I let Lantos' answer sit without response until he felt obliged to explain.

"It's privileged information," he said, wringing his hands nervously. "I can't tell anyone."

Small beads of sweat were beginning to appear on his brow. He wanted no part of this.

I dialed it down a notch.

"That's not exactly true," I said amiably. "There are at least two ways you can tell me. One is: I make a call to the Chairman and ask him to call the U. S. Attorney's Office in Miami and have them send a Federal Marshall over here with a subpoena. Of course if we go to that much trouble, we might as well ask to see everything that might seem relevant or related to this case. We might also want to ask the GAO to come in and audit your records since you seem to have trouble keeping track of your patients. For all we know, you could be billing for people who aren't here. The guys in program integrity would probably want to know that."

Lantos' jaw clenched.

"What's the other way?" he asked.

"You get permission."

Lantos didn't seem to like that option any better than the first. He started to say something and stopped. His mouth opened and closed. His eyes darted left and right.

"Who admitted him?" I asked.

"I don't know."

"Can you check the records and find out?"

I gave him a smile of encouragement.

"I can do that."

Lantos picked up the telephone then thought better of it. Instead, he asked to be excused for a moment. He returned ten minutes later, saying he had asked them to pull the records.

For the next half hour, Lantos skated back and forth between his office and some invisible third party with every question I asked. At one point, he picked up the phone, started to call Rocco's physician then stopped as he considered the implications of what he was about to do.

"The matter is difficult," he said.

"Why?"

"The physician is not a member of the hospital."

"How is it that he has privileges?"

"It's a special case."

The look on Lantos' face said he didn't want to go there so I went around it.

"Is he any good?"

Lantos looked relieved. The tension in his face relaxed. Finally, he had a question he felt he could answer. He leaned forward, closing the distance between us.

"Let's put it this way. If my daughter was sick, I would tell her to go to someone else."

"Does he have a specialty?"

"He is a cardiologist."

A few moments later, Lantos' assistant came in with a thin file - not much of a record for a man who was said to be in and out of there all the time. The discharge sheet said Scarpace had been released at 11:45 AM. An aide had escorted him down to the lobby where he was left to wait for a ride home.

There had been no sign of Rocco in the lobby when I arrived. I didn't bother mentioning that fact. Nor did I bother telling Lantos I was waiting outside and would have seen him leave if what I was being told was true or that I was surprised to see how quickly they had filled the bed with someone else.

Besides, it was it was a quarter after four. By the time I checked in with the office, it would be Happy Hour.

Chapter Four

Richard, call me "Dick," Broadbent had never met a woman he didn't like.

"I can't help it," he often said, "that's just the way I'm bent."

When the call came in, he was at his computer checking one of his favorite sites – StaffAss.com.

Staff Assistant is the name given to entry-level positions on The Hill. These are the people who answer phones, sort mail, greet visitors, and respond to routine inquiries from constituents. It is a tedious job often paying less than $20,000 a year.

As an antidote to her boredom, this one had begun posting descriptions of her private life on the Internet. She confessed she was sleeping with half a dozen men and turning tricks on the side to supplement her income. She provided a running account that left little to the imagination.

"Most of my living expenses are thankfully subsidized by a few generous older gentlemen," she said by way of introduction. "No one can live on what I'm getting paid. I am convinced that the Congressional offices are full of dealers and hos."

Dick had been pulling up her blog when Sartella called. Now, just as he was getting back to it, Brent buzzed in from the front office. She said Alexander was on the line. Would he take it? Christoff, the mole, had picked this moment to step away and Fine was out for the afternoon. He had no choice.

Brent was the oldest and probably smartest of the three women assigned to OSI as support staff. She was somewhere around forty with hair the color of rust. As he picked up the phone, Dick wondered idly if the cuffs matched the collar.

"Where's John?"

Alexander's voice had an edge.

"He is at home helping Pam prepare for their party this weekend," Dick said. "It's the Big Reveal; remember - Macklin's Extreme Makeover. Aren't you going?"

Alexander brushed off the question, focused more on his irritation with John. It was the middle of the afternoon. Congress was six weeks from the end of the session. Members were already starting to tiptoe out of town to campaign. They had less than four weeks to wrap up the investigation and bring it home.

"Is it just me or does John seem to be more interested in his house than his job?"

"I'm not sure it's the house," Dick said.

You didn't have to be a rocket scientist to know Pam needed a lot of attention. One look would tell you she was high-maintenance even before you knew her

———

pedigree. She was a Macklin. Still, he could understand why Alexander was aggravated.

"We just got a call from Sartella," Dick said, trying to ease the tension. "I don't know what you did, but you sure got his attention. He said to tell you: You don't know who you are dealing with. That is a direct quote. I wrote it down. Then, he said: If you push us, we are going to push back."

"That sounds like a threat," Alexander said. "What do you think?"

Broadbent smiled. He could almost see Alexander's lip curl, reminding him as he always did of Clint Eastwood, not the Dirty Harry character blowing everyone away but the one in *Coogan's Bluff* that set up the character to follow like Bogey as Sam Spade in the *Maltese Falcon*, a character so strong it shaped and changed your character until it seemed to play you more than you played it. The scene that came to mind was the one where Walt Coogan, the Deputy Sheriff from the sticks Arizona traveling to New York to extradite the wacko Ringerman, tells the New York cabbie trying to take the rube for a ride to keep the change, giving him a two-cent tip. Broadbent wished he could be that cool but he knew he was more like Dennis Weaver, the guy who played the part as Sam McCloud on the TV. He was earnest and effective but no one had ever called Dennis Weaver cool.

"Sure sounds like a threat to me," Dick said.

"I guess were supposed to be afraid," Nick said.

"Maybe we're supposed to close down the investigation and quit."

"Maybe we should do that."

Dick was new to The Hill. When he arrived, he didn't know how many members of Congress there were or who his Senator was. He was still green enough to be impressed with where he was and what he was doing.

"Or..." he said, and waited.

"Or, maybe it's time to send for the cavalry," Alexander said. "Tell the marshal's office to serve Rocco. I want him here next week if they have to carry him. When you see John tell him I was wondering where he was and thinking of sending the marshals after him as well. Ask him to draft a subpoena for the hospital's records. Tell him to draft it as broadly as possible. Ask for everything but the kitchen sink. Ask for that too if he can think of a reason. And tell Christoff to call Brunner at GAO and ask them to add our new friends to the audit list. I'll run a formal request by Colgate and get it to them on Monday."

Christoff arrived as if on cue. He had a cup of coffee in his hand, his fourth of the day. He signaled for the phone.

"You remember that call I got from Andrews last week?" Christoff said. "He said he was sending me a care package"

___

I said I did.

Andrews was Deputy Commissioner of Health in New York under Kaine. Somehow, he had managed to stay in place under the new administration.

"It arrived this morning. It's a copy of his journal. It shows a lot of calls; letters, even personal visits asking for preferential treatment for Total Health Care. It came from every direction and both political parties."

"How high up?"

"All the way. There are several letters on the Speaker's letterhead. There was at least one meeting in the Governor's office."

"Great," I said. I could already see the flack starting to fall. "Anyone know what you have?"

"No, I don't think so. The Little Byrd has been nosing around. I heard her asking Dick where you were but I don't think she saw this."

"She is the last person I would want to find it. Keep it under wraps. Take it home with you if you have to."

I had my back against the wall in the hospital lobby, facing the Administrator's office, surveying traffic as we talked. You never know. Rocco might still be there waiting for a ride.

Rocco didn't show, but I did see the wiry one again. He left with Lantos at a quarter to five, walking to the right and a quarter of a step behind the administrator as if herding him out.

At 5:15, Esperanza appeared. She had exchanged her uniform for a tank top with a tropical print and a pair of white pants. Neither left much to the imagination. I did my best.

Chapter Five

George Washington was under whelmed when he heard the location of the city that would bear his name. He said, "That Indian swamp in the wilderness?"

Washington was not suggesting that the City was only fit for reptiles - though some might argue that case. He was being accurate. Washington was built on marginal land no one wanted carved out of the least desirable parts of Maryland and Virginia.

For a couple of weeks in the spring and fall, the City can be delightful, but winter can be biting and most of the summer is stifling with heat and humidity in the 90s and air so thick you can bite it. Until air conditioning was installed in the Capitol in 1939, legislators were eager to escape The Hill for the relative comfort of other places.

Good Americans, it was said, went to Paris when they died. The rest went to Washington. It was Hell on the Potomac, devilishly uncomfortable, miserably boring, desolate and devoid of satisfaction. It was a place, as Dickens said, "where few people would live who were not obliged to."

But in one solitary sense the City has always been major league. Every county commissioner harboring a political wish dreams of Washington the way Little Leaguers dream of playing in Yankee Stadium.

At the center of the City, Jenkins Hill rises 88 feet

over the Potomac, creating what L'Enfant called "a natural pedestal" for the Capitol. The Mall is to the west. Residential areas run north, south, and east, forming the community known as Capitol Hill.

The community started with shanties erected to house the men working on the Capitol and the Washington Navy Yard. Over the years, it has grown to become the largest residential area in the City. It is home to about a third of the members of Congress and their staff.

My home is on Constitution Avenue three blocks east of the Capitol, sandwiched between a Federal townhouse and a 19th century manor house. When I bought this place, my friends thought I was something of a pioneer. Now, I live in what is considered a trendy and desirable area.

The cab driver dropped me off late Saturday afternoon. The Rev. Dr. B. B. Maxwell was waiting on the other side of the door. He was sitting on the floor halfway to the stairs.

Most dogs would have come running. Max barely acknowledged my presence. He tilted his head in a look of recognition and then walked toward the back of the house. The door to the staircase leading to the English basement was open. Trish must have given him the run of the house.

A purebred Lhasa Apso, Max is ten pounds more or less depending on the length of his cream-colored coat. I inherited him from my sister-in-law, Marilu. She wanted a lap dog. While he looks the part with a button nose and large dark eyes, he lacks the disposition. Picture a dust mop with teeth. Try to pick him up and he'll take your hand off. From time to time, he has snapped at every member of the household. Lu gave up on him after he treed one of her dinner guests on the kitchen table.

"It's either you or the pound," she said when she dropped him off. "I thought of you because you are a lot alike."

Max stopped halfway through the living room and looked over his shoulder, making sure I was following. He was hungry and expected to be fed. Inside the refrigerator, I found a six-pack of coke, some chips, half a bottle of salsa, and something that looked like it might once have been cheese. All there was in the cupboard was some dry dog food. Max hasn't touched that since he got his law degree.

Max's dish is near his bed in the corner of the kitchen. A dozen framed certificates decorate his wall. His Ph. D. is from Georgetown. The Doctorate of Divinity is from Stanford. His J.D. says Harvard. The medical degree said it came from Yale. Next to that is a framed certificate from the American Kennel Club.

Through the eight-foot sliding glass doors at the back of the house, I could see Trish wearing out the Stairmaster on the second floor of the carriage house. She was moving with fierce determination, pushing herself and punishing the machine. Bruno, the Great Dane next door, was patrolling his yard, pacing up and down the six-foot fence that separated our properties, waiting for her to come out. A massive beast, coal black, bred and trained to work as a police dog, he provided security for the immediate world. He was always outside - rain or shine - probably because there is no room for him inside. His head was as big as Max's body.

I poured some of the dry food into Max's dish, added water, and waited for a reaction. There was a chance he might eat it, I thought, but my hope was short-lived. Max walked to his dish, sniffed disdainfully, and then looked up as if to say, "Surely, you don't expect me to eat this."

When nothing better was offered, Max walked to the door and settled into the guardian position. He looked like a miniature of the Sphinx, paws forward, head up and alert, tail curled back like a bow on his butt, eyes fixed on Trish. I opened a coke and joined him, taking a seat on a stool at the kitchen counter.

While we watched, Trish, formally Patricia Ann Hough, finished her workout, switching from the Stairmaster to a series of floor exercises, twisting her

body into one unlikely position after another. She says it's not yoga but it looks enough like yoga to make it hard to tell the difference.

She came out of the carriage house half an hour later and walked toward the townhouse, stopping to turn on the heater for the hot tub. She moved confidently and deliberately. The image that came to my mind was that of a big, predatory cat. She is five nine in her stocking feet and built to scale, with the kind of figure that made Hefner rich. The narrowness of her waist accentuates the fullness of her hips and exaggerates the differential with her chest, giving her figure almost cartoon dimensions. When she is in shape she comes in at about 118 pounds with a 19-inch waist.

Trish came up the stairs from the courtyard and opened the sliding glass door. A grey t-shirt that looked like it might have been pulled from my closet or snagged from the laundry hung loosely over her black Under Armour. Her skin glistened with perspiration. Her damp hair hung close to her face.

"You look like you were rode hard and put to bed wet," I said.

"Not yet," she shot back, giving me a defiant look, "but the night is young."

Max trotted over to where we stood, took a sniff, and started licking Trish's ankles. I couldn't blame him. A few years back, the Senate Staff Club had named her the best looking woman on The Hill.

When she is fit, which is generally between beaus, Trish is stunning. When she is in a relationship, her weight balloons up. The happier she is the heavier she gets. After each relationship ends, she comes down hard until she bottoms out, and then tries to get herself back together. I have seen her go through the cycle at least a half dozen times.

The last one was the worst. She was convinced he was "the one." They were engaged and living together when he blindsided her, telling her he wasn't attracted to her anymore.

It was New Years Eve. As the clock counted down the minutes and the ball began to drop she was thinking it was time to take their relationship to the next level and he was thinking it was time to get out. He said he had found someone else, someone new, he said, someone thinner, younger, she heard.

She arrived on my doorstep in pieces, clutching her overnight bag and shivering in the cold. She said she had nowhere else to go. After holding her until she had cried herself out, I invited her to stay downstairs while she got back on her feet.

At first she couldn't talk about it. Then that's all she could talk about. Finally, she started pulling herself together. When she asked for the key to the carriage house, I knew she had turned the corner.

"Why do you take so much crap from every one else but never cut me any slack?" I asked.

"I don't know," she said. "Maybe it's because I'm not sleeping with you."

"You're probably right," I said. "I think I would have remembered that."

"You would never be able to forget it."

"That sounds vaguely like a threat. Everyone seems to be threatening me these days."

"I wonder why," she said.

I detected a touch of sarcasm. I'm good that way. After all, I'm a trained investigator.

We are friends without privileges, though she often reminds me privileges have been offered. A couple of years back when we were both between relationships, she invited me to see Springfield in concert. Half way through "This Gun's for Hire," she grabbed my arm tightly, brought her lips close enough for me to feel the heat of her breath on my ear, and whispered, "I sure hope he's not starting something you can't finish."

I didn't. Later that night and often thereafter, I have wondered why I didn't.

"Are you going out tonight?" I asked.

"Yes."

"You have a date."

We both knew the answer to that question but for some reason I needed to hear her say it.

"I have a date. His name is Carson."

I let the significance pass. It was her first date since she had moved in.

"Where did you meet him?"

"At work. It was kind of funny. He came into our

office by mistake looking for Senate Appropriations. I sent him down the hall. He was embarrassed and kind of cute about it. Later we ran into each other in the cafeteria and hit it off."

"What's he like?"

"See for yourself. We are planning to stop by John's after dinner. I want to see what Pam's done with the house."

Max had been sitting at her feet while we talked. Now, he made a low plaintive sound – just enough noise to get her attention. He walked over to his dish and looked back, showing her what had been offered, confident she could do better.

"I'd better hit the shower and start getting ready," she said.

"Please do."

She made that dismissive face women seem to learn when they are five, letting me know she had chosen to ignore my remark.

"You really are in a good mood, aren't you? Is it the party or John's wife you'd like to avoid?"

"A little of both."

When Trish left, Max followed. I heard the shower kick on downstairs. I pulled another coke out of the fridge and sat down to read the mail.

The only thing of interest was addressed to Max. It came from the Chairman of the International Platform Speaker's Association. He pointed out every President going back to Teddy Roosevelt had been a member of the IPSA, along with many Senators, Congressmen, Governors, members of the media and other distinguished souls. The Chairman said he had the pleasure of inviting Max to join this prestigious group.

I thought about it for a while, sipping my coke. Why not, I concluded. Max had as much to say as any of them. Before going up to unpack, shower and change, I spent a few minutes filling out the form. I went to great pains to be as truthful as possible, fudging only where it asked for age - substituting months for years. When it asked for occupation, I wrote 'security consultant.' That seemed close enough to the truth for The Hill.

Chapter Six

The Macklin mansion is located in what realtors call a
transitional area. Some day it will be considered
gentrified but at the moment there are still a lot of
questionable elements hanging around.

After their marriage, Pam began looking for a home
on The Hill that would match her social aspirations
and advance John's career. She had married a staffer
but there was no reason he had to stay one. With his
looks and intelligence, her name, and the magazine's
support, she was confident he had a bright political
future of his own.

She surprised everyone by settling on an abandoned
warehouse three blocks northeast of Union Station.
The building had never been used for residential
purposes but it offered one feature particularly hard to
come by on Capitol Hill – size. It was fifty feet wide
and nearly four times as long, a solid, impenetrable
brick building that dwarfed adjoining properties and
dominated the block.

Pam refaced the front and gutted the interior. She
removed large parts of the center ceiling, creating an
atrium and a natural source of light, and rebuilt from
the inside out around the light source she had created.
From the outside, the three-story structure appeared
largely unchanged. It still looked a lot like the
warehouse it once was; but the inside was completely
transformed. The atrium carved into the center of the
building, divided the property while connecting the

main house with a guesthouse created on the opposite end. Skylights inset in the roof, bridged the residential quarters, illuminating a lap pool, hot tub, and gardens below. Large interior windows and sliding glass doors extended the sense of openness, providing an unobstructed interior view from either end.

The project had taken three months to design and a year to execute. She used the proceeds from the sale of her townhouse, sold his condo, and dipped into one of her trust funds to make up the difference. There was already more money tucked away in Merrill's wealth management program than she or her boys - Mark and Michael - would ever need. This party was the unveiling, the first of many social events Pam hoped to host on The Hill. She was trying to make a statement, eager for people to see what she had done.

Les Tubin had arrived early and carved out a place by the bar. Measured by the standard of who showed up, he thought, the party was already a success. Most of The Hill's beautiful people were there, clustered near the bar and in the dining room overlooking the atrium. They were the privileged ones with big jobs, fancy titles, and full calendars - junior variations of the members they served.

A room full of Mini-mes, Tubin said to himself, hoping as he did that he hadn't said it out loud. He did that sometimes.

He took another sip of his beer, a good dark lager, and surveyed the room. He recognized staffers and former staffers, lobbyist and lifers, pages and cops, spear-catchers and spear-carriers, mopes and mud hens, opportunists and true believers.

Pam was working the crowd. John was following dutifully behind. A red, form-fitting sheath covered her small frame. She looked like a cardinal flitting around. John was dressed in a camel hair jacket over a tailored shirt with an open collar. Between the two of them, he thought, they probably had more on their backs than he had billed last quarter.

Tubin was short and fat with a face seemingly in a constant state of eruption. It no longer troubled him. He knew he was all but invisible to this crowd anyway – no one worth knowing, no one worth getting to know. That was the way it had always been going back to when he started, running elevators in the Capitol. It was as if he wasn't really there. He was just a part of the machinery that got them from where they were to where they wanted to go.

The only foothold he had on power was his cousin's connection with the Sergeant-at-Arms. That was enough - just barely enough - to get him a job on The Hill, nothing more. Still, it had given him a chance to earn his education, doubling up with night shifts when the Capitol was empty and no one else was there or wanted to be there - except cockroaches the size of tootsie rolls and rats as big as cats.

After college, there was law school at Catholic a mile up the road off North Capitol. By then he had enough seniority to reverse the order, working by day and studying in the law library at night. Often he was the last one to leave, staying so late they had to kick him out so they could close down.

Tubin was admiring the big-breasted blonde anchoring the other end of the bar when Alexander came in. A receptionist out of California, she had one of those nose-less, Nordic faces with the perfect symmetry of a plastic plant. She was trying to give the appearance of listening to a thin, hard-looking woman with animated, exaggerated mannerisms. Ms. California nodded her head occasionally while her eyes darted around over the thin one's shoulder, looking for opportunity. He saw her speculative look as Nick approached and wondered if Alexander had ever felt invisible. He doubted it.

"Les," Nick said, extending a hand. "Long time."

"About two years," Tubin said.

"How's it going?"

"Good. Finished law school. Took forever, but I'm done. Passed the bar. Opened an office in the one of the condos across the street from Heritage. Managed to pay the bills last year. Doing better this year. I have a couple of small associations on retainer and some steady clients. I also hire out. Legwork and rundowns. That sort of thing."

...

Even though I had just arrived, I was already wondering how soon I could leave. It was a house

full of strangers. Some I knew. Some I didn't.

As far as I could tell, Tubin was the only real one there. Les didn't take himself too seriously or try to be anything he wasn't. But in five minutes, we had already said most of what there was to say. I consoled myself with the thought that at least the booze was good. I had asked for scotch and was given Chivas, straight up.

I was halfway through my first drink when Broadbent arrived with his new girlfriend. She was 18, if that, with big round eyes and a small round body that stretched the limits of her tube top and paint-on-pants. She looked like ten pounds of flour in a five-pound sack. Flesh spilling out everywhere at every opportunity. Try to undress her and she would probably burst out or her clothes like the Pillsbury doughboy popping out of a tin of biscuits.

Her name was Brandi, she said, spelled with an "i" and dotted, no doubt, with a heart, or, perhaps, a smiley face. She was an intern working at Commerce. It was fun, she said but nowhere near as exciting as what they were doing. Her wide eyes and breathless voice made me wonder what Broadbent had told her. The why of what he had told her was never in doubt.

When Brandi turned to leave, I saw a tramp stamp on the small of her back - two rows of Chinese characters flanking the red g-string visible above the cut line of her pants. It looked like something you would see on a packing crate. "Handle with care," perhaps, or maybe, "This side up."

I was still considering the possibilities when something caught my eye. A swirl of blue. Dress of almost formal length, soft and clinging. Aniston-blonde. Bare back. Bare shoulders. Hair cascading in long loose curls to her shoulders. It was a calculatedly careless look. Without any apparent effort, she seemed to fill the room.

"Oh, my God," Tubin said.

She had the Grace Kelly look, the appearance of being hot while looking cool. There was poise and self-confidence and the strong posture that seems only to come from those funny-named schools where they finish young women, pouring molten iron down their spines, leaving them forever ramrod straight, a young ladies seminary where mornings begin with chapel, lunch is served by maids, dinner is dress, and the curriculum is geared heavily to personal choice.

"She's coming over here," Tubin said, thinking out loud.

The thought made him sweat.

She moved deliberately - one piece, arms close, head straight, legs gliding imperceptibly beneath the long dress. When she got close enough, she held out her hand, palm down. I took it and held it. It was either that or kiss it. It was in wrong position to shake and there wasn't time anyway. She kept coming.

Continuing the motion of extending her right hand, she brought her left hand to my shoulder, using its slight leverage to stand tippy-toe and fix me squarely with dark, mischievous eyes. I saw the fine lines of her fine face, straight nose, and a promising mouth coming close as she gave me a gentle, little sister of a kiss that wobbled my knees.

"Hello, Nick," she said.

A small smile playing on her lips where my lips had just been.

"Dee," I said. "Nice to see you."

And it was. Surprisingly nice, as I remembered the same, warm light seen before in the same warm eyes and the shadow of an always not too distant smile. I found myself angered at just how nice it was.

"You know each other?" Tubin said, a question that was not a question – more an expression of wonder.

"Only if you are being biblical," I said, looking at her not at him.

I saw her confidence waver. She had been so sure, now the doubts filed in, bringing with them the sad-eyed incredibly vulnerable look, the one that kept me up nights. Her smile dissolved into an uncertain movement of mouth. She stood there pained and accusing as I remembered another time and the same smile on the same sad face, feeling already slightly ashamed, wondering why so many of the things I regret are written on the faces of the women I have loved.

She hadn't changed much. She was still about the

best-looking woman I had ever seen. Still slender, maybe too slender for some. Hair, a little longer and with a little more curl, down to and just past the light little mark above her right shoulder blade. She had been taking good care of herself and it showed.

"You look good," she said. "Maybe a little more worn. Maybe a little smaller since I last saw you."

"Clothes will do that."

She gave me her private laugh, the one that belies her demure look, the one closer to her true nature.

"Still the iceman," she said. "God, I was so afraid you had changed."

She stepped nearer, dropping her voice low enough to draw me in and shut others out.

"You could have called, you know. You could have answered my calls. You didn't have to be such a total bastard."
"If I weren't," I said, "whatever would we have in common?"

The dark eyes emptied, then darkened. The smile was gone.

"All right, Nick. Be horrid. Be as horrible as you like. But know this. I'm here and I'm going to stay. You won't chase me away. And this time it's going to be different. No games. Just total honesty."

"Should be a new experience."

Her jaw clenched but her eyes were unwavering.

"OK. Be that way. But I'm telling you the way it's going to be. I tried forgetting you. I tried hating you. I told myself you don't care anything about me and that you weren't worth crying about. And it didn't work."

She moved even closer as she spoke, close enough to smell, close enough to feel her heat, close enough to reach out and grab.

"So, I am coming after you. And this time, I'm going to get you. I know what I want now, Nick. I didn't before. I started lining up a job on The Hill as soon as I heard you were back. That was step one. I'm here. We are together. That was step two. And now I know you still want me…you don't have to say anything. I can feel it. You know I can. And I'm going be here for as long as it takes for you to admit it. That's step three. Like I said, I'm going to get you."

She paused and took a deep breath. Her eyes wavered as I watched. A shadow of doubt flickered across her face as she waited for my response. I let her wait.

"For God's sake, say something!"

"I didn't know they had posted a reward."

Her eyes flashed.

"Damn, you!"

—

"Haven't you forgotten something?"

"What?"

"Your husband."

Her eyes dropped. Color came to her cheeks.

"We're separated."

"Didn't take long."

"I didn't love him. I never loved him."

Her eyes came up earnest and true.

"All I ever wanted was you."

"You could have fooled me…Come to think of it, you did."

Her mouth tightened. There was thunder in her eyes. I knew what she wanted to say and saw her struggle with it. Then, as I watched, the anger in her face dissolved. Reluctant twinges of her mouth broadened and bloomed into a grin as the fire faded.

"It's nice to be back," she said. "I have missed you."

As she said it, she knew it was true. It had always been too easy for her. Men had always pursued her, promised her anything, and given her everything. He was different. He had always been different. She *had* missed him.

"You know what I worried about?" she said. "Oh, I worried about lots of little things, but most of all, I thought I'd come back and find you treating me with some of your remote, cavalier courtesy, keeping me way over there somewhere out of reach and hopeless…It's going to be all right now, isn't it?"

She reached up and wobbled my knees again.

"You don't have to say anything. I'll be around."

Chapter Seven

On the 15th of September, Henry Furth looked out the widow of his study in Middleburg. It was early. The Rodriquez boys had just started working the horses.

In the distance, he could see Sheila Johnson's daughter taking her jumper through his paces. He was dark and sleek and moved with the grace of the champion he was. Furth wondered what it would be like to be able to move that effortlessly.

He had been called many things, but never graceful. He had been a ham-handed, chunky child with a head too large for his body. Lack of restraint had fulfilled the promise of his youth. At 5' 8", he weighed in at 350 pounds.

Largely as a result, he dressed almost entirely in black, cloaking his bulk in darkness. What started out of a necessity created by the limited options he had while he was young had become his trademark. He found the look suited his personality and the image he sought to create.

Furth looked at the messages his secretary had forwarded to him that morning and for the hundredth time since she'd gone realized how much he missed Abi. When the Vice President said he needed a top-notch personal assistant - someone like Abi - Furth knew he meant Abi. The question was the answer.

There really was no choice. Debt and gratitude were

the currencies of his trade.

And as a practical matter, he knew Abi would do more good for him there. Still, he missed her sorely - particularly at times like this. Beau's call had come in late Friday afternoon. People were busy. People were thinking about the weekend, where they wanted to be, and what they wanted to do. No one noted its significance.

Abi would have known. She would have connected Beau's call with the call that came in from Star Services. Melissa, his new executive assistant, had bunched these calls with two dozen others, neither knowing nor noting their significance.

Furth called his office and was pleased to find she answered before the third ring. At least he had to give her that. She was eager and earnest.

"Yes, sir?"

The voice was young, cultured, and refined with a touch of an English accent that suggested class when the reality was far from it.

"I'm on my way in," he said. "Tell the executive staff to be in my office when I arrive."

He didn't bother giving her a time or a reason. He wanted them to be waiting and wondering. Then he called his driver and told him they would be leaving for the office in fifteen minutes. A dark Mercedes sedan was waiting when he walked out ten minutes later.

___

48

Furth spent the hour he was in the car making the tedious commute from the Hunt Country to Washington on his Blackberry checking his network. No one could extend his knowledge and what little he knew was unsettling. His best account was facing a significant challenge to one of its subsidiaries. The threat was coming from The Hill. It was the kind of thing he was paid to prevent.

In the time he had been in Washington, lobbying had changed dramatically. Furth now had more than 40,000 competitors, many of them former members of Congress, his toughest competition. There was a time when members considered lobbying unseemly. The most you could expect was that a member might lend their name in a show of support. Now there was nothing they wouldn't do. Many of the current breed even anticipated this direction as part of their career path - the payoff for a life in public service - seeding it by building alliances and placing trusted lieutenants with influential firms, blurring the distinction between the two to the point where lobbying firms sometimes seemed nothing more than an extension of a member's personal office with staff skating between.

Things could be done in one place that could not be done in another. One step removed from The Hill, staffers could use their positions to gather support for the Congressman's pet projects and raise campaign funds while being compensated far beyond what would normally be possible on The Hill. Salaries there are public and disclosed, by law pegged to that of the members they serve. Effectively, this capped staff compensation at around $150,000.

Off The Hill, key staffers command starting salaries
of more than a half million. Former members
routinely receive retainers several times that - often
from several firms. Robert Livingston, former
Chairman of the House Appropriations Committee,
spoke for the lot when he said, "There's unlimited
business for us out there."

It reflects the changing nature of the political process.
Once politicians were people with ideas who went
door to door, making their pitch like the Fuller Brush
man. All that ended in the sixties when two men
engaged in a Presidential debate and the winner was
the one who looked like he had shaved. Since then,
an unholy alliance between politicians and the media
has emerged. Image is all. Television is king and the
cost of campaigning escalates with every season. As
a result, even members with safe seats feel the
pressure to raise whatever they can, hopefully enough
to scare off any serious challengers.

If money is the mother's milk of politics, lobbyists
are its nursemaids. It should come as no surprise that
more than half the money contributed to
Congressional candidates is raised in Washington.
Payback comes in access, earmarks, invitations to
participate in mark-up sessions, friendly amendments,
letters and calls to the executive branch and
regulatory agencies. There has never been a time
when lobbyists have a greater opportunity to
influence the legislative process. With the right
connections, anything is possible.

Furth knew that if he couldn't protect his client's interests, they would find someone who could. Word would seep out through the air vents. It wouldn't be long before his competition would start circling like the vultures they are. On The Hill you are either at the table or on the menu. Memories are short and client loyalty is an oxymoron.

At 9:45 AM, his car dropped him off at his office on Pennsylvania Avenue across the street from Federal Triangle. Once the site of one of the most successful red-light districts in the country, The Triangle now houses the Departments of Commerce, Justice, Labor, the IRS, and the National Archives along with a number of other federal and municipal buildings. As he entered his building, Furth saw the legend engraved on the front of the National Archives: The Past is Prologue. The irony amused him.

He walked through the lobby, passed his restaurant, Jenkins Choice, and took the elevator to the twelfth floor. Melissa was waiting when the door opened.

"I'm sorry," she said. "I must have missed something."

He hadn't said anything to her directly, but he didn't have to. In truth, there was no way she could have known what the calls implied. Still, she should have known any call from his best client had to be handled carefully.

"In the future," he said, "find me. Wherever I am, find me. If they need a paper clip - find me."

He made no attempt to conceal his displeasure. Star paid the rent. He could not afford to have them doubt him.

Three men and a woman were waiting in his office. They were seated at an antique table Furth had found in the fields of Crumpton, Maryland, a strange place where an endless array of items from the sublime to the ridiculous, hauled out people's basements and antics, are planted twice a week in rows stretching the length of a cornfield that once was, and auctioned off seriatim to the highest bidder. He had bought the table for next to nothing, seeing the treasure it was, and spent twice what he paid Melissa to restore it to its Civil War splendor. It was a butterfly walnut with inlay trim of ebony, sandalwood, and burled walnut, intricately carved.

Furth took his place at the head of the table, leaning back in an overstuffed leather chair, happy to be off his feet. He looked at his lieutenants, flanking him on opposite sides of the table. Jack Rudy and Jeff Tyson sat together. Rudy handled the House while Tyson oversaw the Senate. Frank Mitchell, on his right, followed the Executive Branch. Lynn Pennington sat beside him - but then she always seemed to sit beside him. Furth wondered if they had something going or if she was just using him for cover. That would be more her style. She had worked for the Chairman of Ways and Means until the closeness of their relationship caused enough comment to make it seem prudent for her to find something else to do. Furth hired her before anyone else knew she was thinking of leaving, offering her three times her salary on The

Hill, asking her to serve as liaison to allied groups and affiliated organizations, cementing his access to Ways and Means in the process.

He began without any small talk or preliminary exchanges.

"Anybody know why you are here?"

While he waited for a response, Furth pulled out one of his cherished Cubans, obtained and provided as token of gratitude by one his clients, a prominent member of Miami's Cuban aristocracy. It was a hand-rolled Diplomatico #2, produced at the Jose Marti factory. He wondered idly what they would cost if he could get them legally and had to pay retail. Whatever it was, he decided, it would be worth it.

His four lieutenants looked at each other nervously as he unwrapped his cigar, squeezing it gently with his fingers to test freshness. Each one hoped one of the others would take the lead. Finally, Mitchell did. He had been with Furth the longest. He was as secure as anyone was likely to be with the firm.

"Melissa said it might have something to do with a call about Total Health Care."

Furth absorbed the answer while he began the ceremony of lighting his cigar. His Lamborghini cigar cutter looked like a miniature guillotine. He inserted the head of the cigar into the guillotine, carefully positioning it an eighth of an inch down and methodically chopped the cap off. He watched the tip fall and then held the open end of the cigar over the flame of his butane lighter, enjoying as always the feel of the cigar and lighter in his hands. The lighter was a thing of beauty – a Ligne 2 in black alligator with a palladium finish made by S. T. Dupont in France. It had set him back two grand. The fact that he could afford such extravagance when a simple kitchen match would do was as much a source of satisfaction as the cigar itself. It was the kind of thing he could never have dreamed of doing as a boy.

Furth turned the cigar slowly over the flame priming it for lighting and shifted his gaze toward Tyson.

"Do you know who Total Health Care is, Mr. Tyson?" he said.

Tyson had been recruited from the Senate Appropriations Committee where he was considered Lamar Lewis' right hand.

"One of the largest health care providers on the east coast."

"And…"

That was it. As Furth suspected, Tyson was clueless. He shifted his gaze around the table, throwing the question up for grabs.

"And a subsidiary of Star Services," Mitchell said.

Furth nodded. He brought the cigar to his mouth, holding it at a 45-degree angle over the Ligne's flame, puffing slowly and rotating the cigar until the tobacco around the outer rim began to glow and the smoke began to draw easily. Then he came back to Tyson.

"Do you know who Star is, Mr. Tyson?"

"Our biggest client," Tyson said.

"Do you know why they called?"

The tone of Furth's voice reminded Tyson of one of his professors at prep school. It was condescending and contemptuous. Clearly, he was expected to know. Just as clearly, he did not.

"No, Sir."

"Someone is rattling their dish, Mr. Tyson," Furth said. "Any idea that that might be?"

"No, Sir."

"Why not?"

The question was deliberately combative. Tyson had no response. He knew he was being challenged but he was drawing a blank.

Tyson was everything Furth was not - Ivy League, privileged, fit and attractive. Initially, he thought that was the reason Furth had hired him. Now, he was beginning to think it was because the blob enjoyed making him sweat. He never seemed to miss an opportunity.

"Mr. Tyson, what am I paying you to do?" Furth said,

"Coordinate activities on the Senate side."

"Wouldn't you think that might include finding out if someone over there was coming after one of our clients?"

Tyson looked for help but found none.

"Wouldn't you think we might want to know that? Wouldn't you think we would like to know about it before a Senate investigator appeared at our client's door?"

"Who did that?" Tyson asked, grasping for a straws.

"Oversight and Investigations."

"OSI?" Tyson was surprised and said so. "They haven't done anything in years."

Furth was unrelenting.

"Do you remember what they used to do?"

"Medicaid and Medicare investigations mostly. Medicaid Mills. Nursing Homes. Paper doctors. Clinical labs. That kind of thing; but that all stopped when Moss was defeated.

—

With difficulty, Furth controlled his contempt. Clearly, Tyson had no idea what was going on or what he was supposed to do. Tyson was probably dumb enough to think he was hired because he was a great legislative technician. Arrogance and ignorance. A deadly combination. He would deal with him later. Now, he needed to make a broader point.

"Do you remember who staffed those investigations, Mr. Tyson?"

Again, Tyson looked blank.

"Anyone?" Furth said.

"Alexander," Mitchell said. "Alexander the Greek."

"Right."

"He left with Moss."

"Well," Furth said, "he's back."

He took a long pull on his cigar, savoring its rich flavor before releasing the smoke - deliberately, Tyson thought, in his direction.

After the smoke had settled, Furth said quietly, "Can anyone tell me why we didn't know that?"
Again, there was silence.

Feeling the weight of Furth's displeasure, Tyson felt compelled to say something.

"He's just one guy," he said, and immediately realized he had said the wrong thing.

Furth jumped on him.

"Is that what you think I should tell our client, Mr. Tyson," he said. "He's just one guy?"

Tyson could only shake his head.

"This one guy cost MedTech over $200 million, Mr. Tyson. In less than a month, profits evaporated and shares decreased from fifty to ten dollars. By the time he was done, *Business Week* pronounced the company in 'critical condition.' They still haven't recovered. This one guy cost the Chairman and CEO of MedTech his job. This one guy cost us that account - not to mention the fallout from all the other investigations he led..."

Furth glared at Tyson. His intensity had grown with every sentence. Now again in a quieter, deadlier voice he said, "...And you think he's no threat."

He shook his head. It was beyond comprehension.

"Would you stake your job on that?"

Tyson was afraid to move. He could feel the tension in the back of his neck. There was nothing he could say and he knew it.

Furth took another draw, exhaled, and watched the smoke dissipate before putting the cigar down on one of two crystal ashtrays on the table. Each one was engraved with the Seal of the President of the United States.

He put his palms on the table and leaned forward.

"There is no need to respond, Mr. Tyson. You already have. If we don't get this situation under control, you're gone, and you can take your team with you."

Tyson tried to breathe.

"I know the Staff Director of Government Operations," he said. "I'll see what he can tell us."

"Do that. There are three other members of Alexander's team: Fine, Broadbent, and Christoff. See what you can find out about them as well."

If his subordinates were surprised that he knew more than they did, they didn't show it.

"All of you. I want to know whatever there is to know about these people. I want to know what they are doing. Everything. I want a full threat analysis - risk assessment, points of access and vulnerability. Now go. Tell your people to get busy."

Furth's cigar had suffered from neglect. He took his lighter from his vest pocket and relit it while his lieutenants hastily gathered their papers. He stopped them at the door.

"Mr. Mitchell, Mr. Rudy, Ms. Pennington, if there is any doubt in your minds, what I said to Mr. Tyson applies to all of you as well. Do whatever you have to do to get this situation under control."

Chapter Eight

From the air, the Capitol looks like a wedding cake surrounded by shoeboxes. Over the years, the shoeboxes have multiplied - Senate Office Buildings to the North, House Office Buildings to the South. Government Operations is on the first floor of Dirksen, the middle box on the Senate side, past the elevator, two thirds of the way down. The Permanent Subcommittee for Oversight and Investigations occupies the last office in the suite.

I came in a few minutes before nine. Broadbent was already at his computer. He had the look of an adolescent caught doing something he knew he wasn't supposed to do.

"Pam's party made StaffAss," he explained.

There was something close to awe in Dick's voice. The thought boggled his mind. She had been where he had been. He had undoubtedly seen her, but which one was she? The blonde by the bar? The exotic one on the deck with the kind of legs you normally see wrapped around a pole? He would have remembered her even if she hadn't dressed to be remembered with a tight green top and a skirt the size of a postage stamp. It started low and ended high, stopping just short of the promised land. What if it was Alexander's roommate? He couldn't believe

Alexander wasn't tapping that. Maybe one of the girls in the pool towards the end of the night, stoned out their minds, or the brunette getting into the scene in the carriage house where the two pages put on their show. He got hot just thinking about the possibilities.

"Partied with DA last night," StaffAss wrote. "Cool place in NE. Work fun. Everybody was there. Got keyed up. Couldn't sleep. Called LM. He came over. Did it missionary. He finished before I started. With a condom!! Frustrating. Who the hell comes missionary anymore?!"

Who was she? Dick wondered. It was impossible to know. Maybe he could start a pool and enlist the staff in helping him find out. Someone had to know who she was.

John's desk was on the opposite side of the room. It was still vacant. Christoff was at his desk in the third of the four cubicles in the office. A basic room divider separated them. As usual, he was focused on his work, ignoring everything else.

Christoff, a CPA and a lawyer, had never learned to type. It was probably just as well. No machine would ever be able to keep up with him. His left hand was sweeping across one of the legal pads on his desk, disregarding the margins, filling the page with his tiny back-slanting scrawl to within a half inch on either side of the page, an inch top and bottom.

Exhausted pads were stacked neatly on one end of his

desk. Half a dozen clean pads were stacked on the other end. Five, fine-point, red Bic pens were centered at the top of his desk, lined up head to toe. The only other thing on his desk was a telephone.

My desk is in the back right corner of the office - a five-foot section of kitchen counter top stacked on two three-door filing cabinets, raising it chest-high. I walked passed Broadbent, ignoring his screen, and dropped my bag on the bar stool I perch on when company comes. I rifled through the messages stacked on the desk. Most of them were from lobbyists. I pulled out one from Katherine Catlett and dropped the rest in the trashcan.

Christoff had placed three messages from Bill Byrd, Government Ops' Staff Director, to the side. One of them was marked urgent. I dropped them in the trashcan as well and logged on to the Senate's computer system. There were 310 new messages in my in box. A couple were from Byrd's office. I logged out without opening anything I had received and began pulling up my notes from Florida. I had scheduled a staff meeting at ten.

Fine arrived just as we were preparing to go down. It was ten to ten. His eyes were red and heavy lidded. He seemed to be having a hard time adjusting to the light. He looked like he had partied through the weekend.

Politics makes strange bedfellows. My team proved the point. They could not have been less alike. Christoff had the look and intensity of a rabbinical scholar. Broadbent was blonde with a Wild Bill

Hickock mustache and thick glasses that magnified his pale eyes. A Deputy Sheriff in Colorado before coming to The Hill, he still dressed the part – belt, buckle, and boots. He had a janitor's or jailor's key ring clipped to a belt loop on one hip and a Blackberry with Bluetooth strapped to the other. Fine, out of Northwestern, was long and lean and impeccably dressed. He wore a dark, three-piece suit, with a pinstripe shirt and a solid tie. From all appearances, Christoff didn't care what he wore. He had one suit in multiple colors. Today, he wore brown.

We met in the Senate cafeteria in the basement of Dirksen. To compensate for the lack of natural light, mirrors had been attached to every vertical surface, including support beams. It doesn't take long to figure out that if you pick the right seat and check reflections you can see everyone at any of the other tables in room, as well as anyone coming and going.

We sat two thirds of the way back on the right side. A plump brunette with a pale friend occupied a table two over. Broadbent picked a seat where he could see them both - one head on and the other reflected in the mirror. A two-tripper with a mud hen, he thought. Still, the fat one had a sensuous mouth. The skinny one had good legs. I picked a seat with my back to the wall. John took the seat to my right. Christoff put his back to the girls. He pulled up the table between them so that he would have a place to put his files.

It was too early for lunch. In an hour the crowd would begin to gather. A half hour later, the place would be packed and so noisy you couldn't hear yourself think.

"Let's move through this quickly," I said. "Where are we?"

"We know Total Health Care controls 20 hospitals, 95 nursing homes, and at least 200 clinics, pharmacies, and urgent care facilities in New York and New Jersey," Christoff said. "We know they operate throughout the east coast but we don't know the extent of their holdings in other states. That's one of the things we asked GAO to find out."

"Does Dershowitz still have control of Total Health Care?"

"When the company was purchased, Star put Paul Ricca on the Board but apparently he's just monitoring operations," John said. "The original management team is still in place. Dershowitz, his wife Ann, daughter, Marta, half-sister Jeannette, two sons, Stanley and Meyer, and his son-in-law, Steve Herriman are all still involved."

"Anything new on Scarpace?"

"We found a witness who says she overheard Scarpace chewing out Delta for losing his luggage on a flight from New York to Florida," Dick said. "She says he was particularly concerned about a package with Dershowtiz's name on it."

He felt obligated to explain.

"We think he has been laundering money for Dershowtiz in the Bahamas."

"What does GAO say?"

"They say Dick is probably right," Christoff replied. "Dershowtiz's accounts show monthly deposits and withdrawals in amounts as high a $100,000."

He pulled a folder out of his briefcase.

"In addition, the Bank of New York found 30 of the 57 checks we subpoenaed. As you can see, 22 of the 30 were made out to Dershowitz."

Broadbent smiled, feeling vindicated.

"No wonder they didn't want to produce the checks when we asked for them."

"I have been reviewing the cash receipt books," Christoff said.

He pulled out another one of his folders.

"So far, I have found about $2 million - $2.2 million to be precise - paid out to people identified only by initials."

"Whose?"

"No way to be sure, but some of the initials match Dershowitz, Dershowtiz' wife, his sons, and your friend, Rocco. There is another three quarters of a million paid out without any notation at all."

"Any idea where that went?"

"No one knows."

"Best guess?"

Christoff had been working for the New York Attorney General's Office when we met. After that, he served as Kaine's Administrative Assistant, essentially running the Governor's office. He knew the state as well as anyone.

"Best guess. Protection. Dershowitz couldn't get away with this stuff as long as he has if he wasn't covered."

"All right. Enough guessing. What else do we have?"

"You remember the subpoena we issued to the insurance company Dershowitz uses?" Christoff asked.

I did.

"New York Security."

"It's a subsidiary of Grand Brokerage out of Bermuda. Steinberg and Espinoza are listed as directors."

"Both of them?"

"Both."

The brunette had become aware of Broadbent's interest. She crossed her plump legs, hiking her short skirt well up her fat thighs. She was glancing his way often enough to make it hard for him to concentrate on what was being said.

"So what?" he said.

Christoff looked at him with the impatience. As far as he was concerned, Broadbent was dead weight, a political appointee who knew nothing and did nothing.

"Stanley Steinberg is Speaker of the New York Assembly, Ben Espinoza is the Minority Leader," Fine said.

He had taken Broadbent under his wing when he arrived and still felt responsible for him. He quickly changed the subject.

"There has been a shakeup at NME," he said.

Broadbent looked blank.

"National Medical Enterprises," Fine said.

The faster he shoveled the deeper Dick got. He was beginning to think Christoff was right.

"Do we know what happened?" I asked.

"Merriman says Cannistracci was forced out. He was

accused of embezzling. Cannistacci said the Mafia was extorting him. He was scheduled to testify before the organized crime strike force when he disappeared."

"Disappeared or disappeared?"

"We don't know," John said. "The Bureau has an informant who says he was probably dropped in the river."

Chapter Nine

When I returned from the cafeteria, I found the Committee's Chief Clerk, Patricia Byrd, at my desk.

"The Staff Director is looking for you," she said.

She looked flustered and a little sheepish.

"You mean your husband?" I said and watched her face turn red.

It's a thin face on a long neck attached to a thin body. Her hair is almost always pulled back in a bun, stretching her pale skin across her bony cheeks. Disney would make her a crane – a skinny bird with big eyes.

A career staffer, unmarried and probably unbedded, she was stuck on the ladder that gives administrative staff proximity to power, watching others - younger, more attractive, and more aggressive - leapfrog over her until the Big Byrd came into her life. When the Senate turned over and Byrd found himself staffing the majority, he brought her on to manage the office. An Army brat, she brought military commitment and a librarian's sense of humor to her job.

"Mr. Byrd would like to see you," she said firmly, but she could not hold my eyes.

Something was stuck in her craw. I waited.

Finally, she said, "I found the messages you threw away."

She'd been fishing. It was nothing new. She often did, looking for incriminating information and justifying it by saying she was looking for waste. Occasionally, she found a paper clip someone had thrown away and made a production of it.

"If you are going to go through our trash," I said, "try Broadbent's. I think you'll find it more interesting."

"He's disgusting," she said and shuddered.

Still, she could not or would not leave.

"Is there something else?" I said.

Large splotches of red began to appear at the base of her throat. With shaky hands she held up a letter and shoved it at me.

"You can't talk to constituents this way."

"Why not?" I said as soon as I recognized the document she had pulled from my outgoing mail. "Wouldn't you want to know if some idiot was sending your Senator letters and signing your name?"

"You can't say that."

"I thought I did."

"It's on Committee stationery."

"It's not on your stationery," I said. "It's on mine. If you don't like it, take it up with the Chairman."

The rash on her throat spread to her neck and ears. She took a deep breath, fighting for control. Daddy would have been proud.

"What do I tell him?" she said, biting out the words.

"Who?"

"Mr. Byrd," she said firmly.

"Tell him I've gone to lunch."

...

Katherine Catlett was waiting at the Monocle. Another Nick and another Greek had parked her at a booth in the back next to the Magnuson table. There was a time when more appropriations were settled there during his midnight gin games than when the committee was in session.

Kat's hair is so dark it almost seems black. It surrounds a fine face with features drawn from Ireland and the Baltic States. Her skin is fair, almost porcelain, with eyes that curious shade of gray that sometimes seem a darker shade of blue. Oversized dimples that start just below her cheekbones and deepen with even the slightest movements of her mouth enhance the overall effect.

She has been with the hospital association as long as we have known each other. It is no secret I find her attractive. She knows it; just as I know she is attracted to me. Neither one of us has ever done anything about it though at least once month one of us finds an excuse to get together for lunch. More often than not, I let her buy because I know it gives her a way to explain our relationship. Plus, I know she enjoys using the company card. It is one of the few perks they give her.

Kat is smart and straightforward. She has an interest to represent but she is never overbearing about it. We have never had trouble finding other things to talk about. Today she was all business.

"You're about ready to go, aren't you?" she said.

"Why do you say that?"

She watched him closely. Nothing. You could never tell what he was thinking.

"You're making a lot of people nervous."

"I didn't know I was that popular."

Again nothing. He was dancing around her.

"That's not the word I would have picked," she said and smiled. "Do we have any reason to be nervous?"

"No," I said finally. Clearly, this was important to her.

"I had to ask," she said, sorry now she did.

"If anything, your people have every reason to applaud what we are doing."

"I know you believe that but not everyone would agree. People define their self-interests differently."

"That's what makes life interesting."

"Sometimes you make it more interesting than it has to be."

"Perhaps." I tried to think of a way to put her at ease without going places I didn't want to go.
"You remember clinical labs?"

She nodded.

"The Clinical Laboratory Association, which, if I recall correctly, is one of your affiliates, brought the problem to our attention. They helped identify the bad guys and testified against them. They lost a couple of dues paying members in the process but they got a lot of positive press in return. I thought Legorio was going to wet his pants when he saw himself on 60 Minutes."

"He passed out copies of the tape as a Christmas present."

"I don't blame him. He had every reason to be proud. They helped us put some crooks away, clean up their industry, and save the taxpayer a bunch of money. In return, they got to help us come up with a legislative remedy that made sense. They deserved a lot of credit when all was said and done. The AMA, on the other hand, has been against every progressive health reform you can name - including Medicare – all in the name of preserving the sanctity of the doctor patient relationship. You can admire one; the other is hard to respect."

"Aren't you being a little hard on the AMA?"

"Do you think so?"

I saw John Valanos approaching. He stopped at a respectful distance, waiting until he caught my eye.

"Welcome back," he said.

John's father, a CPA, started the restaurant more than fifty years ago. Noting the paucity of watering holes on the Senate side, he tried to convince his clients that opening a restaurant there would be a good investment and wound up taking his own advice. Under his genial guidance, the Monocle grew so popular the Senate had it wired for bells so that members who frequented the establishment wouldn't miss too many votes.

When John inherited the restaurant it was a gift of dubious value. The Senate was in the process of acquiring the property as part of its endless expansion. At the last moment, someone inserted an amendment designating the building a historic landmark. As a result, the Senate now owns a building it can't do anything with. The only thing that made sense was to lease it back.

"Greek salad?" John said.

I nodded.

"And for the lady?"

"Crab cakes," she said, choosing one the Monocle's signature dishes.

John smiled his approval and discreetly withdrew to expedite the order.

"Does the fact that the AMA helped defeat Moss have anything to do with the way you feel about them?" Kat asked when John had gone.

"Only as it reflects their mindset. They took him on because he exposed bad docs, phony docs, and the crooks running Medicaid mills. You'd think that would be something they would support. Instead, they contributed a bundle to his opponent, organized against him, and celebrated when he lost. The truth though is that it probably wouldn't have made any difference if it weren't for Howe."

"These things are not always logical, you know. Some people are always more afraid of the cops than the crooks," she said. "And if Howe was that toxic why didn't Moss walk away from him?"

"Howe said he was set up. He was innocent."

"Isn't that what they all say?"

"Moss believed him."

"Do you?"

———

76

"You have to remember where they come from. Most of these guys couldn't get a date in high school. They get elected to Congress and all of sudden they are swimming in women who look like you. They are like kids in a candy store. Howe wasn't like that. He had a wife he loved and a family he cared about. Besides, you would have to be a few bricks short of a load to think you could pick up a hooker in Salt Lake City without being noticed. In DC or LA or even Des Moines, you might get away with it, but not in Salt Lake City, not when you are one of four Federally-elected officials in the state."

"So you believed him?"

"It doesn't matter at this point. The jury didn't. Moss did and he paid for it."

The conversation had gotten heavier than I wanted. Fortunately, the waiter arrived with lunch and gave me a chance to change the subject.

"How are you doing?" I asked.

"About the same. I still can't crack the boy's club. They pat me on the head and say nice things but they don't take me seriously and probably never will."

"Have things gotten any better at home?"

"Better? I guess."
She made a face, wondering if this was the time to tell him. She sampled the crab cake and then came out with it.

"I filed for divorce."

She waited for a reaction. As she feared, he didn't give her one. Maybe he just needed time to sort out the implications of what she had just said. Still, it would be nice if he would give her something to work on.

"You've been talking about that as long as we've known each other," he said.

His response was flat. Factual. No emotion.

"I know. Still, it's hard."

"Why?"

"There's nothing wrong with him. For a while I thought there was something wrong with me. But the truth is there is nothing wrong with me either. We just don't work."

"As I recall, you were together a long time before you got married."

She nodded.

"We started dating in college."

"It can get to the point where it just seems like the thing to do."
"I'd say that sounds like the voice of experience but I know you've never been there."

"No, but I have been close enough to know it can be hard to find a reason not to take a relationship to the next level. That's the social expectation. Even if it means you are marrying the wrong person for the wrong reason."

"Do you really think there a right person for every one?" she asked, still hoping for a sign.

"If not, what's the point? You just have to be picky and patient."

"I'm not sure how picky you've been but you've certainly been patient."

She dropped her eyes. When she looked up, mischief lurked there.

"Some people say you are a closet case."

"Do they? What do you think?"

Her laugh was long and hearty. When she stopped, her dimples still creased the corners of her mouth, suggesting another laugh was lurking not far behind.

...

When I returned to the office, I found a message from Dee waiting. My email address is not listed in any of the directories. How she found me was a mystery. I thought about the difficulty with which we parted and remembered how easily we had come together the last time I came back to The Hill.

I had gone calling on old friends. On impulse, I stopped in to see her, half expecting her to be gone, quite sure she would not recall my name if she were still around. To my surprise, she remembered better than I could have hoped what little there was to remember. I was surprised at how much she remembered and how much, at her prodding, I was able to recall as well. We talked only a moment or two, agreeing to catch up over coffee. She took the lead from there, calling to arrange lunch, then dinner and then more suddenly than I could have imagined we were involved.

The last time we reconnected she said, "What took you so long to get around to me?" Now, she asked simply: "When can I see you again?"

Chapter Ten

Oliver Wendell Holmes called it. He said,
"Politicians are like fish in a fish market crawled over
with flies."

It's still the best analogy. The more seniority a
member has the more flies he is likely to attract.
When members leave The Hill, the host becomes the
parasite and the cycle is complete.

Plato was said to have had a single volume of
Aristophanes under the pillow on his deathbed. Were
a lobbyist detected in that improbable situation, the
volume would be the Congressional Directory. A
Blackberry would be on his nightstand.

The best of the breed are considerate and inoffensive,
ever accommodating, ever persuasive. They
ingratiate, store indebtedness, and contribute like a
relative. In best Dale Carnegie, they know how to
win friends and influence people. "You can catch
more bees with honey," Carnegie said and the honey
flows, individual contributions like drops of rain
forming streams and rivers that flow toward The Hill,
drawn by the gravity of self-interest.

By every account, Henry Furth was among the best.
He perennially made The Washingtonian's most
influential list. His firm, HFC, ranked fourth among
the top lobbying firms in town, behind Patton Boggs,
Atkins Gump, and Ogilvy. He was known for his
political generosity, rarely turning down a request,

making the maximum personal contribution to more than two hundred Congressional candidates in each cycle.

"Money is like manure," he explained. "You have to spread it around."

Knowing the more he had to spread around, the more potent he would become, Furth began bundling contributions from his clients and targeting distribution with position more than political persuasion guiding his gifts. Star had been particularly generous. Under his direction, they had spent millions to help elect candidates nationwide. Harvey Davis, Star's CEO, had personally donated more than $7 million to federal and state campaigns, putting him in the company of Eshelman, Adelson, Soros, and Bing.

In addition, Star had seeded The Center for Health Policy, a 527 front Furth set up to support candidates with favorable positions and attack adversaries. Under federal election rules, there is no control on the source or limit to the amount of money 527 advocacy groups can raise and little control of how that money is spent. It was a loophole Furth had often exploited to his advantage.

Tuesday morning as he gazed out the window of his penthouse suite, Furth felt the City was his to command. The Capitol marked the horizon to the east. The White House, to the west, was hidden from sight, obscured by the Treasury Building and the lay of the land, but the Washington Monument was clearly visible to the south. He was where he had always wanted to be with income, influence, and power beyond anything he could have imagined growing up in Detroit.

Mitchell, Pennington, Tyson and Rudy were waiting in the conference room. As he prepared to join them, he thought about the distance he had traveled, how hard he had worked to get where he was, and how difficult it had been to be an outsider in an insider's town. What had been political was now personal – a threat to all he had achieved. Colgate and Alexander were coming after him. He was determined not to let them disrupt the life he had created for himself.

His subordinates were sitting as if assigned where they had sat the day before. Pennington and Mitchell had their heads together, whispering to each other. Tyson was visibly nervous. Nine in the morning and he had already begun to sweat. Rudy was leaning away, trying to distance himself as much as possible.

The meeting began without formality as soon as Furth settled into his seat. Again, Mitchell took the lead.

"This is a consolidated report," he said, handing Furth a copy of the threat analysis they had prepared. "Its drawn from all sources at our command - public records, newspaper reports, Dunn & Bradstreet, staff contacts on The Hill and in the Executive Branch, input from allied organizations, and Saveco. Saveco's agents explained their interest by saying they were conducting background checks for security purposes. Confidence is high. Areas of uncertainty are noted.

"Key points: Colgate took over Oversight and Investigations at the beginning of the last term. John Fine was his first hire. Fine came by way of the Better Government Inc., the Chicago watchdog group. He was their chief investigator. Barbara Benson, a Colgate family friend, founded the BGI. She recommended him. Fine is out of Yale and Northwestern, top of his class, editor of the law review. His core expertise is corporate law. A year ago, he married Pam Macklin, the only daughter of the magazine Macklins. First marriage for him, second for her. Two children from her previous marriage, Mark and Michael, ages nine and seven. Fine formally adopted them six months ago.

"Richard Broadbent is a former deputy sheriff out of Colorado. He was hired at the beginning of the year. Three months earlier, he had the good fortunate to pull over a vehicle driven by Paul Paulsen's youngest daughter. We were told she was speeding and driving under the influence. If so, this was not the first time. Court records show three previous convictions – DUI, possession of a controlled substance, and reckless driving.

"Somehow she talked Broadbent out of giving her the ticket that would have suspended her license and probably persuaded her family to send her to see Betty Ford. A month later, they eloped. They were married in Vegas. Our sources say the family was so unhappy about it that Paulsen pulled in a chit to get Broadbent out of town. Paulson and Colgate were roommates at Harvard. She stayed in Colorado and has made a show of becoming involved in the brewery but she still manages to party enough to make the rags from time to time.

Broadbent was disciplined twice by the Sheriff's office while he was there. Once for misconduct involving a minor. That case is sealed because of the child's age. The second case involved a complaint of sexual harassment from a co-worker. She also filed a civil suit. Both were withdrawn about the time Broadbent came out here. A settlement was probably involved, but Saveco cannot find a record of one. So far, the woman has refused to talk about it. She told Saveco she was trying to get the matter behind her and get on with her life.

"Bill Christoff was hired by Alexander. We know the most and the least about him. He is a CPA and a lawyer out of Columbia. He worked for Kaine when he was Comptroller and then the Attorney General. Apparently that's where he was when he met Alexander. When Kaine was elected Governor, he brought Christoff on as his chief of staff. We know nothing about Christoff's personal life, apparently because there isn't much to know. In New York, he is known as a paper-eater. He is a workaholic.

"Alexander came back in May. Sources in Colgate's office say it took several calls and a face-to-face for Colgate to persuade him to return. Colgate and Alexander had some contact when Colgate was in the minority. Still, it's a strange match. Their backgrounds could not be more different.

"Alexander came here for college, started working on The Hill while he was at GWU, and joined Oversight and Investigations after law school. He has stayed with it except for a couple of years in the military, where he was assigned to the Pentagon's Counterintelligence Force. We don't know what he did there.

"When he was discharged, Alexander returned to OSI as Counsel and Director of Oversight, working for Moss. He left when Moss was defeated. After that, he focused on real estate. He has been buying and managing properties on The Hill for years. Before returning to OSI, he sold his investment properties and most of his business to Denton. We don't have a number yet but we know he did well enough to be assured he didn't come back to The Hill because he needed money.

"As you know, Oversight and Investigations is under Government Operations – at least nominally. The Staff Director is Bill Byrd. He was Minority Staff Director under Stallsmith. When Stallsmith opted for Commerce, he persuaded Pete Popper to let Byrd stay on through the end of his term. Popper has announced he will retire at the end of this session. Byrd is already looking for a place to go. That may be something we can work with."

"Based on the information we have, it seems reasonable to conclude Alexander would not have returned unless he was given a free hand. One of our colleagues calls him the last of the virgins. He is a true believer. It's also reasonable to conclude he has a personal agenda. The speed with which things have developed supports that conclusion. He ordered a series of GAO audits immediately after he came back."

"This is unfinished business, revenge, or both. Alexander knows what he is looking for and he knows where he wants to come out. That's significant. It is the difference between an objective investigation and an investigation with an objective. Based on his track record, what he is doing is looking for a way to reinforce conclusions he has already formed."

"In all probability, Alexander will engage the media in this effort. His pattern in the past has been to selectively involve correspondents on the front end, giving them a lead so they will buy into the investigation, and tee it up for others. In the clinical laboratory investigation, that meant setting up a storefront with *60 Minutes*. "Paper doctors" concluded with an FBI sting of phony docs, and a *Dateline* segment. The pacemaker investigation was capped with a segment on *20/20*.

"You will recall the way that one unfolded. The first our client knew what was happening was when Alexander called the chairman and CEO to advise him that his firm would be mentioned at a

Congressional hearing and invite him to appear and respond. It is worth emphasizing Alexander made that call personally. It tells you something about him. Someone who knows him intimately said he is the kind of guy who would kick the devil in the balls --"

"That would be us," Rudy said with a smirk.

"That would be us," Mitchell said, deadpan.

Mitchell didn't find it funny. From the look on Furth's face, he didn't either. Rudy's stomach fell. He should have known better than to call attention to himself.

"I don't have to tell you the way it works," Mitchell said, looking directly at him. "Alexander didn't have to make that call. He didn't have to go looking for Rocco. He could have had a secretary call about the hearing or sent a marshal after Rocco."

Rudy dropped his head.

"It also worth remembering the way he set up the MedTech hearing," Mitchell said. "The first we heard of it was when the call came late Friday afternoon. That left us a weekend with an angry client and nothing to do about it. The hearing was on Wednesday. *20/20* ran the night before. Effectively, we only had, two days of response time. By Wednesday morning, we were dealing with saturation press. All we could do at that point was bail and try to keep our client afloat. It was too little too late."

"The same thing happened with Mills. Moss, Alexander and the Capitol Hill cops he pressed into service to pose as Medicaid patients were on the front page of the *Times* above the fold two days running. As usual, everyone followed the *Times*' lead. By the end of the week, the investigation was on the front-page of every daily in the country."

"Senator Colgate compounds our challenge. He presents a potentially lethal combination of aggression and ambition. He can't be influenced and he can't be bought. That makes him a dangerous man. Members of his personal staff believe Alexander was hired to help position him for a run at the White House. Colgate's wealth and business experience guarantee him the backing of established interests; but he will have to broaden his support if he is to succeed. Based on the way he has campaigned for the Senate, he knows that. He has sought every opportunity to identify himself with the common man."

"In sum: We are facing a political perfect storm. We have a staffer with a messiah complex working for an ambitious man who can't be bought. The threat is intense and urgent. It may even be personal. We don't know if Alexander knows about our role in setting up Howe or how deeply we were involved in bringing Moss down, but it's possible. Bottom line - it probably doesn't matter. He is coming after us. If he succeeds, Colgate's intent is clear. He will try to ride us into the White House."

Mitchell paused, looking for a reaction. All he got was a puff of smoke and a wave of the hand. He put down his notes, sat back, and waited.

Most of what Mitchell had said Furth already knew. Beau had briefed him earlier but there was no reason for his subordinates to know that.

"Has Colgate introduced anything relevant?" he asked.

"No."

"Is he preparing a package?"

"If he is, no one knows anything about it," Tyson said. "If something appears, we will have an opportunity to address it in Committee. Most likely, that would be Government Ops. I've talked with Byrd. He has promised to give me a heads up if something develops. Depending on what's in the package, we might also have a chance to get at it in Finance or Appropriations."

"Are all of you in agreement with this assessment?" Furth asked.

His eyes circled the table. When there was no dissent, he nodded.

"Then we all know what we have to do. Before you leave there is someone I'd like you to meet."

He buzzed Melissa. When she answered, he said, "Send him in."

A large man came lumbering through the door. He was awkward and self-conscious. He would probably look uncomfortable in any environment but he looked particularly uncomfortable here, as out of place as a pair of Crocs with a tuxedo. He was breathing heavily. His shirt was soaked with perspiration.

"Gentleman, Ms. Pennington, this is Les Tubin," Furth said. "I have just retained Mr. Tubin to help us. I have been persuaded he can be of great assistance."

Chapter Eleven

At 10:00 AM, a Federal Marshal escorted Scarpace into the Committee's conference room. He filled the door.

Rocco's face said he should have learned to duck. His body said maybe he couldn't move that fast. His movements were deliberate, like a dump truck in low gear. He looked like the kind of guy who would take your best punch and just keep coming until he could grab you by the throat with one hand and beat you senseless with the other.

When they found him at his home in Boca Raton, Rocco said something obscene and threw the subpoena back in the Marshal's face. Cop that he once was he soon realized it was better to comply than face the contempt charges that would certainly follow.

The marshal followed Scarpace into the room and took a position near the door. Without being told, Scarpace walked to the conference table and took a seat next to the stenographer. He raised his right hand and took the oath that could send him to jail if he lied and the Committee could prove it. He looked like he'd like to see someone try.

From across the table, I could see a scar over Rocco's left eye. If the news reports were accurate, there were a couple of others hidden from sight, remnants of ancient wounds from a fire fight in the Bronx that earned him the mayor's citation as a "Hero Cop." There was a soft whiplash collar around his Hulk Hogan neck.

"My name is Michael, M-I-C-H-A-E-L," he said, like a man accustomed to the circumstances. "The middle initial is T. The last name is Scarpace, S-C-A-R-P-A-C-E."

I let Fine take the lead.

"Why did you fail to appear for the deposition last week?" John began.

"I was hospitalized."

"For how long?"

"A couple of weeks. Off and on."

"Did you have any medical procedures while you were there?"

"Yes."

"What procedures did you have?"

"I was anesthetized."

"For what reason?"

"For my prostate."

"Why?"

"They said it was enlarged."

"Was it?"

"No."

"Was that it?"

"I also had a vasectomy, which was not completed."

"Why?"

"I changed my mind."

Rocco's face was impassive.

Christoff picked up the questioning.

"What do you do?"

"I'm retired."

"When did you retire?"

"About seven years ago."

"Do you know Rabbi Daniel Dershowitz?"

"Yes."

"How long have you known him?"

"About nine years."

"What is the nature of your relationship?"

"We're friends."

"Have you ever been in business together?"

"No."

"Were you ever employed by any of Dershowitz' nursing homes, clinics, or other facilities?"

"No."

"Did you ever receive a loan or consideration of any kind for services rendered to Mr. Dershowitz?"

"What?"

It was hard to tell if he was genuinely confused or just trying to avoid the question. While Rocco's movements were slow, his eyes were quick.

I spelled it out.

"Mr. Christoff is asking if you were ever employed, directly or indirectly, by Mr. Dershowitz personally or by any of his related corporations."

Rocco looked directly at me for the first time. There was something bordering on malice in his eyes. He knew I had come looking for him.

"Sorry. I didn't understand the question," he said.

His voice was measured and controlled but his

---

nostrils flared. The shape of his mouth approached a snarl when he spoke.

I met his gaze and held it.

"Do you understand the question now?"

"Yes."

"Then answer it."

Rocco's eyes flared again, but his face remained impassive. It was like watching from a distance while someone lit a campfire on the side of a mountain.

"I was employed to perform security work."

"For how long?"

"I don't remember. Off and on for a while."

"Do you know Meyer Lansky," John asked.

"I never met him in my life."

"Do you know Paul Ricca?"

"I do not know Paul Ricca," Rocco said.

I took note. He had repeated the question in his answer. It was one of the signs of deception.

"Al Diamond?" John said.

"No."

The process was too tedious for Broadbent, the only non-lawyer on the staff.

"We are told you work for Joe Colombo," he said.

"That is not true."

"Do you know Joe Colombo?" John asked, shooting Broadbent a look.

"Yes."

"How do you know him?"

"As a friend."

"How did you come to know him?"

"As an American of Italian extraction. He was one of the founders of the Italian American League. I am proud to be a member of that group – in Boca and New York. I was instrumental in building the House of Italy in the Bronx. I raised a quarter of a million dollars for that project."

His pride was obvious and sincere.

"Did Mr. Colombo contribute to that effort?" I asked.

Rocco turned his eyes toward me like gun turrets.

"He may have," Rocco said evenly. "I don't remember."

"Was he involved in the effort?"

"Yes."

"How?"

"I just told you. He was one of the leaders of the League."

"Were you close?"

"With regard to Italian civil rights, we were close."

"What did you call him and what did he call you?"

"I called him Joseph and he called me Rocco."

"So, you are telling us you don't remember if your friend made a contribution?"

"It was a while ago. There were lots of contributors."

"Are you sure you don't know Paul Ricca?"

"As sure as I can be."

"What do you mean?"

"It's a common name. There are a lot of people named Ricca."

Any attempt to remain impassive had disappeared. He was defiant. His body language said you can haul me in, you can keep me here against my will and sit on my chest but you can't make me say "uncle." As much to aggravate him as anything else, I kept him there for the better part of the morning.

Reluctantly, Rocco admitted being employed intermittently by Dershowitz throughout the years of his retirement from the NYPD. He admitted Dershowitz had given him a personal loan to start a private detective agency and a security protection service. He admitted making several trips a month back and forth between New York and Miami. He admitted accepting free room and board in the penthouse of one of Dershowitz' apartment buildings during his visits and riding with Dershowitz in his car to check out satellite operations.

"How did your professional relationship with Dershowitz begin?" Christoff asked at one point.

"After I retired, I took a job with Star Linens and Laundry."

"What is the nature of their business?"

"What do you think? It's a laundry service."

"Who do they serve?"

"What?"

"Who are their clients?"

"Doctors. Dentists. Medical clinics."

"What was your position with this firm?"

"I was in sales."

"What was your commission?"

"Sometimes 6, 8, 10 percent. Whatever I could get, but I never got it."

"What do you mean?"

"I never sold anything."

"Did you try to sell Dershowitz?"

"No."

"How did you come to work for him?"

"He hired me to find out who was stealing from one of his clinics."

"I thought you said you never worked for his clinics."

"He hired me personally."

"How did he hear about you?"

"I don't know."

"Do you know who owns Star Linens?" John asked.

"No."

"Who hired you?"

"Steve Herriman."

"Was he one of the owners?"

"I don't know. He was one of the bosses."

"Was Dershowitz one of the owners?"

"I don't know."

"Was your friend Joe Colombo one of the owners?"

"I don't know."

"You said Herriman was one of the bosses. Who were the others?"

"I don't know them all."

"Which ones do you know?"

"There were a couple of guys from Chicago."

"Who are they?"

"I don't know their names."

"Did you ever travel to Chicago for the company?"

"A couple of times."

"Did you meet them there?"

"I don't remember. I may have."

"Would it surprise you to learn Star Linens is a subsidiary of Star Services?"

"No."

"What are Star's other services?"

"I don't know."

"Have you heard of Star Financial Services?"

"I might have."

"What do you mean?"

"I am not sure. My memory is not so good these days."

"Would it surprise you to know Star Financial Services is a subsidiary of Star Services?"

"No."

"Were you ever employed by Star Financial?"

"No."

I picked it up.

"How long have you lived in Florida?"

Again, the guns turned.

"Four or five years."

"What do you do there?"

"What do people from New York do in Florida? I'm retired."

"Are you saying you don't work in Florida?"

"I do a little security work."

I picked up the pace, shooting another question at him as soon as the last one was answered.

"For whom?" I asked.

"Cruise ships mostly."

"How often?"

"Maybe once a month."

"What's the name of the cruise line?"

"Santa Cruz."

"Are they tourist or gambling boats?"

"Show boats don't need security."

"Where do they run?"

"Around Miami."

"Do they ever go to the islands?"

"Sometimes."

"Would that include the Bahamas?"

"Sometimes."

"What about the Cayman Islands?"

"Sometimes."

"Who do you report to at Santa Cruz?"

"What do you mean?"

"Who tells you what to do?"

"Frank Caprice."

"How do you know him?"

"He is a friend of a friend."

"Is he a member of the Italian American League?"

"Yes."

Rocco had no problem keeping up. He was not as dumb as he looked.

Chapter Twelve

Bill Byrd was waiting in the hall when we left the conference room. It was around noon.

"I was hoping to see you," he said.

He made it sound like he had just stopped by on his way to lunch.

"Then, this must be your lucky day," I said.

Another message from Byrd had been waiting on my desk when I arrived that morning. I had thrown it away like the rest.

The Hill operates on a feudal system. Each Member of Congress is a Lord with an empire established by seniority, position, and power. In his heyday, Carl Hayden, then the Senior Senator from Arizona controlled over 5,000 jobs on The Hill. He had been on The Hill since Arizona was admitted to the union. When Lyndon Johnson was Majority Leader, his fiefdom included over 100 rooms in the Capitol reserved for his personal use. It is the only workplace in the United States where staff can be hired without question or qualification and fired without cause. Staff serve at the members' pleasure – often literally.

For those caught up in the system, this presents a peculiar situation. Even among colleagues who are amicable – and Byrd and I were far from that - there is always some infighting as staffers jockey for position. Byrd saw me as a threat to his security. I saw him as a waste of the taxpayer's money.

He is a large, portly man with heavy jowls that seemed to shrink his eyes and sink them deep in his face like marbles in a bowl of batter. Add a constant five o'clock shadow and a permanent scowl and you get a face that resembles the cartoon character Black Bart. Put twenty pounds on Fred Thompson and you'll get the general idea.

"I want to know where you are," he said.

"I thought we had established that."

"You know what I mean."

I said nothing.

"Look, there are Committee resources involved. I have a right to know what you are doing."

"A wish is not a right. We both know OSI has a specific allocation."

"As part of the Committee's budget. I have to account for what you are doing."

"If I were you, I would be more worried about accounting for what you are doing with the rest."

Byrd flinched as if he'd been struck. Maybe he didn't know discontent with his leadership so was prevalent staff turnover was attributed to 'Byrd Flu.' Maybe he didn't know a petition had been filed with the Chairman, charging him with misuse of Committee funds. Maybe he didn't know his incompetence had been a significant factor in Colgate's decision to ask me to return. And maybe he did.

"What's the focus of your investigation?" Byrd asked as firmly as he could ask anything,

"You mean your wife hasn't found out? She has gone through more trash than the cleaning staff."

Byrd's fat fists clenched. He pushed his chest forward, puffing himself up like a blowfish.

"Mr. Alexander, you'd better be careful," he said.

"Why."

"Some of the areas you are pursuing are very controversial. The Committee is already getting a lot of calls expressing concern."

"I wasn't hired to be careful."

"Do you expect to go to hearing any time soon?" Byrd demanded.

"That's up to the Chairman," I said.

I left Byrd where he stood. I could feel the heat of his eyes on the back of my neck as I walked away.

The Big Byrd didn't hire me and couldn't fire me, but he could make life more difficult. I was certain he would try. There was nothing new in that.

Chapter Thirteen

Desiree Amidore called at 2:15 PM. We were planning travel and setting up interviews. Fine's ties to Chicago made him the obvious choice to lead there. Dick would go with him while Christoff and I made a run to New York.

"Have you thought about what I said?"

"Thought about what?"

My head was in a different place. There was a lot to do, not much time, and there had already been too many interruptions.

The first was a call patched through from the Chairman's office. There was a persistent woman on the phone, they said. She had a problem. She had been calling all week. Translation: She is a constituent who won't go away. Get her off our backs as nicely a possible.

The problem turned out to be an insurance issue. The woman, Connie Fischer, had a daughter born with a chromosome defect. As a result, she had systemic failures. She couldn't hear or speak and suffered from heart, kidney, and intestinal ailments.

Mrs. Fischer said her husband was a postal employee. Even though they were entitled to help under his insurance policy, they took care of Katherine by themselves for 15 years. When it became more than they could handle, they asked for assistance. As soon as they did, the policy was changed.

That didn't seem fair, Fischer said. They had paid the premiums for years and never filed a claim. Now when they needed it, the benefit was taken away. She had called everyone she could think of and no one would help. Everyone told her to talk to someone else.

I listened to her story. I couldn't do much at the moment but I could do that. I asked a few questions and told her I would follow up. I was completing my notes when Allison called from the front office. Allison was all of nineteen and on her first job that didn't involve burgers. She had been there six months but still looked like a deer in the headlights from time to time.

"There is someone named Esperanza Torres on the phone," Allison said. "She says she knows you. Should I take a message?"

Her tone suggested she hoped the answer would be "yes."

I could only think of one Esperanza. The last name might be Torres. I took the call.

"I've been fired," she said. "They said they're going through some sort of reorganization, reducing staff, and cutting expenses, and had to let me go."

"How many people have they let go?"

"As far as I know, I am the only one."

"Interesting."

"That's why I called. There was a big fuss after you left. They turned the place upside down and asked a lot of questions. They asked me if I met you and what we talked about."

"What did you tell them?"

"The truth."

"The truth?"

"All they needed to know."

"Sounds like I may have cost you your job."

"Who cares? I was thinking of leaving anyway. That place gave me the creeps. People coming and going. You never know who's in charge or who you're talking to. Who needs it?"

"What will you do?"

"Querido, I am a nurse. I can always work. I can go anywhere and find a job."

There was a small pause.

"I was thinking I might come up there."

"Nice thought but it's probably not a good idea at the

moment. It's better if you stay away from me for a while."

"I was afraid you'd say that."

"If you are looking for something to do, I know a guy at Miami Children's. His name is Chad Perlyn. I think you would connect."

She didn't need much persuasion. I promised I would call Perlyn and put in good word for her and did, focusing on her professional qualifications. I didn't bother to mention the package wasn't bad either. Chad could figure that out for himself.

So when Dee called, the last thing I needed was another interruption.

"I want to see you," she said.

I told her I was busy and couldn't talk. She responded by coming by at the end of the day. Can we talk now, she said. She stood tall, arms folded, proud and demanding. Maybe we can have dinner?

Reluctantly, I agreed. She suggested the Monocle, a place where we were sure to be seen. I wondered what kind of statement she was trying to make, wondered even more when she took my hand while we waited for Nick to seat us, and sat next to me instead of across from me in the horseshoe booth in the back room across from the Magnuson table.

She wore a cream colored dress with fluttery sleeves

and an uneven hemline. It seemed draped around her body, flowing with her every move, revealing and concealing, managing to make her look at once innocent and provocative.

"I thought about us a lot, Nick," she said when we had settled into our booth.

She turned toward me, placing a thigh against my thigh, a hand on the arm I had resting on the table.

"Even though you were gone somehow I felt connected to you. Damn you, Nick. How could you just walk away like that?"

Her dark eyes were fixed and intent.

"Why couldn't we have talked about it?"

"Mother told me never to speak to strangers," I said and watched the corners of her mouth tighten.

"If I was, it wasn't my idea," she said. "I wanted to be needed; I wanted to be as close to you as I could be. But you never let me near. I used to think it was just a matter of time. I thought it was just the front door that was barred and after hanging around for a while, I'd find a backdoor or something, some way to get close. But you never let me in, Nick. There was always some part of you tucked away somewhere, someplace I couldn't go. You only gave me just so much. And it was so little. The rest was marked private…"

She took a breath, waiting for a response. When none came she pressed closer, her right leg crossing over her left, her foot coming to rest against my calf.

"I'm not trying to be critical," she said. "Maybe we were both at fault. Maybe we just didn't trust ourselves and what we were feeling. When I thought about it, I found I wanted a lot of things but I wasn't sure why most of the time." She laughed. "Mother used to say that all I ever wanted was all I ever wanted. Maybe she was right."

She held her smile for a moment, looking for a reaction. When she didn't get one, she quickly continued.

"He has given me whatever I have asked for but he can't give me the only thing I need. The rest just doesn't work without you. I know that now. That's why I'm here. And I'm not worried any more about why or how or what anyone might say. I'm not even worried about how I know. I just know. I want you. I have since the first time I saw you. Somehow, I know I always will."

She was intense and earnest. Clearly, she had been working up to this.

"If I had any doubts, it ended Saturday."

"What happened Saturday?"

"I saw you. And I met your roommate – Ho."

"It's pronounced "Huff.""

"I know," she said with that small smile. "I didn't like seeing her, but I found I felt too sorry for her to be really jealous."

"Why would you feel sorry for her?"

"Because I could see what you were doing to her."

"And what's that?"

"What you do to everyone. The shrinks call it inconsistent stimuli - at least, that what mine said. Like my girlfriend who loves cats, she loves them so much that, of course, she had to marry a guy who can't stand them, the kind of guy who spent his whole little life tying tin cans and firecrackers to their whatevers. She has these three beautiful Persians. They are just gorgeous. Whenever she is around, he pets them nice, nice, and as soon as she steps out he is swatting them around and bouncing them off the wall, only quietly, you understand, cause if she ever caught him something else would be bouncing…Anyway, you should see those poor cats. Every time he reaches for one of them, they quiver."

"Sounds like there is a moral in there some place."

"Don't…Don't get defensive. Lord knows I have my faults too."

Her eyes broke away, looked up and to the right, searching.

"Anyway, it doesn't matter now. All I am saying is

that until I saw you I didn't know how important she was."

"You could have asked."

"I didn't have to."

She touched my arm again, reassuring.

"Those who matter leave their mark, Love. The only marks on you are mine."

"Maybe I feel I've been marked enough."

"Don't," she said again, increasing the pressure on my arm. "Don't do that. I'm trying to be completely honest with you."

Her eyes blinked and broke away, then came back. There was some uncertainty or nervousness there.

"At least, I mean to be...What I'm trying to say is that I know what I want. So, it's your problem now. You are the one who will have to decide if I can be trusted."

"I'll trust you now and then," I said, taking the offered line. "That's your problem - knowing when."

She remembered and smiled, another one of her small smiles that somehow lights up the room, making you wonder what the full force of her smile would do and how you could bring that about. It can get to be a full-time preoccupation - gathering remnants and scattered incidents, thinking this will please her, storing stories, spending hours dreaming up some little thing, some special way of saying something that would purchase an extra millimeter of that smile.

Looking at her now took me to another place, another time. I remembered how good we were together and how in sync we seemed to be, how she could read the weight of my eyes, her body sensing and lifting imperceptibly in recognition, knowing not only that eyes were on her but whose eyes and from where, standing with that strong straight posture a little straighter, almost leaning back, her body tense and receiving. She says she always knows. After many demonstrations I became convinced it was true. It is one of her mysteries.

"So, I have decided, Nick…Nick, where did you go? Did you hear me? I said I have decided…I am going to hang around, wherever you go, I'm going to be there, looking forlorn and sad, and touching and as pathetic as possible until you understand how it is with me. And until then, I'll take whatever you will give me. I'm still looking for that door, Nick. I'm not worrying about protecting myself any more. I'm not holding back. Maybe that makes me vulnerable. I don't know. I don't think so. I've never felt stronger or surer. Somehow, I have never felt as free as I do right now. All I want is to be with you…Nick, will you say something! I can hear myself talking and talking and you are just sitting there letting me babble. Say something!"

"Don't you think you should get a divorce first?"

She gave me an elbow and turned away. After a moment, she looked back, stopped, and looked beyond. I saw her mouth tighten, her eyes shift. She had been intensely with me. Now she looked like she wanted to bolt. I wondered what had changed, who had walked in. There were a couple of tourists at the bar and an assortment of staffers but no one I knew.

Out of nowhere, she suggested we cut dinner short and go for a ride – somewhere quiet where we could talk. The restaurant had become "stuffy" and "confining." I paid the bill and we left - our dinners unfinished on the table. I saw John's look of concern and went to assure him there was nothing wrong. When I returned, she had bounced back from wanting to hide to wanting to a public display of affection. As I draped my jacket over her bare shoulders, she turned and kissed me, firmly and deliberately, fully on the mouth.

I drove down by the Tidal Basin, taking the loop passed the park exit four times, battling her busy hands. Now that we were alone, she seemed determined to get as close as possible. Finally, she couldn't stand it.

"Nick, if you don't park this thing somewhere soon," she said, "I'm going to come in my pants without you even touching me."

I picked the boatyard - somewhere near the place where the nation's first female journalist lay in wait for President Adams as he bathed in the nude, sitting on his britches until he granted her an exclusive. She took the initiative. She made all the moves. I sat back, semi-detached, watching myself, watching Jefferson, watching her, feeling her and my response to her, of two minds, wondering why I couldn't accept what was so casually being offered. For a while I thought I could - because I have always found her attractive, because I missed her, because she made me feel things I hadn't felt in a while - but I couldn't. Half the time she seemed to be throwing out ideas to looking for a reaction, checking the tension on the line. Half the time she seemed to be trying to close the distance between us by being physical, becoming increasingly, deliberately, indiscreet.

In the heat of the moment, these thoughts seemed a bit cold-blooded. It was not what I wanted to think, but what I couldn't help thinking. There was too much calculation in everything she did. Her little speech at the Monocle seemed a little too pat, practiced with poses rehearsed. The overwhelming passion, the little girl lost in something beyond her control, didn't fit the woman I knew or the one I once thought I knew so well.

Huffing like a furnace, mouth puffy, eyes slack, she demanded we go back to my place. I dropped her off across the street from her car instead. She made no attempt to hide her displeasure. Still, she recovered quickly enough to stop under the street light at the entrance to the Senate parking lot, the guard not more than ten feet away, and mouth words of love.

It was like watching a movie trailer. There was so much deliberation in it, it rolled like the second reel of something rank.

Chapter Fourteen

Amtrak is the only civilized way to get from Washington to New York. The Acela express leaves Union Station, a block from the Capitol, and arrives downtown at Penn Station in two hours and forty-five minutes. The shuttle will get you from Reagan to LaGuardia in an hour, from time to time, but you can't count on it. When you factor in weather, driving, parking, clearing security, picking up a car and fighting your way into town, the minutes even out. The pay off is in stress reduction and productivity.

We took the 9:00 AM Wednesday morning, arriving at the station early enough to find a seat in the cafe car. I had my laptop and cell on the right side of the table between us. Christoff had pulled one of a half dozen legal pads out of his briefcase. He sat centered, the yellow pad squarely in front of him. One of his red pens was placed on the left side, cap off, point down. A half empty Starbucks was on the right, lined up with the corner of his pad. I marveled at his precision. Every time he picked the cup up, he seemed to be able to put it back in exactly the same place.

I leaned against the corner on my side of the table, back against the wall, facing away from the window where rundown houses and dingy industrial parks whizzed by. A carrying carton with two Cokes and a

cup of ice rested near my laptop. One end held down the stub of my boarding pass.

"There's something I wanted to talk with you about," Christoff said.

We had been talking about work for nearly two hours. This had to be personal.

"Sure."

"I fired Olivia."

There weren't many women in Christoff's life; none, in fact, that I knew by name so it didn't take long to figure out he was talking about the woman he hired to clean the condo he had rented a block from the Senate. Christoff's place was so sparsely furnished I couldn't understand why he had hired her let alone what she could have done to make him believe she should to be fired. Still, it didn't surprise me all that much. Christoff was a particular man.

The first Sunday of every month since he moved in he had called and asked me to help him rotate his mattress. When I asked him why, he said it was the only way he could be sure it would wear evenly. In the four months we have been doing this, nothing in his apartment has changed. Boxes with his personal things remain where the movers placed them, stacked three high against the interior wall between the kitchen and dining room. At first I thought this was because he was uncertain how long he would stay and wondering if it was worth the trouble it would take to unpack. Then I noticed an Oriental rug he had purchased rolled up near the fireplace. It rests on one edge of a carpet pad that dominates the center of his living room. When I commented on it, Christoff rolled the rug out so I could see what it looked like. Then, he carefully rolled it up again. He said it is placed in position for special occasions but I can't imagine when that might be.

Once, when the closet in Christoff's bedroom was open, I got a sense for just how meticulous this man is. There were a half dozen suits, a dozen shirts - either solid blue or white - and number of ties evenly spaced on the closet rod. The ties took up half the closet. They were draped over the closet rod facing out, backs threaded, ends together. Six pairs of Johnston and Murphy shoes - two pairs of the same style in black, brown, and cordovan - were paired up, toes together, laces tied, and placed on the floor directly beneath the suit they matched.

Maybe he decided Olivia wasn't needed, I thought, but then he would not have made an issue of it. He would have simply let her go.

"Why did you fire her?" I asked.

"She was stealing?" Christoff said.

I couldn't imagine what there was to steal – any more than I could imagine what there was to clean.

"What?"

"Stamps."

"Stamps?"

"I always leave a roll of stamps in the corner of my desk drawer, on the right side, with the last stamp on the roll folded back so it's easy to tear off and ready for use. The stamps were moved. The stamp on the end was flat. It looks like there are at least a half dozen stamps missing."

"That's it?'

"No."

"What else?"

"A pillow case."

"You're sure about that?"

"Yes."

I wondered if he had any idea how odd this sounded. Christoff didn't seem to be concerned.

"Anyway, here's my question," he said. "Should I tell John?"

"Why would you?"

"I think he would want to know."

"You think he would want to know Olivia was stealing stamps?"

"Yes."

"Why?"

"He recommended her. He said she had worked for Pam for years. If she's stealing from me, she's probably stealing from them. I think I should tell him, don't you?"

Fine was in Chicago with Broadbent. They had flown up the night before. I told him it could probably wait.

We were half an hour from Penn Station. I pulled up my messages to see if there was anything I needed to tend to before heading downtown. The only ones that interested me came from Broadbent and Fine. Fine's was most recent.

John said they were checking corporate records. Broadbent was at City Hall. He was at the Secretary of State's Office. The Secretary of State, Mark Everett, had won the right to oppose Governor Welch in the general election and was inclined to be helpful. He had given Fine full access and provided programmers to help run names and check the State's corporate computer banks.

"It looks like Star is in acquisition mode," John said. "They have acquired three chains in the last 16 months. The company is closely held with a pattern

of interlocking ownership. The same people are listed as principles in all of their subsidiaries. At least on paper, they swap roles - the president of one is secretary of another and so on. Merriman says it is an open secret the Governor is in bed with them."

"Can we prove it?"

"Maybe. Merriman has a source - George Jeffers - that might be willing to talk. Jeffers worked for the Bureau of Quality Control until he started making waves. Merriman has agreed to make an introduction. He said he will hold his story in return for an inside if we take his lead."

Broadbent's message was sent an hour earlier. It was a broadcast email. While John was doing his job, Dick had transmitted the latest entry from StaffAss.

"I just took a long lunch with BA," she said, "and made a quick $400. When I returned to the office, I heard that my boss had been asking where I was. He probably had the same idea. What a loser."

"Who would have believed it," Dick said. "Whores on The Hill."

Chapter Fifteen

George Wilson was in his office at Manhattan south when we arrived. He is a hulk, 6'4", with close cut grey hair. We had formed an alliance and then a friendship during the Mills investigation. The Department of Health had been reluctant to have a bunch of Senate investigators running around town pretending to be Medicaid patients. They concluded nothing could come of it but embarrassment. When they declined Oversight and Investigation's request for assistance, Wilson stepped in providing Medicaid cards, backup, and support. In return, I promised I would refer any potential criminal investigations coming out of the investigation to the U.S. Attorney's Office.

Wilson was still mining this field. Jonathan Stack and Mark Egberg were the latest casualties. They owned eight medical centers affiliated with Total Health Care. Until their conviction, they employed 200 people and ran an operation that grossed more than $12 million a year. Wilson said the grand jury had concluded at least half of that was stolen.

Stack and Egberg were defiant the first time we met, denying any wrongdoing and refusing to appear before the Committee. Now, they were more than willing to cooperate. A long sentence and a little time in jail will do that.

Wilson escorted us to a conference room on the third floor of the US Attorney's Office. Stack and Egberg were waiting. Stack was average in height, rotund and reticent. Egberg was smaller and more forthcoming.

"You have to understand," Stack said defensively, once the hand off had been made and Wilson departed, "we weren't doing anything everyone else wasn't doing. All the docs are writing down extra visits and services here and there. No one has a problem with it. Until now, the worst thing that could happen is that somebody might ask you to give some of it back."

He was middle-aged, dark and brooding. Confession did not come easily to him.

"All the docs?"

"All the docs we know," Egberg said. "Some of them are a lot worse than we were."

"You'd think someone would have a problem with it."

"We were told to."

"It was company policy?"

"Yes," Egberg said. "Everyone was told to do it. And everyone did it."

"Everyone was bragging about it, too," Stack added, still pleading for understanding.

"Why?"

"It was so easy. It was like finding a wallet. If you find a wallet on the street with $100 bills in it, what are you going to do, turn your back on it?"

"And it was safe," Egberg said.

He seemed anxious to please.

"Nothing ever happened. Nothing ever came up. But if it did, THC told us all we had to do was deny it."

"What do you mean?"

"Think about it," Stack said, arrogant as ever. "What are the investigators going to do? No one knows what you do in your practice. The nurse - is she going to argue with you? Besides, she won't even be in the room when you see the patient. So it comes down to the patient. He's going to say what? At worst, it is his word against yours. If they ask you, 'Did you ever put down for a patient you didn't see, you say, 'I don't recall. If they ask you, 'Would you do that? You say, 'No, that's dishonest. I am a doctor. All I am interested in is good medicine. I wouldn't even think about something like that. Did you do these procedures? Yes, but that's not my handwriting. The girl did the paperwork. I should read it more carefully. There was no way anyone could prove a thing."

"If it's that easy, maybe we should get in the business," Christoff said.

Egberg took him seriously.

"One of the clinics in the Bronx is for sale," he said.

Christoff may have been kidding but his suggestion immediately struck me as a good idea. We knew most of these places kept two sets of books. Maybe they would show a prospective buyer the real set. There were some obvious dangers but I didn't think about that then. Instead, I let Christoff continue questioning Stack and Egberg and called Fine to check their progress and tell him what I had decided to do.

"I just met with the Secretary of State," Fine said. "I talked with the Comptroller earlier. Jeffers appears credible. I'll know more tomorrow morning. We've set up a meeting at the Big Eye."

"Everything else on track?"

"Yes, but – particularly in light of what you just said – I think you should know they know we are here. If they know we are here, they probably know you are there."

"What makes you think they know you are there?"

"Someone has been asking about us. Frank says they are trying to figure out where we are and what we are doing."

"Who are they?"

"Don't know."

"Where is it coming from?"

"Don't know that either. I'll let you know if and when we find out. So far, we don't have a clue."

I considered the possibilities. It could be coming from anywhere but the leading candidates would be Total Health Care, Star, the Governor or Speaker's office. The former would be interested in knowing what the Committee knew and doing whatever they could to thwart the investigation. Theirs would be a defensive battle. The latter would take it a step further and try to derail or defuse the investigation. They would either take the fight inside and work the members or launch some sort of pre-emptive strike. That would be hard to do in New York; but Illinois was a different story. If the Governor announced a massive attack on fraud on Saturday night, the Chicago end of the story would move from page one to the obits. It would be tough to keep the press in line.

NBC had the lead with a segment on *Dateline* Monday evening. They would follow with "day of" coverage. The *Tribune* in Chicago, the *Times* in New York and the *Post* had the lead Tuesday morning – the *Times* because it was the *Times*, the *Tribune* because of Merriman's involvement, and the *Post* because hometown coverage was imperative. It was a delicate balance. They would all bolt before risking the loss of their story. If they did that, the impact of the hearing would be blunted.

As we were preparing to leave, Wilson returned. He asked us to stay a moment. He looked beat. He sat down, took his jacket off, and loosened his tie.

"Sorry to keep you," he said, "but I thought you should know what's going on."

He handed me a FAX. It was an AP report on the gangland style killing of Don Bowers, an *Arizona Republic* reporter. He had been killed by a car bomb that exploded as he went to meet an informer.

"I have been on the phone with the state police in Arizona most of the day," Wilson said. "Bowers was investigating an insurance company called Arizona Security. It is a subsidiary of Grand Brokerage."

Chapter Sixteen

Broadbent and Fine arrived at the Big Eye at 9:00 AM Thursday morning. Better Government Inc. is on Michigan Avenue on the 20th floor of the Benson Building. They have a modest suite in what once must have been a grand building. The grandeur has faded with time but the building still provides a commanding view of the river and the magnificent mile. Ted Marcus buzzed them in and escorted them back to the conference room. Merriman and Jeffers were waiting.

Marcus had taken over as Chief Investigator for the BGI when John moved to Washington, just as John had inherited the role from Merriman when the *Tribune* offered him a byline. Marcus was young and looked it. He had a slight build and sandy hair. Merriman, in his '50s, was known for his dry wit and self-deprecating humor.

"It was a good story," he would often say when complimented on his Pulitzer. "It would have been better if it were true, but it was a good story."

Merriman looked more like a history professor than a reporter. Jeffers looked like a throwback to the 60s. He had a long lean frame, dark hair pulled back in a ponytail, and frameless, Lennon glasses.

When Merriman asked Jeffers to tell his story, he began slowly and nervously. Perhaps, the big eye etched in the glass conference door over his shoulder intimidated him. Perhaps, it was because he knew he was crossing the Rubicon. He had hoped to make a career in public service. With this, any chance of that was gone. Still, he said, he couldn't stand by idly and watch what was happening. Criminals aided by corrupt politicians were taking over health care in Illinois.

When John asked him if he could be more specific, Jeffers handed him a blue binder. There were twenty tabs, each dedicated to a firm he had flagged while working with the Bureau of Quality Control. John thumbed through the binder. Each tab contained a complete corporate rundown - ownership, clients, revenue, percent of revenue from Medicare and Medicaid, other sources of income, participating physicians, related parties, suspect activities, and a projected fraud factor. There was enough there to keep several grand juries busy for months.

"Have you given this to anyone else?" John asked

"Up front, you will see a letter of transmittal," Jeffers said. "It's dated six months ago. I prepared this for the Governor's Task Force. When I was appointed to that, I thought it meant something. They ignored it. I turned it over to all the appropriate state officials after that. Copies of my letters are included at the back. No one seemed to care. Nothing happened."

There was more than enough information to warrant bringing Jeffers before the Committee. The story line was clear and compelling, but Fine needed to know if he could sell it. There are three constants in press coverage of Congressional hearings: quantification, characterizations, and conclusions. Could Jeffers give the media the sound bites they needed? Would he hold up or wilt under questioning?

"Give it to me in one line," Fine said. "How would your summarize your findings if you were asked to testify today?"

"Medicaid isn't medicine," Jeffers said. "It's all about the money. That's two lines but it should work."

"You went to a lot of trouble to put this together, but I have to tell you it is doubtful our members will have the time to read it. We will and their staff might, but they won't. If you had to focus their attention on one thing, what would it be?"

"The red tabs. The worst offenders are factoring firms. They control the money and that drives everything else."

"How would you explain that to the dumb kids in the class?"

"Just think about it this way. There is a stream of money flowing from the government to the doctors. Factors control the faucet."

"Give me an example."

"Sure. Say you are a doc with a modest practice. You've got $10,000 coming for your week's work. You know it will take at least 6 months for the state to pay you. Meantime, you've got bills to pay. You want to live. You can't afford to wait so you sell your receivables to a factoring firm. You tell the factor I will give you the right to collect the entire $10,000 I have coming if you will give me $8,000 today. The factoring firm advances $8,000, collects $10,000, and keeps $2,000 or 20 percent for their trouble."

"So you are saying it's like a payday loan with 20 percent of the taxpayer's money winding up in the pockets of middlemen who do nothing."

"Maybe more."

"How is that?"

"Read this."

Jeffers pulled an affidavit out of his folder.

"It's a sworn statement from Carl Hester, a physician in Oak Park."

"Two years ago a salesman from Star Financial Management walked into my office," Hester wrote. "He told me that he could help me get paid promptly for my services. He picked up the telephone at my desk and called Springfield. He was able to tell me immediately my public aid department profile and the amount of money due me. This is confidential information. It is more than I could have found out myself. He told me his company could make sure I was paid quickly and eliminate my denials. He said they could collect 150 percent more than I could on my own and he threw around the names of several politicians he said were close to the Governor. A week later, I was invited to a party sponsored by Star with a lot of other doctors. The guest of honor was a man who processes bills for public aid. He gave a speech and told us we would be much better off using the factoring system and the only factor he would recommend was Star Financial."

"What Hester didn't know," Jeffers said, "is that the salesman was a convicted felon who had previously pled guilty to bribing pubic officials. The guest of honor was probably J. M. Kilbreath. Every one in the office knows he's tied in to Star. But he's just the tip of the iceberg."

"Are they all dirty or just Star?"

"All factors are dirty; Star is just the dirtiest. They have leverage and muscle. They know they are protected so they are pretty brazen about what they are doing. They are bribing State employees to make sure their bills are processed rapidly. If a doc doesn't cooperate, they put a freeze on him. His invoices wind up on the bottom of the pile and six months becomes a year. What's he going to do about it - complain to his Congressman?"

"You say they can get more than 20 percent?" Broadbent asked.

"Yes."

"How?"

"The faster they are paid the higher their rate of

return. Most of the bills handled by factoring firms are turned around in 30 days or less. So it is not a 20 percent annual rate, it's a 20 percent monthly rate. They are turning the money over at least 12 times a year. If you look at the printouts, you will see Star does better than that."

Fine pulled up the printouts and scanned them quickly.

"Looks like they are averaging payment in about two weeks."

"Sixteen days, to be precise. Plus, as I said before, they kite the bills."

Broadbent was still playing catch-up.

"What do you mean?"

"If you go to Hester's file, you'll see his invoices for December came to $12,500. Star gave him $8,000. His W-2 says he was paid twice that amount. That's key to this thing. He has no way of knowing what is being billed in his name. He has no control. He is just a pawn. He signs the invoices blank. He never sees the bill Star submits. He never sees the check that comes back. It goes to Star. Star pays the clinic manager; the manager takes his cut, and passes what's left on to the doc. They can do anything they want and he is the one who was legally liable."

"Why did he agree to this?"

"He had to. The factor has to have a power of

attorney or they can't collect for you. Once you give them that, they've got you by the short hair. They own you and if anything happens, you're the one who goes to jail."

"Why doesn't Hester walk?"

"He said there was a guy he knew in the clinic who was a real pig. Every patient he saw got every test imaginable. After a really big month, he decided to move to California. He sold his paper to a factoring firm and pulled out. A month later, he died. They said he had a heart attack. Star made sure everyone knew about it."

"You say they are connected?"

"Everyone in the Department knows Harvey Davis, Star's CEO, is close to the Governor. They were the largest contributors to his campaign."

"If it helps any, our investigations confirm what Jeffers is saying," Marcus said. "Factoring is nothing more than legalized loan sharking. All the firms we reviewed are tied to crime syndicates."

"Who is involved?" Fine asked.

Merriman laughed.

"It would be easier to say who isn't," he said. "There's so much money floating around they are fighting for it. They are all trying to get a piece of the action, muscling in on clinics all over town."
"Besides Jeffers, what do we have?"

"Skinner," Merriman said and handed Fine a release. "He indicted Eugene Feinstein a couple of weeks ago."

The release said a federal grand jury had indicted 16 providers and six pharmacies in a Medicaid fraud scheme that ran well into the millions. Feinstein and 12 of his associates were among those named in the suppressed documents. Skinner was quoted, saying the indictments resulted from an 18 month long investigation. More indictments were expected in the next few months.

"Alexander has talked with Skinner," Fine said. "He is on board. What about Feinstein?"

"I don't think so," Merriman said. "He stonewalled the grand jury and he won't talk to us. He is either too dumb or too scared to cooperate."

They were halfway into the noon hour. Merriman and Fine took Broadbent to Uno's for pizza before going their separate ways. They call it pizza other places, but anyone who has been to the original knows it's not the same.

Chapter Seventeen

"I was in it from beginning," Ricca said.

It was late Thursday afternoon. Ricca was driving his black Continental through the Bronx. I was on the passenger side, a German shepherd on the floor between my legs, the dog's head inches from my crotch.

"I was one of the pioneers," Ricca said. "People thought I was crazy."

One of us is, I thought. Ricca was carrying a handgun in a shoulder holster. I was carrying a recorder.

"Up until Medicaid and Medicare came along, I never made $100,000. In my first year, I made a half million."

That morning I had called Ricca's clinic, running the call through a secure line arranged by the GSA so that the source could not be traced.

"I'm Tom Clancy," I said. "I understand this clinic is for sale. Can I talk with someone about it?"

The receptionist put me on hold. In a moment, a flat, nasal voice came on the line.

"Ricca," he said. "Who is this?"

I repeated the fictitious name I had selected for this stunt, wondering again why I always picked on the Irish.

"Who did you say are you with?"

I hadn't mentioned a company. There was none to mention. I improvised.

"I am the east coast representative of Comprehensive Health Care.

The name was generic enough to sound plausible. It was vaguely familiar. Hell, there probably was a company by that name somewhere.

"Where are you based?"

"Chicago," I said and quickly asked a question of my own before I could get backed into a corner.

"Are you the one selling the clinic?"

"Yeah."

"I'd like to come out and talk with you about it."

"I'm busy. I have other places to be. But I can give you a few minutes. Around 2:00."

It was more than I had expected, but the timing was tight. I found a cut-rate printer on 42nd Street and had business cards made for the company I had just created. I gave it an address on Michigan Avenue and used the Better Government Inc. backup number

John had arranged for cover. While the card was being printed, I sent John a text, giving him the specifics. Then I went looking for Wilson.

Wilson was still in court when I arrived at Foley Square, but he had left a message saying if I needed something to ask for Carl Bogan. I passed the note back to the receptionist and waited while she pressed a couple of buttons. A few moments later, a tall, bald, ageless man came forward from the back door of the inner sanctum.

"Nick?" he said, extending a hand. "Carl Bogan. Come into my office."

Bogan was a veteran of some thirty years on the force. He had worked all the rackets, first for the city, then the DA, and now the U.S. Attorney. There was a faded picture of Telly Savalas over his desk. It was autographed, "From Kojak to Kojak."

Bogan asked where I was going, what the circumstances were, and how long I would be out. When I told him I had Paul Ricca on the line, he gave me a big, beautiful smile.

"I was going to ask if you wanted the KEL or a Nagra," he said, "but you'd better take the Nagra. It's bulkier but you're big enough to carry it. It is made by Kudelski. The model we use is a variation of the one President Kennedy had made for the Secret Service. It has stereo mikes and a 1/8 of an inch tape. It can record two people talking at the same time and will give you twice the run of anything else in the shop. It's the kind of thing you need for a job like this."

Bogan opened a desk drawer and pulled out what looked to be pocket warmer sewn into a canvas belt.

"You can wear it under your arm, place it in the small of your back, or wrap it around your waist," he said. "I generally clip it inside the belt of my pants. I put the recorder in the small of my back and run the cord down my trouser leg."

Bogan held up three feet of cord attached to a small mushroom-shaped microphone.

"Cut a hole in the bottom of one pocket and feed the cord through. Once you start it, push this tape over and seal it. Don't try to start and stop it. If the tape cuts in and out, it's dead. We'll never be able to use it in court. Got it?"

I said I did.

"You sure you don't want one of our guys to carry the wire?"

"No. I'll do it."

"Do you want a backup?"

"Got one. He is arranging transportation."

"OK. Don't do anything stupid. If something goes wrong, I don't know how I would explain this."

"Thanks for the concern."

Bogan smiled again.

"Give me a call later and let me know how it went."

...

We arrived at the clinic an hour early and circled the area until we knew the lay of land. After a couple of passes, Christoff found a vantage point where he could park the surveillance van we had borrowed from the IRS.

We were in the area once known as Fort Apache. So many buildings in the community had been torched locals called the police station in the precinct the Little House on the Prairie. For a while, it was the only thing standing for blocks. Now it looked like any beaten up commercial district in any third world country.

After experimenting, I had taped the recorder to the back of my right calf and ran the cord up my trouser leg. I thumbed it on as I left the van and pressed the tape over as instructed.

When I walked into the clinic, I was struck by how dark and depressing the place was. There was little to suggest it was a medical establishment other than the patients – a couple of women, five children, and a number of young men - waiting to be called. I asked for Ricca and was told to join the waiting ones.

At a quarter after, Ricca came out. He was deeply tanned or unusually dark-skinned. His black hair was combed straight back and slicked down. Despite his best efforts, curls had broken out near the back of his head, extending down to his collar. He wore a dark two-toned suit, shiny enough to appear iridescent. His maroon shoes were patent leather.

All he needs, I thought, is a girlfriend with a beehive and five inch heels.

Ricca examined my card and put it in his pocket.

"I'm really rushed right now," he said. "I have an appointment downtown but I'll give you a quick tour."

He was curt and abrupt.

I tried to slow him down by asking questions, hopefully the kind of questions a prospective buyer might ask: How does this place operate? Why should I buy this business?

"Here's the way I run this place," Ricca said, "I make sure my administrator goes around and sees to it that every patient that walks in the door sees every doctor here. Whether they have a cold or a bunion – doesn't matter. You can get on the front or the back end of the merry-go-round. It's still the same ride. I like to keep everybody busy."

"How much do you pay them?"

Ricca looked at me with disdain.

"They pay me. I get $1,000 a month from the dentist and the pharmacy, $1,500 from the pediatrician, podiatrist and chiropractor. The internist is the gatekeeper. He pays $2,000 a month."

"That's it?" I tried to sound unimpressed. "That's your take?"

"Of course not. We split everything they bill 60-40."

"Who gets 60?"

"You do."

"Do they have a piece of the gross?"

Ricca shook his head. Disdain had become disgust.

"No. No. No. I don't know how you do things in Chicago, but here these guys are just puppets. They are just here. They are workers and you are the boss. They're all on oral agreements. If you don't like them, they are out."

His tone made me wondered how I could have asked such a dumb question. I tried another.

"What does it cost to run this place?"

"Eleven fifty a month."

"Plus utilities?"

"With utilities."

"What's the net?"

"Half a million. Minimum."

"Minimum?"

"Minimum. This is Medicaid land. Anything goes here. And nobody ever bothers me."

"Sounds like a good business."

"It is. I'll guarantee you it's a better return on your money than Wall Street. I'll show you my books if you are really interested."

"I'd like that," I said and meant it.

Ricca paused, looked at his watch, and looked away.

"Look, you've got me over a barrel," he said. "I'm really rushed right now. I have somebody waiting for me downtown at a quarter after. If I don't leave right now, I'll never make it. Let's get together later. I'll check you out and then we can talk - OK?"

I made a mental note to shore up his flimsy cover and took a chance. I told Ricca I had arrived by cab and asked if I could hitch a ride downtown.

"Maybe we can talk along the way," I said.

"Great," Ricca said. "That's the best idea yet. Take a ride with me."

I followed him out the back door to his car,

wondering if Christoff could see us leave. The German shepherd was curled up and waiting on the front seat. He came to attention when we approached and turned toward me, watching my every move. On command, he backed away.

"Don't worry," Ricca said. "He's friendly."

As I inched my way in and on to the seat, the dog took a position between my legs. His head was about four inches from my groin, close enough to the recorder to hear it hum. If he gets hungry, I thought, I'll do more than that. The thought was still with me when I saw the handgun. It was plainly and maybe purposefully visible as Ricca slid in on the other side.

It looked like a Glock - 22 or 23. Safety features make most handguns hard to operate in a hurry. Glock makes it easy. If your finger is on the trigger, the safety is off - which is probably why it is the weapon of choice for law enforcement agencies around the world. It's the kind of gun you carry if you never know when you may have to use it.

Ricca eased the car into traffic, checked his rear view mirror twice, and headed toward the Concourse.

"If business is so good," I said, "why are you getting out?"

"What makes you think I'm getting out? I'm just thinking of selling this place. If I get my price, I'll do it. If not, I won't. I don't have to sell."

"Sounds like you've done well."

"I've done very well. I have interests from here to Miami and all the way to the west coast."

The further we got from the clinic the more relaxed he seemed to become.

"This is the wild west out here," he said, gesturing to the right. "Everything else burns down, but our office will never burn down."

He took his eyes off the road long enough to look directly at me, sending me a message or anticipating a reaction.

"You can make a nice buck in insurance though if you want to."

The tape around the recorder was beginning to cut off my circulation. My leg was starting to cramp. I shifted positions and the dog came to attention.

"Do your other clinics operate the same way?"

"Right. But in Miami it's all Medicare. There's no dental. It's radiology, you know, very heavy EKGs. Everybody's into internal medicine, cardiology."

"Any other differences?"

"Medicare is harder because you've got Americans - mostly Jews. In New York, you've got mostly Puerto Ricans. In California, you get Mexicans. It's a hell of a lot easier working with Mexicans and Puerto Ricans than Jews. Especially, old Jews - they can be very tough."

"What's the volume in Miami?"

"Three quarters of a million. If you're interested, maybe we can work out a package deal."

I said I was and watched Ricca warm to his task, like a fisherman trying to set the hook.

"If you've got the manpower there is no limit to what you can do. The government is printing money and practically giving it away. All it takes is a small initial investment. You may also want to get some union business."

"How does that work?"

"You talk to Tony Peters. He is the head of the local. I'll introduce you. You give him a few bucks and he puts you on a panel. That's all there is to it."

"What's he going to want?"

"Can't say. You've got to cut your own deal. For all I know, you could have a recorder on you."

I laughed and fought the impulse to check for protrusions.

"I take it he's not going to dent the bankroll."

"Not if your bankroll is as big as you say it is."

"Anything else I should know?"

"Yes, but I've got to be careful. A guy like you approached me a few years back. It's a funny thing. He was from Chicago too. I had a very nice deal for him. Unfortunately, something happened and the guy disappeared. Never saw him again."

Ricca brought the car to a full stop. We were in a parking garage across the street from the New York Hilton.

"Anything goes here," he said. "If you want to do something, you can do anything. It's an unlimited situation."

"Sounds like a blank check."

"It is. A blank check for as much money as you want to make."

I had a wild thought. It would be fun to bring Colgate or Mancini into the mix. Maybe, Mancini would be best. Colgate was too recognizable.

"Would you be willing to help me sell this to my directors?"

"If you're really interested," Ricca said, "but I've got to know who you are first. I'm going to make a couple of calls. Let's talk next week. If you are on the level, we'll sit down and make a deal. I'll make you an offer you can't refuse."

Was he sending a message or trying to be funny? I wasn't sure.

I left the garage with the parking attendant eyeing the dog and trying to summon up enough courage to move the car. Ricca walked toward the Hilton. I walked the other way.

When I felt safe, I called Christoff and told him where I was. He was still waiting in the Bronx and didn't seem all that concerned. Then I called Bogan and told him what I had.

"You're beautiful," Bogan said. "Drop the tape off and we'll get on it."

I walked the rest of the way back to the Marriott, mulling it over. By the time I arrived, my leg had cramped so badly I had to cut the recorder free with a pocketknife.

Chapter Eighteen

Dee surprised me in New York, of course. I say "of course" because she said she would and I didn't believe her.

Christoff got her call and was cagey. The suite was registered in his name. He didn't know why anyone would be asking for anyone else. He asked if there was a message. She declined. Fifteen minutes later, she called again.

This time I picked up. She was down the hall, flushed and breathless like in the movies. An adventure. When could I come down, she wondered. When could we be alone?

Again with the games. Again I wondered why.

In many ways, we were much alike. We were both independent. We were both largely self-sufficient. We both lived by they own standards. The difference, I thought, was there - in those standards. Sometimes I wondered if there was anything she would not do.

She lied – to me and who knew how many others. She had been unfaithful – God knows how many times. She would not hesitate to take whatever she wanted. In a rare moment of candor, she had confessed she ripped off Macys for more than $5,000 a year as a teen. She said she was not proud of it, but it came with no apparent regret either.

She was very cool, very calm, thoughtful, and organized. She had presence, nerve, and a poker face – enough to have brazened her way out of several arrests, once after being caught putting a thousand dollar dress in a garment bag, with a straight face and an indignant lie.

She talked of poverty and excess growing up, alternating between her father's lavish lifestyle and her mother's meager means. She lived with her mother after their divorce but clearly favored her father. She had a set of credit cards for boutiques in each of the major cities.

She traveled at will and, apparently, rarely alone. She talked at length about the men she had known – men, she said, that didn't matter - talked in a manner vaguely reminiscent of the locker-room, detached, uninvolved, clinical, and depressing. Yet, she could be warm and giving, curling up into you completely, like a trusting child.

I took her to the Top of the Sixes for a drink and tried to explain where I was. She said she heard what I said. She said she understood. Yet, she would not be denied. She would not believe I would not bed her.

I wore a black sport coat over a white turtleneck. When we returned to the Marriott, I kept my coat on and my hands off. She wore a lace bodysuit over a black silk mini and started undressing before the door was properly closed. I left her on the bed in her underwear in disbelief, left her feeling foolish, self-conscious and not a little embarrassed, kicking myself down the hall for playing the tin-plated knight.

I half expected I'd never see her again - the other expectation, that we would see each other once in a while in the halls of the Senate where we would pretend not to notice each other. Five minutes later, she was tapping on my door. She stood barefoot, looking small in the hall, dressed as I had seen her last, seemingly unconcerned for what anyone who saw her might say or think.

"Please come down," she said. "Can't we talk about it?…Even if I promise not to seduce you?"

A strange phrase, I thought.

"Forget it!" she said when I did not respond.

I watched her stomp down the hall, wanting to call after her, knowing there was no way to make her understand. You have to go with what you've got. I would not play the fool for her or any other. I would not make something I could not respect of myself.

Repeatedly, she had said, "You'll never get to smell the flowers if you spend too much time trying to untangle the roots." Take what's given was what she meant. Grab what you can get. A popular philosophy now more than ever that now more than ever I find hard to accept.

Less than twenty minutes later, there was another

phone call. She did not understand. Why not? Come down. It seemed such a shame to waste the opportunity to be together. I didn't know how to answer her, what to say I hadn't already said. I only knew there was no way I could walk out of there again.

"I'll call you in the morning," I said.

"Don't," she said, resigned for the moment. "Just come by whenever you're up. I'll wait for you in bed."

I had a vision of what that promised. An hour later as I tried to find sleep, I heard footsteps. A note was slipped under my door.

"It's been so long," she wrote. "I sometimes wonder if you are real. I can't help feeling I'm writing a letter to Santa Claus – like a child. You put your heart and soul and desires in it and send it out into the unknown. Who knows who ever reads it? Where in the world is the North Pole anyway? We used to be able to talk. We used to laugh – we laughed so much when we were together. Perhaps there will be times when neither of us will laugh, but I beg you – Please, let me see you."

She had penned in "The Lesson of the Moth," by Don Marquis. From memory, perhaps. Some of the words were missing. It's me, she said. "We get bored with the routine and crave beauty and excitement. Fire is beautiful and yet we know if we get too close it will kill us."

In the morning, I deliberately slept late, staying in bed beyond necessity.

"Who is it?" she asked, when I finally knocked on her door.

Who would it be - Santa Claus?

She let me in real or feigned confusion, apologizing for her near nakedness as she headed for the bathroom. I couldn't help noticing she took her time. There was a breakfast tray on the bureau, a laptop and Blackberry on the bed.

In a moment, she came back with a bra added to the panties she'd been wearing. "Dressed now," she said. A nightgown was added as I watched. She sat on the bed, legs crossed, leaning back, eyes inviting my eyes.

"What kept you?" she said.

I sat in the single chair by the dresser. Within moments, she was in my lap, delighting in my manifest response to her nearness and warmth and near nakedness. I hid behind my clothes and humor until she wearied and had weighed my resolve – firmer than I'd have thought.

I waited while she dressed - openly in front of me - and thought how strange it was. When she undressed, she focused entirely on me, monitoring my reactions, every movement calculated and deliberate. When she dressed, it was as though I wasn't even there.

I took her to the Carnegie Deli for lunch for old time's sake, remembering a time when I believed everything she said, thinking how hard it was now to believe anything she said.

"I think I'm just as glad now you did what you did," she said two hours later when we boarded the train heading south. "Now I'll have something to look forward to."

Chapter Nineteen

If you work The Hill long enough, the telephone can begin to resemble an instrument of torture. The phone rings constantly. At its best, it is suffocatingly harmless, like walking through a swarm of gnats. At its worst, it's like swimming through a pool of piranhas. There are times when it seems everyone wants a piece of your hide.

The hearing announcement and the witness list had been released at the end of the day Friday, meeting Senate rules but effectively diminishing response time by two days. It was a simple release – date, time, and topic - as few specifics as possible. It largely escaped notice until Monday morning. Now, the lobbyists were weighing in with a vengeance.

All of the Committee's lines were lit. As soon as one was answered, another call came in. A man named Prendergast called repeatedly from New York: Could he testify? Could he have some input? Would the Chairman agree to see him? It sounded like he was trying to earn his retainer. The morning was filled with people just like him. We told them all the same thing. The witness list was set. The Committee would keep their interest in mind.

The hardest people to say no to are constituents. There are always "friends" of the Senator and groups from home you don't want to offend. One of them was a consortium of Pennsylvania health facilities represented by a barracuda in a blue suit. Sent down by Colgate's office, he paraded uninvited into OSI's cubicle and demanded to be heard. I told him what I had told Kat earlier. Before he pushed too hard, he would be wise to consider how closely he wanted to associate his clients with the targets of this investigation. The barracuda took the hint. After thinking it through, he decided he would wait and submit a statement for the record.

Former Senator Lawson, the "L" in L.A., Inc., didn't bother with staff. He called Colgate directly. He told Mary Jane, Colgate's Chief of Staff, that he knew Dershowitz to be an outstanding citizen. There had to be a misunderstanding. He was sure it could be cleared up if Colgate would meet personally with his client.

At 11:00 AM - 9:00 AM Chicago time - Evan Jones, head of the Illinois Department of Public Aid, called. Press reports that his former employee would testify had angered him. Christoff took the call. Jones expressed his displeasure forcibly, using small words. Christoff was unimpressed. He had grown up in Brooklyn in a neighborhood where obscenity seasoned every conversation. He listened quietly, which only seemed to provoke Jones more. Jeffers was unstable, Jones said. He was a kook. He was on a witch-hunt. He couldn't believe OSI would take his testimony.

While Christoff was occupied, a page came in with a message from Colgate's office. She was seventeen, trying to look twenty-one. Dick remembered seeing her at Pam's party, a young face in the small crowd enjoying the entertainment in the carriage house. She wore blue slacks and a white shirt, the required uniform for Senate pages on duty. Off duty, she had looked like a tart in training, dressed in the kind of outfit you often see on the young ones these days, the kind of thing that makes you wonder if she has a mother until you see the mother and then you want to do them both. The thought raised Dick's blood pressure. He wondered if Brandi would go for that. She was green but eager. Based on last weekend, he thought she would probably go along with anything he asked. The page said her name was Patty. Perfect, Broadbent thought – Patty cake.

The envelope she handed him had Alexander's name on it but it wasn't sealed. The note said the Governor of Pennsylvania had called Colgate to express his concern. He said the Party had enough on its hands with the scandal in the liquor commission. They didn't need any more problems at the moment.

Scrawled along the bottom of the message was a cryptic note from Mary Jane.

"Nick, this is starting to get hot," she said. "I sure hope you can put your money where our mouth is."

The phone calls continued through the morning. Dick was glad to escape at half past twelve. Alexander was waiting in the Plastic Place. He wore a dark blue blazer over a white T. He looked cool and comfortable.

"How's it going?"

"I think we have their attention," Dick said with a smile, a remembrance of an early conversation.

"What are we going to do," he asked, a naïve question from an outsider to the insider who had just been named is his boss. He couldn't see how a couple of people could force change in such a change resistant environment. It would be like pissing on a forest fire.

"First you get a two-by-four," Alexander said, "then you soak it in creosote so that it won't bend, break, or splinter. And then you hit them over the head with it until you have their attention."

When Dick smiled, he looked like a younger version of Wilfred Brinley, forty pounds lighter with lenses thick enough to magnify his eyes to bug size. Dick had his failings to be sure. He was easily distracted and would chase anything in a skirt. He could be brash and insensitive, but for all his faults he had one saving grace. He desperately wanted to be one of the good guys - even if he sometimes went about it with the clumsy enthusiasm of a white Lab.

When Christoff and Fine joined us we walked through what needed to be done by morning. Skinner, Jones, and Brunner were veterans. Their testimony needed to be reviewed but they would need little guidance. Dershowitz would respond to allegations. I asked Fine to prepare questions for the Committee to ask Jones and Skinner. Christoff took Brunner and Dershowitz.

Jeffers and Hester were the biggest challenge.

Testifying before Congress was a new experience for them. They would need direction. I spent the rest of the afternoon walking them through their testimony. Like most people unaccustomed to appearing on The Hill, they tried to say too much and talked too long. I told them their oral statements had to be short and to the point but they resisted any effort to chop up the words they had so carefully crafted until I reminded them where they were and asked them to think about their audience.

"You are being naïve if you think a half a dozen Senators are going to sit through an hour of testimony," I said and added a bit of theatrics. "Calculate what you think a Senator's time is worth and multiply it by 6 to 12, the number likely to be present, add staff expense and support costs and then take another look at what you have written. See if the third paragraph on the 15th page is worth anywhere near what it will cost to listen to it."

Jeffers' testimony was so strong I had to ask him if he had thought through the consequences. Jeffers said he did. He had tried going through channels only to be ignored. Something had to be done. Still, you don't accuse a sitting Governor of corruption without inviting a discussion – particularly if the Governor is from Illinois and up for re-election. Jeffers finally got the message and went through the statement again. He made a few changes but not enough to alter the substance of his remarks. I hoped he could withstand the firestorm I knew it would start.

Chapter Twenty

At five, Colgate's office called. They said the Chairman would be ready to go at six. A half hour later, I left to pick up my car. At five to six, I pulled into the circular drive on the east side of the Russell building and waited for my boss to arrive.

Colgate looked like he came from central casting - tall, dark, and handsome, with a boyish smile. He was the sole heir to the Colgate Company, carrying the name of the grandparent who started it all – J. Carlson Colgate. He was talented enough to do just about anything he cared to do and rich enough to do nothing at all.

Some said he chose to run for office because he had an ego the size of Kansas; some said he had a deep desire to serve. While there was probably some truth in both perceptions, I thought the principal attraction was elsewhere. Colgate had the double Y chromosome. He was the most aggressive animal I had ever seen. He loved competition. Whatever he did, he wanted to play the best and he expected to win. My job was to make sure he was armed and prepared for battle.

After Colgate stowed his briefcase in the backseat. I handed him the hearing package. Colgate read while I drove. He glanced at the witness list first, read the press release carefully, and then began digesting the briefing memo, his eyes flying over the pages:

Hearing Background:

The Federal health programs enacted in the mid-60s were the result of five decades of debate. Though the initial response of the medical community to a national health program was favorable, the AMA soon retrenched, stating unqualified opposition to any form of health insurance controlled or regulated in any way by the state or federal government.

The balance turned during the presidential election of 1960. Kennedy made health insurance a principal part of his campaign. Nixon responded in kind but both made a critical compromise to ease the opposition. They backed away from a comprehensive national health program to endorse health insurance programs offering partial coverage with eligibility restricted by age and income.

In the five years that remained before the enactment of Medicare and Medicaid further compromises were made. All of them have come back to haunt us.

One of the fundamental disagreements was whether the state or federal government should run the new program. Either option would have been preferable in the long run to the solution Wilbur Mills devised that essentially divided authority and responsibility.

The second compromise was even more costly. The purpose of Medicare and Medicaid was said to be to make "mainstream medicine" available to those who couldn't afford to pay for it themselves. To accomplish this, doctors were assured they would be paid their "customary fee", whatever that was or whatever they wanted it to be. In either case, payment was made virtually without review.

To perfect the disaster, the Feds agreed to insulate the medical community from the disgrace of receiving money directly from the government. The possibility of contamination was avoided by passing the public's money through intermediaries created and controlled by hospitals and physicians. In short, organized medicine asked for and received a blank check as a condition for their participation.

It should not have been a surprise that within a year of the program's initiation, the government had to increase Medicare taxes by 25 percent in order to meet the unexpectedly high costs of the program. Within five years, there was evidence that Medicare and Medicaid were in serious difficulty. Costs were running at about twice their predicted levels.

Key Statistics:

- *When Medicare and Medicaid were created, health care expenditures accounted for less than 10 percent of our gross national product.*
- *Health care expenditures now approach 25 percent of GNP.*
- *According to the Congressional Budget Office, health expenditures will double by mid-century.*
- *Much of this is waste. OMB reports improper billing costs for Medicare now exceed $27 million per day - about $11 billion annually*

- *Medicaid is even worse. OSI's investigations indicate there is reason to think that as much as half of the money we spend for Medicaid is being stolen or wasted.*

The bottom line as one witness will testify is that "Medicare and Medicaid are raining money. It's only a question of who has the biggest bucket." The worst thing that has happened to the worst offenders is that they have been asked to pay back some of the money they have stolen.

The Committee's response:

These problems are well known and well documented. Literally, hundreds of hearings have been held by OSI and other committees without significant improvement. Changes made have been incremental and by and large ineffective, at best redirecting abusers to more fertile ground. Investigators call it the waterbed principle - push down here and they pop up there.

What is needed is a comprehensive and focused effort to address systemic problems, "shock" the system into alignment, and fix oversight with one agency, an Inspector General who can be held accountable. The special attorney general for Medicare and Medicaid fraud in New York offers a model.

Historically, most significant reform legislation has passed in the last 6 weeks of a session before the opposition can mount a fatal challenge. Accordingly, OSI must move swiftly and decisively.

Witnesses:

<u>*Felix Brunner, GAO*</u>. *Four months ago, OSI asked GAO to examine financial transactions at targeted health care facilities in New York. These facilities are part of a chain (Total Health Care) controlled largely by Rabbi Daniel Dershowitz and his family. Total Health Care owns and operates hospitals, nursing homes, urgent care facilities, and community clinics with a concentration in the northeast. A number of clinics associated with Total Health Care were the subject of investigation by OSI as part of our inquiry into Medicaid Mills. Star Services subsequently purchased Total Health Care last year but the management team remains in place.*

The GAO will testify Total Health Care's books are not in conformity with accepted accounting principles and are often illegible. There are unidentified entries, questionable accounts, loans and exchanges between related parties, and irreconcilable differences. The government has improperly been billed for liquor and wine; contributions to unions, religious and political organizations; and personal expenses in excess of a half a million dollars. Some two and half million dollars is missing from Total Health Care's accounts. Another $2.2 million has been paid to Dershowitz, his relatives, and relatives of his associates for unspecified services. In addition, the value of each facility has been inflated at taxpayer expense by "churning" – repeated sales to related parties. One facility in the Bronx has been sold 34 times since 1979, increasing its value and the cost to the taxpayer from $250,000 to $5.7 million.

*Sam Skinner, US Attorney, Chicago, IL. Mr. Skinner
has recently indicted 16 people for defrauding
Medicaid, racketeering and mail fraud. As part of his
indictment, Skinner asked for the confiscation of all
the assets of 30 related clinics and pharmacies. The
owner of these clinics is Eugene Feinstein, one of
those indicted. He is the son of Alan Feinstein, one of
the founders of National Medical Enterprises, the
Chicago focus of OSI's Mills investigation.*

*Charles Hester, a physician practicing at one of the
clinics named in Skinner's indictment, is cooperating
with the authorities. He will testify his billings were
kited and falsified by the clinic in collusion with Star
Financial Management, a factoring firm and a
subsidiary of Star Services.*

*George Jeffers, former Section Chief, Bureau of
Quality Control, Illinois Department of Public Aid.
Jeffers will reinforce Skinner and Hester and place
their testimony in context. He will testify fraud is
rampant in Illinois, costing the taxpayer more than
$300 million a year. He will say the major reason
this waste continues is the direct interjection of
politics into the administration of the program.*

*Hugh H. Jones, Jr., Assistant Director of the FBI's
Criminal Investigation Unit. The FBI launched an
extensive investigation of criminal conduct in the
Medicare and Medicaid programs earlier this year.
While the investigation is still young, Jones is
prepared to say the Bureau has concluded corruption
has permeated virtually every area of Medicare and
Medicaid. The FBI opened twenty-two cases in the
first three months of operation.*

Rabbi Daniel Dershowitz. Rabbi Dershowitz left the country when OSI initiated this investigation for "an extended vacation in the Holy Land". He returned last month after other corporate officers, included two family members, were deposed. He has said he will deny all charges. Since Medicare and Medicaid were enacted, Dershowitz' personal fortunate has increased from $30,000 to over $80 million.

Carlson put the documents back in the envelope and said nothing while he processed the information. After a moment, he looked up and smiled.

"This is going to be fun. What's the push back?"

"So far, minimal. We have been flying low. I blocked out a tentative hearing schedule when I arrived under the same lead the Committee used last year: The Future of Health Care Policy. I hoped this would encourage the belief we were continuing along established lines. We have let the previous dates slip with no explanation, suggesting we haven't been able to get our act together. That changed Friday. After tomorrow, the bounce will be intense."

Most members would have been intimidated at the prospect. Colgate relished it.

"Member issues?"

"None that we can identify. FEC and Senate records show industry contributions to half the Committee but they come from groups that like to spread it around. That is also likely change tomorrow. Hopefully, fallout from the hearing will be heavy enough to

170

persuade members this isn't something they want to defend going into an election.

"On the other hand, political pressure is already mounting. It's going to get worse, but Paulson and Mancini are with you. Paulson because he asked for the audit Welch's people squelched; Mancini because he was personally involved in Mills and wants to see it through. Plus, we have given him an Arizona angle to ride. We have not spoken with any other members directly but staff response indicates strong interest and a good turnout."

"When does the legislation drop?"

"We are ready when you are. I was going to suggest tomorrow after the hearing but if we waited a day or two it wouldn't hurt and might provide a hook for a follow up story. Either way, a statement has been prepared for you. There are two pieces: one changes the false claims statutes to allow private parties to sue on behalf of the government and keep 25 percent of whatever they recover. The second authorizes state and federal agencies to contract with private firms to audit high profile targets on a percentage of recovery basis."

"So what we are saying with the legislation is that because the government is unable or unwilling to do its job and protect the public's interests we have to privatize the effort and provide an incentive for action."

"In a nutshell, yes. That's what the record shows and these hearing demonstrate. The third piece, the creation of an Inspector General for Medicare and Medicaid, is hiding on the House side. Congressman Dennison introduced it in June as part of his reform package. He has been minimally involved in health since he took over Rules so no one has paid much attention to it. Hopefully, that we will continue.

"If and when we get traction, they are set to pull our piece out of the package and attach it to whatever vehicle is viable. Rinehart is handling it. You may remember him. He served as a fellow with Oversight and Investigations a few years back. He is now on Dennison's personal staff."

NBC was waiting when we arrived at Colgate's townhouse in Georgetown. They were set up in the library. Sarah Patterson was the correspondent. Caroline Colgate, the Senator's elegant wife, was entertaining Patterson. She gave Colgate a hug while I greeted Sarah and then left.

Sarah asked her crew if they were ready and got a nod. While they did a white balance, wired Colgate, and got their levels, she said, "Senator, as you know, we are running a piece tonight about your hearing tomorrow. We just want to get a couple of comments to use as a lead."

I checked messages while they moved Colgate into position. They set him up in an armchair near his desk. They had taken the pictures of his wife and children from his desk and placed them on either side of the bookcase behind him.

"When Medicare and Medicaid were enacted the great fear was we might be moving toward socialized medicine," I heard Colgate say. "The reality is we haven't so much socialized medicine as industrialized it. The entire focus of our health care system has shifted from social, ethical and moral considerations to those of business: income, expense and profit. As one of our witnesses will testify tomorrow, Medicare and Medicaid are raining money. It's falling from the sky – free for the taking. The only question is who has the largest bucket."

A perfect fifteen-second sound bite. It's something you can't teach. I didn't have to be told the last three sentences would introduce Sarah's piece that evening.

Patterson and Colgate chatted while the camera crew broke down what they had spent the last forty-five minutes putting up. He had that compelling personal chemistry every good politician needs. She was drawn to him, hanging on every word even though nothing of real consequence was being said.

A flood of messages popped up on my cell as it came alive - a sure sign things were heating up. Two were from Dee. One was sent at 4:15 PM; the other was at the top of my inbox and must have just arrived.

The first said simply: What will make you happy? The second conveyed a nude image discreetly photographed to reveal assets while concealing identity.

Chapter Twenty-One

On the 23rd of September, the line started forming at the Senate Caucus Room three hours before the hearing was scheduled to begin. By the time I arrived to check the set, lobbyists and the placeholders hired by lobbyists were cued up, waiting to get in.

The Caucus Room is the Senate's most historic hall. On April 22, 1912, a week after the Titanic went down, a special Senate subcommittee opened the first investigation held there. Officials of the White Star Line, a British firm, were called to testify and explain the loss of 1,500 American lives.

Twelve years later, Senator Thomas J. Walsh conducted hearings in the Caucus Room on what came to be known as the Teapot Dome Scandal. Secretary of the Interior Albert Fall was found to have secretly leased naval oil reserves, receiving over $300,000 in cash and securities. The hearings discredited the Harding administration and sent a cabinet officer to prison for the first time in American history.

The Caucus Room was the site for the hearings examining Wall Street practices leading to the Depression and responsibility for Pearl Harbor at the beginning of WWII. Subsequently, it hosted the Army-McCarthy hearings; the McClellan investigations; Watergate; and Iran-Contra.

I had used the Caucus Room for every significant inquiry I led. I liked the tradition and grandeur of the place. Any other hearing room could be anywhere. This was unmistakably the United States Senate.

When I left to get the Chairman, the line waiting to get in stretched to the end of the corridor. Kat was about halfway back, wearing a black pantsuit and a grey turtleneck. Both fit her well, I noticed, as did the man behind her, a thirtyish yuppie with blonde hair. He was trying hard to get her attention. She appeared equally determined to ignore him.

When I returned with Colgate at a quarter to nine, the placeholders had been replaced by the people who hired them. Those far enough back to fear they might be closed out were working the line like scalpers at a sporting event. I wondered what the going rate was. Kat would know. I made a mental note to ask her when I got a chance.

Like moths, members of Congress are drawn to the light. More than a couple at a hearing is a sure sign cameras are present. This morning, we had a full house. Every member of the Committee was present. They and their staff filled a third of the room. The press filled another third. There were three dozen cameras - networks, independents, and affiliates - set up to the Chairman's right parallel to six of the twelve Corinthian columns along the wall that flanks the three French windows. C-SPAN had one camera on that side and another at the back of the room. Radio and print correspondents were stationed at a table that started where the cameras ended and ran the length of the room to the wall.

When I started out on The Hill, I was taught to recognize members of Congress by their name, party, and state. That was much too easy now. I played the insiders variation, identifying them by their dominant interest. It had become more than a game for me. It was a necessity.

Your best friend on one issue was likely to be your worst enemy on another. I had learned that the hard way. I routinely began every investigation by looking for ties to the Committee. If there was one, and more often than not there was, my first task was to find a way to neutralize it. The sad reality is that everyone on The Hill is in someone's pocket. Some are in more pockets than lint.

The members were seated by party and seniority - Democrats to the Chairman's left, Republicans to right. First was Don Hubbard, the farmer's friend; then Ernest Burdett, the banker's boy; Tom Claggett, known as the Senator from Lockheed; and Joe Bennett, who answered a magazine's survey a few years back by saying the most important political influence in his life was his church. Where half the Senate complained their biggest problem was keeping current, he bragged he hadn't read a book in years and said his favorite painter was anyone who used Bennett paint.

Bennett was talking with Jack Buchanan, a professional non-professional whose chief vocalized virtue was his amateur standing among pros. He ran for office as an outsider and tried to maintain that posture after he was elected. It was rather like the hooker who swears this was her first time and she wouldn't be doing it at all if you weren't so special. Buchanan was on his third term.

The last two Republicans were Ray Mancini and John Talbot, the marine merchant's man. Contributions from maritime interests constituted nearly seventy percent of Talbot's campaign fund. Mancini, the junior Senator from Arizona, was up for his second term. We connected when Mancini learned I had family in Phoenix. He became personally involved as a result, using his experience with Oversight and Investigations to leverage his position on Budget. He is one of the party's rising stars.

Ethan Paulson, the boy wonder, was to Colgate's left. Paulson had worked his way up from the stockroom to become CEO of a Fortune 500 company by the time he was thirty. He ran for the Senate as soon as he was eligible at the age of thirty-six. Then came Lou Roche, the pharmaceutical industry's friend and Jonathan "Drill Baby" Foster, the oil industries angel.

Foster was seated next to Vince Hartlett. Hartlett had the distinction of being voted least ethical Member of Congress three years running. In a world looking for people to use, Hartlett is a volunteer. He seems to get reelected largely on the electorate's belief that there was no point in ruining a new man.

Paul "The Face" Lauer, Jack Wayson, and Jay Sadowski completed the set. Lauer, the lawyer's advocate, is a humble one who won't go to the john without sending an advance man and spends $250 for a haircut. Wayson, a self-made man, is best known for hiring all his secretaries personally. On more than one occasion, his questionable screening process has left candidates rushing from his office in tears. Sadowski, a former longshoreman, has the union label stamped on every move he makes.

The hearing was convened precisely at 9:00 AM. In the interest of time, Colgate asked the members to submit their statements for the record, sparing the press and the public the agony of watching a parade of egos. The only ones disappointed were staffers deprived of the pleasure of hearing someone read their words into the record.

"First we will hear from a distinguished panel," the Chairman said, "representatives of the FBI and the General Accountability Office joined by the US Attorney, Northern District, Illinois."

Felix Brunner had the lead. He was coming up on 20 years with the GAO. What was left of his hair was crew cut, a style he has sported as long as I have known him and, knowing him, probably as long as he has had hair to cut. After Brunner had summarized the GAO's findings and submitted their report for the record, Colgate held up one of Dershowitz' expense sheets.

"Have you seen this before, Mr. Brunner?" he asked.

"Yes, sir."

"Where?"

"We discovered it during the course of our audit."

"Can you explain this notation: POA 2x P.W. $2,000."

Brunner smiled.

"Yes, sir. Piece of ass. Two times. And the amount."

"Who or what is P.W.?"

"Those are the initials of a state contract officer."

"Was this expense passed on to the government?"

"Yes, sir."

"Nobody caught it or questioned it?"

"No, sir. Not until we did."

Skinner and Jones followed, reading their testimony. When they concluded, Colgate asked them both to summarize their findings, going for the statement he knew the press wanted – what's this about in 30 seconds or less.

Skinner was one of the youngest US Attorneys in the system. Jones was nearing retirement, one of a half dozen agents allowed to represent the Bureau on The Hill.

"I believe we are witnessing the greatest rip-off in history," Skinner said. "Literally millions in hard-earned, sorely needed tax dollars have been squandered, wasted, and stolen from federally funded health care programs."

"I would have to agree," Jones said. "I have never seen anything like it in my twenty years with the Bureau."

"Mr. Skinner, can you quantify the amount of waste?"

"A FAW factor – that's fraud, waste, and abuse - of twenty-five percent would be a conservative."

"Twenty-five percent of total expenditures?"

"Yes, Sir."

"Mr. Jones, Oversight and Investigations has been looking for one Joseph Cannistracci in conjunction with this hearing. He seems to have disappeared. Can you shed any light on this matter?"

"Mr. Chairman, the gentleman in question has been a subject of interest to the FBI for some time. He has a history of arrests that include extortion, theft, and other white-collar crimes. Unfortunately, I can't tell you where he is at this moment. Rumor has it he is underground and unavailable for comment."

One by one, the members took their turn questioning the witnesses, covering and recovering the same ground, hoping to find the magic sound bite that would make the evening news or – failing that – be picked up for play by their hometown affiliate.

When the panel was dismissed, Daniel Dershowitz was called to the stand. I had considered saving him for last, but that would risk pushing his appearance dangerously close to the cut line for early press. He entered surrounded by a phalanx of black-robed, bearded aides. They formed a moving wedge with Dershowitz at the center, convoying him to the witness table and shielding him from the press.

Dershowitz had begun his career as a chaplain in a nursing home on the East side. He was now sixty-three and a multi-millionaire. Some said he was a fine gentleman, others called him a merchant of misery who preyed on the old, the sick, and the dying. All of his facilities had been cited for providing substandard care at one point or another - many, repeatedly.

I couldn't help thinking how different this must feel for Dershowitz than his last appearance before Congress. At that time, some six years ago, he had been given the rare privilege of opening a session of the U.S. House of Representatives with a prayer. The fact that his father had just been being arrested in France for trying to smuggle heroin into the United States, concealing the drugs in compartments cut out of prayer books, was glossed over. The elder

Dershowitz said it was merely sand from the Holy Land. He was convicted, sentenced to two years in prison, and then extradited to the United States where he joined his son's business.

In the movies, the part of Dershowitz would have gone to Sidney Greenstreet. He was as round man - a round face on a round body. There was a thin wisp of beard on his lower lip. A yarmulke fit neatly over the bald spot on the back of his head.

"Only God in heaven knows that I am not guilty," he told Fox before the hearing began. He said he had come to Washington to "cleanse his reputation."

Dershowitz ignored the cameras and surveyed the Committee as if taking note of who was there. As his escorts pulled back, Christoff approached the dais and handed me a well-worn copy of the Book of Common Prayer.

"If he takes the oath, let him take it on that," Christoff said. "If he takes it on a Bible, it doesn't mean a thing."

I passed the Book on to the clerk and watched as the Little Byrd ceremoniously placed it on the witness table. She hated me and hated what we were doing, but, conscious the cameras were on her, relished the moment.

Dershowitz looked at the Book as it was placed before him and paused. He took the oath in a voice that was barely audible and sat down deflated. The bravado he had displayed earlier had disappeared. He said he had decided to assert his Fifth Amendment rights on the advice of counsel. Curiously, his lawyers were nowhere in sight.

When Dershowitz left the hall, he took most of the cameras with him. Most the Committee followed, leaving staffers to track events and pull them back if there was a need or an opportunity. Only Colgate, Paulson and Mancini remained to hear Hester and Jeffers.

Hester testified first, describing his personal experience. After all our preparation, Jeffers decided to simply submit his statement for the record.

"As a boy," he said, speaking from the heart, "I remember watching the Watergate hearings held in this very room. It's humbling to be here. I wish it were under better circumstances. Watergate was about power. This is about money. The common thread is corruption."

"According to the Department's records, there are only eleven factoring firms in Illinois. My computer analysis has found more than thirty. Most of the factors operating below the radar are controlled by a holding company called Star Services.

"These factoring firms are paid more and paid more promptly. They also submit an extraordinary number of bills marked with an override code designed to bypass all computer checks and validations. These bills are paid immediately and without question. One of these factors inflated half of the 4,000 invoices they presented for payment. They collected $15 million in two years without a single denial."

"Based on your review, can you estimate the magnitude of this problem?" Colgate asked.

Jeffers was quick with his response. Maybe our preparation was wasted after all.

He said, "Fraud is rampant in Illinois, Senator. It's costing the taxpayer more than $300 million a year and the State is doing nothing about it."

"Why?"

The question was obvious, the answer unexpected. Even with all our preparation, none of us thought Jeffers would go directly after the Governor.

"The most significant reason," he said, "is the interjection of politics into administrative process. There is no secret most of the people perpetrating these abuses are connected to the Governor."

Governor William Welch was on the phone before the sound died in the room. He wanted Colgate.

Chapter Twenty-Two

Just before the hearing began, Governor Welch had received a "courtesy call" from Senator Paulson. Paulson told the Governor he felt obligated to brief him on the nature of the hearing. Welch had taken the hint and was watching on C-SPAN.

It was deftly done. Welch had been set up. He was livid.

As I left to take the Governor's call in the back of the room, I heard Paulson say, "I have just been handed a note by staff indicating that the Governor has called..."

The cameras ate it up. Later, a close reading of the transcript would show Paulson doing more damage than Jeffers. All Jeffers had to say was, "No, Senator; yes, Senator; so it would seem, Senator." The conclusions and characterizations were all Paulson.

Allison's eyes were wide, her face pale as she handed me the phone. She said the Governor was shouting, stating the obvious. He could be heard ten feet away.

"What the f--- is going on down there?" he said. "What are you trying to do to me? I want this hearing stopped. You can't let that nut testify. He is making wild accusations that are not true."

A few months before, Jeffers had been a member of Welch's administration responsible for supervising

200 employees. A computer whiz, he was among those appointed by the man who was now calling him a nut to what he then called a blue ribbon panel charged with cleaning up the state's Medicaid mess.

"The Medicaid Task Force was a sham," I heard Jeffers say.

"What do you mean?" Paulson asked.

"It was a public relations stunt. The Governor created the task force to blunt the impact of the GAO audit you requested. The State spent a million dollars over six months on salaries. They hired a Director, 15 investigators from the Department of Law Enforcement, 11 agents from the Illinois Bureau of Investigation, 9 state policemen, a dozen auditors from the Illinois Department of Revenue, and two dozen others employed by Department of Health. Their only accomplishment was a 36-page report. And that was inaccurate and purposely misleading."

"Stop this hearing," the Governor demanded.

"We can't do that," I said.

"You mean won't. How could you do this without checking with me first?"

I couldn't help wondering what he would have done if we had.

"We checked Jeffers allegations rather thoroughly, Governor," I said. "There's a lot of fraud in Illinois and not much evidence the State has done anything about it."

"That's not true," Welch said. "I've made it one of the priorities of my administration."

His voice got louder.

"Jeffers is under oath," I said as quietly as possible. "If he is not being truthful, he will be prosecuted."

"I can't believe I'm getting stuck with this!" Welch said and added a string of obscenities. He used them with the ease and confidence that suggested this manner of expression came naturally.

In contrast, Jeffers spoke flatly and without emotion.

"Millions of dollars are being ripped off by factors and corrupt vendors. They are engaged in wholesale fraud. The State of Illinois has not only covered it up; it has facilitated the process."

"You are being used," Welch said. "Why don't you look around and see who put Jeffers up to this?"

"A half dozen people vouched for his credibility, Governor, including his former supervisor, the Secretary of State, and the Comptroller. Are you saying they all lied to us?"

"They are all Democrats, aren't they?"

When I returned to the dais, the hearing was wrapping up. The three remaining members were searching for a way to characterize their reaction to what they had heard vividly enough to capture the interest of the five remaining cameras.

 "It's too bad it takes this kind of attention for us to look at the heart of the problem," Paulson said, "which is the way we reimburse for health care."

Mancini took a different tack.

"I know there are a lot of representatives from the medical community present," he said. "As you go forward and consider how you react to this let me tell you nothing could be less rewarding, less useful, than a parade of excuses, buck-passing, and the tired explanation that there are only a few isolated cases of abuses. I encourage you to look inward. This committee has provided the examining room. It is up to the physician to heal thyself."

Colgate was about to close the hearing when Lester Sweet arrived. He was flushed and clearly agitated. As soon as he sat down, Sweet, Government Ops' Ranking Member, asked for a point of personal privilege. In a voice trembling with emotion, he began taking OSI to the woodshed.

Sweet said he had just received a call from Governor Welch and was appalled by what he heard. He expressed his deep concern, saying it was inappropriate for the Committee to be playing "gotcha." He said the staff had gone too far.

Byrd appeared from the holding room and moved in

to take a position behind Sweet on the dais as he spoke. Byrd clearly enjoyed the moment. His response was predictable but I couldn't help wondering why Sweet, a Democrat, would come so forcibly to a Republican's defense. Not until later were we able to find the connection. Sweet and Welch were friends. They started out together, practicing law in J. C. Penny's corporate office.

Colgate listened quietly while Sweet spoke his piece. When he had unloaded, Colgate calmly refocused the hearing.

"I can understand my colleague's concern," he said. "We certainly want to be fair but we need to fair to everyone – including the taxpayer. What struck me as we listened to this testimony is how much we heard about money and how little we heard about the patient. I think we've got our work cut out for us."

As the Chairman adjourned the hearing and the audience stood to leave, Dee caught my eye and smiled. She was wearing red and hard to miss. She had come in when Dershowitz left and the crowd thinned out, taking a seat two rows from the back. Ironically, Kat was on the opposite end of the same row.

Dee's smile didn't register until I returned to the office, wondering where to eat and how to get away from the mob that followed us. I found a shopping bag waiting on my desk. It contained a bottle of wine, fresh rolls, cheese, fruit, fresh pastries, and a box of oversized cookies.

As she no doubt had intended, Dee was the topic of conversation for some time. Allison ate lightly. Brent asked pointedly why all the presents and what I did for her. Dick offered a few lewd suggestions. Fine focused on the quality of the wine. Christoff ate little and said nothing.

Chapter Twenty-Three

On the 24th of September, Dershowitz made the front page of the *New York Times*. The photograph was taken from behind. He was shown in silhouette taking the oath. Colgate was facing him, framed nicely between Dershowitz' head and outstretched arm.

The Chicago papers ran Jeffers page one. Dick stopped by Annie's newsstand on the way to work and picked up multiple copies. The *Tribune* headlined: "Governor Charged with $350 million Waste." A two-column story with Merriman's byline followed.

A quote from Joel Workman, director of a state bipartisan investigative committee, had been pulled out, boxed, and set in deep type five paragraphs down.

"For years we have known there was some kind of a cover up going on," Workman said. "Now that the heat is on, a lot of stuff is going to finally come out into the open."

A side bar reported Welch's denial. He was quoted as saying Jeffers was unbalanced and delusional, a disgruntled employee seeking retribution. He accused Colgate of grandstanding.

The Senate receives an average of 1,000,000 e-mails and 83,000 thousand pieces of mail a day. The flow follows the calendar and the consideration of controversial measures. When I arrived at the office, it looked like a disproportionate share had landed on my desk.

Christoff had pulled two items and placed them on my keyboard for immediate attention. The first was a note from Jay Constantine saying he wanted to talk about the reform package. The second was a CYA from Paulson. Paulson had been briefed on the front end and gotten more than his share of press at the hearing, but now he wanted to "lay out his concerns for the record."

I called Vernon, Paulson's legislative assistant, and took it to him.

"Yes, I've seen the letter," Vern said. There was no explanation, just a restatement parroting the letter. After listening to Sweet, the Senator had some concerns.

The message was clear. If things got rough, Colgate was on his own.

Tubin called at 10:00 AM.

"I just wanted to know if anything is going down," he said.

"Just what you've seen in the press," I replied, wondering why he was fishing.

After a moment, Les answered the question I hadn't asked.

———

"I got a copy of Paulson's letter to Colgate," he said.

How did that happen? I wondered. What looked like a CYA could well have been repayment of an IOU.

"I've started to do some consulting work for a couple of big firms," Tubin said. "If it works out, I'll be set."

I wished him luck. The fact that Les hadn't identified his new clients gave me pause. Was he appealing for help based on our friendship or giving me a heads up?

Broadbent handed me a copy of a letter from former Senator Lawson sent down from the Chairman's office. First Lawson had vouched for Dershowitz. Now he came to Welch's defense. It was a personal note - "Dear J.C" - one colleague to another.

"I've just discovered some information that might be of interest to you," Lawson said.

There were two enclosures. One was a letter from Star Services, carefully distancing itself from the operation of its subsidiary, Total Health Care; the other was an attempt to discredit Jeffers by someone identified as one of his former co-workers. The cover letter was signed "Larry." The last line was most interesting.

"If I may, I will call you on my return from New York," Lawson said.

Until he was defeated, Lawson chaired a

subcommittee of Appropriations. He was close enough to the Chairman, Lamar Lewis, to have exchanged staff and bold enough to tell it as it is. "All we do up here," he said, "is transfer money from one group of people to another." He had made a career of taking care of his friends.

John arrived at 10:45 AM. Again, he looked like he had partied long and hard. I left shortly thereafter, leaving the three of them to respond to the incoming calls.

The calls could roughly be divided into thirds - press looking for a follow-up, people who saw an opportunity, and irate callers looking to vent. I told Brent to feed the irate calls to John. That would sober him up. I directed the press to Christoff. Broadbent got the rest.

Constantine's office was on the fourth floor, a cramped cubicle on the front end of the Finance Committee's suite.

"I have found an alternative to Viagra," he said when I arrived. "It's called that girl. All I have to do is look at her and I get hard."

Jay ran the Health Subcommittee. That girl was his receptionist, Gail Sutton. He is short, dapper, and slight of build. She is tall and built to old school standards. If they stood toe to toe, his face would be buried in her cleavage – a fate at least one of them would enjoy.

Sutton had heard enough of Jay's off-color jokes and sexual innuendo to seem oblivious to them now. Or, perhaps, she tolerated them because she knew that beyond the burlesque image he projected was a professional whose uncompromising nature had saved the taxpayer billions. He was the gate through which those who would feed on the federal trough must pass.

"You've made a good start," Jay said, "but you know you will have to feed the fire. It's a lot easier to stop something up here than it is to pass anything. The opposition will pull out all the stops now."

"The next round is already lined up."

"Yeah, but this time you won't have the element of surprise."

I found myself wondering if I ever did. Just as I was about to voice my feelings, Sara Grafton popped in. Grafton, a lobbyist with a downtown firm, specialized in health issues and is known to be one of the more aggressive females on The Hill. She wore a tight knit top, showing more cleavage than anyone cared to see and a skirt pasted to her ample hips. It was a look she probably could have gotten away with when she started working The Hill. No one had bothered to tell her that time had passed.

"This looks interesting," she said. "Can I join you?"

"It's kind of crowded in here," Jay said without missing a beat. "The only room is under my desk. Given your size, it will be tight fit but from what I hear you'll love the view."

Grafton was still trying to decide how to respond when Gail caught up with her, easing between her and the door.

"I told you he was in a meeting," Sutton said.

There was enough heat in her delivery to back Grafton away.

"Sorry, Boss," Gail said when Grafton had gone. "She came nosing around right after Nick arrived. I told her you were busy. She must have waited until I went to the copy room."

Gail closed the door firmly behind her when she left.

"Rinehart is ready," I said. "He plans to pull the provision creating an Inspector General for Medicare and Medicaid out of the reform package and tack it on to the Omnibus Reconciliation Bill scheduled to move this week. Dennison will bring it up under a closed rule. With the heat the hearing has created, he feels there is a good chance they can blow it through the House."

"Good. When will Colgate's package drop?"

"Tomorrow."

"That should provide a distraction. Tell him I'll be ready."

The phones were still ringing when I returned to the office. I let the others handle it until Sarah called. She was looking for a follow-up. I told her the *Times* had the New York angle covered. Now there was blood in the water, they would be all over it. The breaking news was probably in Chicago. I suggested she follow Skinner's lead and see what she could find there.

A few minutes later, Kat called.

"Congratulations," she said. "And thanks for the advice. We'll probably submit a statement for the record when things settle down. Right now everyone is running around in circles trying to figure out how to respond to Mancini's challenge. We are getting a lot of flack from our members. As you probably know, all of Total Health Care's hospitals belong to the association. We are getting calls asking what we are going to do about it. We are also getting a lot of calls from people afraid they'll be next. I'm trying hard to be a good soldier but I can't work up much sympathy for them. They deserve whatever they get."

I pulled up my mail while we talked. There were over five hundred new messages. One of them was from Dee. As far as I could see, it was the only one unrelated to the hearing. I didn't bother looking at the rest.

"I went to the Kennedy Center last night," she said. "What a kick in the ass!"

She said she had port at intermission and it messed up her mind. She loved the opera but hated the guy she was with. He kept going on and on about the costumes and the scenery until she was ready to hit him over the head with her program.

Then, she spoke of love.

"It is extremely difficult for me to let go and give myself," she said. "I don't mean in a physical sense – that's different – sometimes more than I care to admit. But deep down sometimes I wonder if I've ever loved anyone, really lay-down-your-life love. I think not. I have not had to do too much sacrificing and it's probably a good thing for I truly love my creature comforts. But sometimes I think if I don't let anyone know the real me, my life will be wasted…Maybe there is no real me."

Distracted by Dee's note, I lost track of what Kat was saying so when she suggested we get together sometime soon it caught me by surprise. It was a departure from our usual routine. I managed to pull it together in time to say that would be nice, but not soon enough to keep her from wondering if I meant it. I could hear the doubt in her voice as she hung up.

At a quarter to five, there was a knock on the door to our suite. The door is unmarked. It is only used by staff, and rarely then. Fine opened it. He stepped aside quickly as he recognized the face before him.

"Tiny" is a nickname you give someone who is unusually large or unusually small. He was neither. He was flanked by a couple of muscle men wearing identical suits that barely fit in all the wrong places. I couldn't help wondering where the workout twins got their uniforms and if they came with the job.

Tiny walked passed John without looking at him and handed me a card. It said, Anthony Peters, President, Local 1122, United Service Employees. His flunkies took positions on opposite sides of the door.

"I hear you are looking into health rackets," Peters said. "Take my advice. These are the guys you should go after."

His voice was flat. There was nothing menacing in what he said but something about the way he said it made the hair on the back of my neck stand up.

Peters presented me with a professionally prepared binder, containing a series of affidavits fingering National Medical Enterprises, Eugene Feinstein, and Sam "The Snake" Siciliano. I didn't bother asking him how he'd found us or why he had bypassed the receptionist three doors down. The message was clear. Instead of meeting with my directors, Ricca had sent one of his own.

Chapter Twenty-Four

When I came downstairs Thursday morning, Trish was in the kitchen. She was dressed for work. She wore a dark sweater and pants tight enough for me to notice she hadn't put on any weight. Max was curled up on his bed facing the deck. He didn't bother to get up.

"Biddy was looking for you," she said.

"What did she want?"

"She's upset about the Claytons' dog. She says he has been barking non-stop the last few nights and she's tired of it. She can't sleep. Her cat is so terrorized it is afraid to leave the house. She says Bruno is a public nuisance. She wants you to join her in signing a complaint."

Clayton was Marie Clayton, my neighbor on the left. Biddy was Beverly Turbiddy, my neighbor to the right. Turbiddy was part of the gentrification movement. Clayton was among those being gentrified, the last of the residents living on the block when I moved in. Their animosity was deep and long-standing.

"Is Bruno keeping you up?" I asked.

"Can't say he is. I know he's not bothering you. You haven't been around enough lately to bother."

"Did you have something in mind?"

"Would it do me any good?"

I let it pass.

"I thought you were pretty well occupied," I said.

"Not so much."

Her eyes dropped.

"He is not wearing well."

"Something to talk about?"

"Probably. But not now."

You can't force it. I knew she would talk when she was ready. I said "OK" and let it go.

"Meanwhile," I added, "if you see Turbiddy before I do, tell her I'm on Bruno's side. I've never been able to warm up to her cat."

When I got to the office, I called Hugh Jones. I told him Peters had come calling.

"Send me a copy of the file," Jones said. "In the meantime, you might want to talk with Father Phillip Carey, Director of Xavier's Institute of Industrial Relations. Tell him I told you to call. He knows Peters as well as anyone. He will tell you what I can't right now."

I called Carey and left a message. Then I called Wilson, thinking George would want to know about Peters' visit. When I was told Wilson was unavailable, I asked for Bogan.

"I was just getting ready to call you," Carl said. "All the more reason now. You remember Keller?"

I said I did.

"Somebody tried to take him out last night. He missed dead by about a quarter of an inch."

I was stunned. It was too close for comfort.

"We pulled Ricca's records. He has a number of arrests. No convictions. Charges were always dropped. People got lost. People changed their minds. That kind of thing. The Bureau's files say he has "social ties" to Columbo. That means they've got pictures or wire of him going to weddings and baptisms and coming over to the house for dinner," Bogan explained. "They think that may mean there is some sort of relationship.

"We have Keller dead to right on multiple felony counts. Stack and Egberg gave him up. We thought we could flip him and set him up to deal Ricca. When he wouldn't bite, Wilson arranged for him to go before the grand jury. He subpoenaed Ricca, as well, and had him waiting so that he would witness Keller's arrival.

"Keller took the fifth, but Wilson kept him there for

more than two hours anyway, asking him everything from where he got his shoes to what he thought of the Yankees' chances. Ricca knew none of this, of course. All he knew was that Keller was in there for a long time. I watched him sweat it out through the one-way glass.

"We took Keller out the back door before we brought Ricca in. When Ricca took the stand, Wilson followed the trail on your tape. He also used some of the information we got from Stack and Egberg. Wilson made it clear we knew a lot about his operation. As far as he could see there was only one way we could know everything we knew."

"That's quite a stunt."

"Yeah, only Ricca was not amused. They go to all the trouble of setting this thing up to look like the guy's spilled his guts and then they're surprised when someone takes it seriously. Imagine that. Last night, the schnook is driving home when a sedan pulls up beside him, a window comes down and somebody tries to put a bullet in his brain. It was a game, I guess. Now they hide the poor SOB across the river."

"Did they recover the round?"

"I don't know. Why?"

"Ricca carries a Glock."

"Good to know," Bogan said. "I'll check into it. Meantime, Nick, be careful. Normally, these guys just kill each other but with the kind of money that's on the table anything is possible."

Chapter-Twenty-Five

Colgate called at 2:15 PM. He was in Philadelphia for a speaking engagement.

Later, I learned there was someone waiting for him in his office when he left to make the noon train. The passenger came along for the ride and went back alone. Whoever it was, his name wasn't blocked into Colgate's appointment calendar.

"Welch has been working The Hill," Colgate said. "He has Sweet on my tail. Paulson is backing away. They want an immediate hearing. Can we do that?"

"We can, but what's the hurry?"

"Sweet says the Governor feels it is essential that this thing is cleared up before the election."

"All right," I said, thinking quickly, "but if we are going to go to all the trouble of rearranging the Committee's schedule for the Governor's convenience, why don't we tell him his personal participation will be required?"

Colgate liked it. He asked me to run it by Paulson. Paulson loved it. He knew there was no way Welch would expose himself by testifying under oath. The pictures alone would kill him. Refusing an invitation to appear before the Committee would be almost as bad.

The invitation was on the Telex in the front office

when Goldberg called demanding we stop it. There was no need for it, he said. Somewhere - I wondered where - the Governor had learned about our plan in time to thwart it. There was no way to be sure but I thought the answer was probably sitting about 50 feet from the telex.

Goldberg said there was no guarantee Welch would be able to appear but he would do his best to be there. Since they were the ones pushing for an immediate hearing, that wasn't saying much.

I took some small satisfaction in knowing we had raised Welch's blood pressure again, but the bottom line was they had won this one. The hearing would be all his way. There was no way to avoid it. The only way to cut our losses was to get the Governor's people on the record and freeze their position.

When you can't duck, you take the punch and roll with it. I told Fine to call Jeffers and ask him if he would be willing to take a lie detector test. It proved nothing, of course, but it didn't have to. We were not in court. We were in a battle of momentum and public opinion. As far as the public is concerned, the lie box is a pretty reliable gauge of whether someone is telling the truth. All you have to do is look at Maury, Wilkos, and Springer.

There was only one downside. Jeffers might fail. If that happened and word got out, the Governor and his friends would have a field day. The solution was to ask him to take the test privately - somewhere out of state, across the border in Indiana, perhaps - and stipulate that the results be given directly to him. If all went well, we could block the Governor's counterattack by leaking the fact that Jeffers had passed a lie detector test. If not, no one need know anything about it.

Meanwhile, the Byrds were apoplectic. The Big Byrd didn't know whether to panic or rejoice at the thought of another hearing. Nothing could serve his purpose more than to have the investigation blow up in our faces – as long as he could get out from under. Little Byrd was running around like a chicken with its head cut off. Every call that came in from Chicago, New York, or Pennsylvania sent her into a tizzy. She didn't know what to do or how to respond.

With all this, it was late afternoon before I got word Father Carey had returned my call. He had left a cell number. When I caught up with him, I learned Carey had played a pivotal role in cleaning up the waterfront. At that time, Tiny was a bodyguard for Joe Curran, head of the Maritime Union. Carey said Curran was tied to Columbo. Peters was his connection.

"Peters was forced out after one of Curran's rivals was killed," Carey said. "There was no way to prove Tiny did it, but everyone knew he did. It looked like him - brutal to the point of being disgusting. The

union paid him $500,000 to leave. I think they hoped the smell would follow him. Peters used the money to buy into 1122."

"What's he doing there?"

"The usual stuff. Dipping into the pension program. Kickbacks. Sweetheart deals. These guys aren't that creative."

"What's the health connection?"

"Peters sells what he calls insurance. It's just a variation of the protection game. But he works both ends. If you are a member of the union, you have to have his policy if you get sick. And he makes sure members know that if you don't have his policy, you can get sick real fast. On the other end, if you want to open a clinic on his turf you have to pay him off. He takes a percentage. If you do well, he takes a bigger percentage. Pretty soon he owns you."

"Anything else I should know?"

"Yes. You are dealing with a truly evil man."

Chapter Twenty-Six

I was up at 5:00 AM Friday and in by 7:00 AM.
Christoff was there when I arrived. Broadbent came
in an hour later; Fine half an hour after that. It was
becoming a pattern. He was the last one in, first one
out.

The testimony from Welch's team had arrived late the
night before - 6 inches of it, with supporting
documents - limiting the time we had to go through it
and analyze the Governor's response.

John left at 9:00 PM. Pam had been giving him hell
most of the day. He said she was feeling neglected.
There was some discussion the job had become more
important than their marriage and a suggestion that, if
things didn't change, he might have to come looking
for her. The rest of the team stayed later – Christoff
making notes on his legal pad, Broadbent on the
computer, half the time on sites no one else cared to
see.

In the morning, we picked up where we had left off. I
spent the two hours I had drafting statements and
blocking out questions for Colgate - questions he
never saw. Colgate arrived at 8:55 AM. He
convened the hearing and left, spending most of the
day skating in and out. It helped that the Delta relief
bill was on the floor, providing an opportunity for
him, as one of the bill's sponsors, to disassociate from
what was going on in the hearing room.

With Colgate gone, Sweet assumed the chair much of the time, Paulson only when Colgate and Sweet were both absent. There were no other members present. The press was all Chicago. There was no reason for anyone else to be there.

Sweet made the most of it.

"Were you notified in advance of Jeffers' charges?" he asked each rebuttal witness. "When were you first contacted by Oversight and Investigations?"

He implied impropriety, challenged procedure, and seemed to be setting up some future action. He seemed genuinely outraged. Colgate stood his ground and responded well. From then on Sweet picked his spots, laying his concerns on the record when Colgate was out.

Welch did not appear. Instead, he sent a letter and a lawyer. Goldberg delivered the letter and sat in the back of the hearing room monitoring events and calling Springfield after each witness. To a man, Welch's people denied Jeffers's allegations. To hear them tell it, nothing Jeffers said was true.

James Tobias, Director of the Department of Health, took the lead in presenting the State's case. Tobias questioned Jeffers' mental stability. He denied the existence of substantial fraud in Illinois, accused Jeffers of unauthorized investigations, and characterized any losses as an honest difference of opinion.

Evan Jones, Director of the Department of Public Aid followed Tobias. Jones walked a thin line, maintaining there was no fraud in Illinois while claiming the Governor's task force had uncovered all kinds of it. He concluded by saying Welch would be appointing fifty new investigators to solve a problem that didn't exist.

There was nothing I could do but watch the events play out and try to anticipate Welch's next move. Welch had his hands full at home; but if he felt strongly enough he could follow Sweet's lead. He could work the party, criticize staff, question OSI's motivation, or ask for someone's head.

When the hearing was over, I asked Christoff to block out discrepancies in the testimony presented by Jeffers and those he accused. Somebody lied. As every President since Nixon has learned, lying under oath will get you into more trouble than any high crime or misdemeanor.

I spent the afternoon drafting a letter of transmittal to the U.S. Attorney and memorandum to go with it. I copied Sweet and attached a cover letter. "It was nice having you with us," I said. "You may find the memo attached of interest." I couldn't resist the barb even knowing that in all probability Sweet would never see it. Whether he did or not, it served another purpose. If Sweet continued to press OSI, we could release the memo with a note saying the matter had been submitted to the proper authorities for investigation. At worst, it would buy some time.

There was a chance Sweet would back off after he

cooled down – particularly if he read the memo and realized what he had stepped into. Even if you accepted the most charitable interpretation, he was used. He had walked into this thing out of loyalty. That was understandable - even admirable. But he had never asked for a briefing. He never attempted to find out exactly what was involved. He had never asked us if the Committee could support its conclusions. In fact, he had never expressed the slightest interest in what the Committee was doing until he was persuaded to carry Welch's water. If he was still inclined to play that game after reflection, there would be no choice but to take it to him.

Chicago was imperative now - even more than when I told Sarah to follow Skinner. New York had its own momentum. Thanks to the GAO the facts there were not in dispute. In Illinois, the GAO's inquiry had been thwarted and the Governor's people were pushing back. The only good news was that they were now on record denying the existence of any substantial fraud in their State. They had marched up to the precipice like good soldiers, stuck their necks out, and upped the ante. All we had to do was lay it at their feet. The Governor owned whatever we found.

With that in mind, I put in a call to Patterson to see where she was. Jeffers called while I waited for her response.

"A friend of mine in the Department said the Governor's people are calling me a lying homosexual," he said.

You didn't have to be an investigator to know he was angry and upset.

"Relax," I said. "You had to know they were going to deny everything. As for the other matter, it is either true or it isn't and who cares one way or another?"

"It isn't," Jeffers said, still agitated. "By the way, the test went well."

As I hung up, an instant message from Dee popped up on my screen. She was in Georgetown shopping. Having fun. Could I get away?

I wondered how many staffers on The Hill have that much flexibility. I pulled up the green book out of curiosity and saw her listed as a consultant. That would explain it. Consultants set their own hours. They can also work for more than one member – she was associated with two – and avoid the salary cap. Her take home pay was greater than either of the people she worked for.

Patterson returned my call at 4:35 PM.

"Nick," she said without waiting to hear why I called, "did you know what you were getting me into when you sent me up here?"

"What do you mean?"

"Feinstein's father was shot and killed last year. A few months later, his partner was killed."

"Uh huh."

"It was in December after you left The Hill. Three months after the Mills investigation," she said. "You must have known."

"They ran National Medical Enterprises. We found Feinstein when his name popped up as a high-biller. NME was pulling in upwards of $50 million a year. Unfortunately for him, he was dumb enough to boast about it. We caught him on tape as part of a sting we organized. Somehow word got out during the media blitz that followed Mills. Shortly after that, a gunman wearing a stocking mask walked into his clinic, bold as brass in the middle of the day, pulled a shotgun and blew Feinstein's head off."

"What about his partner?"

"He told Skinner a syndicate out of New York was trying to move in on their business. He said he wanted to cooperate and help catch the killers, but they got him first. He was closing up shop. Someone called his name. He turned and caught a shotgun blast in the chest."

"Who did it?"

"The Chicago police say a young black man named William Hill. They said it was a hit ordered by Max Kaye, a dentist working for NME. They said it was a personal dispute - an argument over money. They said Kaye felt he was being cheated."

"What did Kaye say?"

"He had a heart attack right after Hill was arrested."

"And died…"

"You got it."

"How convenient."

"More than you might think. Kaye was in his thirties. No history. No autopsy. A doctor in the clinic signed the death certificate. The body was cremated."

"What happened to Hill?"

"He got life."

"You know, you could have told a girl some of this before sending me up here."

"Hey, you're a trained reporter. I knew you'd figured it out."

"Yeah, right." She was unimpressed. "Add this. The guy who signed Kaye's death certificate was William Guthrie."

"Was?"

"Was, as in no more. We were supposed to talk this afternoon. He was found dead this morning. The police are calling it a suicide."

"You say that as if there is reason for doubt."

"His throat and wrists were slashed. Sometime after

that, they say he jumped out a window and fell nine floors to his death."

"You have to admire his determination. Not many people kill themselves twice."

"Yeah, and if you believe that, he was also something of a track star."

"What do you mean?"

"Most jumpers land feet first on the sidewalk. Guthrie was either a long jumper of Olympic caliber or somebody really strong shot put him out the window. He planted his face in the pavement right in front of a Chevy Tahoe doing 40 in a 25-mile an hour zone. The driver hit the brakes so hard he got rear ended by a Mini Cooper. Messed up traffic for hours."

"And the Mini, probably."

"Right."

"Anything else?"

"They found Guthrie's razor on his dresser."

"How far was it from the window?"

"At least ten feet."

"Any blood on it?"

——

216

"Not so as you'd notice."

"Neat."

"No. Determined and neat."

Chapter Twenty-Seven

At 11:00 AM on the 29th of September, John called from Chicago. He had taken a direct flight that morning out of Reagan with Broadbent for backup. John said he was encountering resistance at Public Aid. Evan Jones called as soon as he arrived and told him to go home.

Given the headlines over the weekend, I wasn't surprised.

On Saturday, the *Tribune* ran two columns on the front page below the fold reporting Welch's defense. Next to it was a story with Merriman's byline reporting Jeffers had taken and passed a lie detector test.

But the big news came Sunday. The Attorney General charged the Department of Public Aid with obstruction of justice. He said the Department had been sitting on evidence of massive fraud for more than a year. The case involved a group of pharmacies controlled by Star Services.

"The evidence of wholesale fraud was so obvious it was visible to the naked eye," the Attorney General said. "Additions were made in handwriting visibly different from the physicians and in ink of a different color."

"The Department of Public Aid has impeded this investigation in every way possible," the AG noted, "denying the problem, fighting a subpoena, and then reporting the files in question were missing."

Goldberg responded for the Governor. He was quoted as saying the Attorney General was piling on and playing to the headlines. His charges were politically motivated.

Jones was now at the center of the bull's-eye. He wasn't taking it well.

"He told me we would be wise to take the next plane back to Washington," John said. "He said, 'You wasted the taxpayer's money getting here. You're not going to get any information from my Department.' Then he added a threat. He said, 'If you know what's good for you, I suggest you stop bothering our people and get on a plane and fly back to Washington.'"

John wanted to know how hard to push it. They were jerking us around. What did we want to do about it? The vendor reports he was sent to review were supposed to be open for public inspection.

"Tell Jones they can give you what you asked for now and save everyone a lot of trouble or they can give it to you later. It won't help his case any if the press reports he stonewalled the Senate and made us subpoena public records."

I told John I would get a subpoena authorized and have the marshals deliver it as soon as possible. Mancini, Sadowski, Hubbard, and Roche were quick to agree. Ben Schneider from Talbot's office said he had just returned from a holiday and would get right on it. Rick Baird said he wouldn't be able to get to Burdett for another hour. Dave Rust said he hadn't talked with Foster, but he was certain Foster would want to support the Chairman. I could count him in unless he heard something to the contrary before the end of the day.

Vernon tried his best to remain civil, but it wasn't easy. He said Paulson was upset. He had read the *Tribune*. He knew he'd been left out of the loop and why. Apparently, Paulson was blaming Vernon. He didn't like the way he had handled the situation. Vernon said he wasn't sure about the subpoena. I took that to mean he wasn't going to bring it up.

Still, we were nearing a majority when Brent called on the intercom. She said Broadbent was holding. She said he sounded distressed. For some reason, she found it amusing.

John had asked Broadbent to find Jonathan Nussbaum, one of the doctors indicted with Feinstein. Nussbaum was a foreign medical school graduate, like many of those who practice Medicaid medicine. Unlike most of the rest, however, Nussbaum had not passed the equivalency exam. As a result, he was not licensed to practice in the United States. That meant every bill he submitted while working for Feinstein was fraudulent. He was facing more felony charges than he could count. If we could get to him, there was a good chance he would cooperate.

Dick was making his case when one of Nussbaum's neighbors came tapping on the door.

He said, "Tell your friend his car just blew up."

Dick said he didn't know what to do. I told him to call the cops.

"Don't get paranoid," I said. "Bogan says these guys mostly kill each other."

"Mostly," Broadbent said.

He didn't seem reassured.

Burdett and Talbot came through shortly after lunch. The subpoena was authorized and en route by 2:00 PM. Miraculously, the files appeared before the subpoena could be delivered. Still, they had chewed up a day of our time.

...

Dee arrived as I prepared to leave. She said she was on her way out as well. Her excuse for stopping by was something she wanted to show me – a silver ankle bracelet bought for a girlfriend. It was engraved. Three initials outside. Two names inside. One I didn't recognize. She said it came from Beladora in Beverly Hills.

Our conversation was strained and awkward. There were extended periods of silence. We were uncomfortable with each other and ill at ease. Christoff walked in, assessed the situation, and walked out. She had no reason to stay but seemed unwilling to leave.

To break the silence, I offered her a drink. She refused.

"I'll be in Bermuda for a few days," she said finally, "at the Princess," wondering if I remembered, knowing I did.

When there was no response, she announced, "I've changed my mind."

"About what?"

"About the drink."

She settled in to Christoff's chair, obviously meaning to stay. I took a bottle out of the bottom drawer of the filing cabinet that held up the right side of my desk.

"What is this?"

"Remy in a paper cup."

"Geez, you're impossible. I want to know what's what."

"What 'what' do you mean?"

"First, you wouldn't screw me, and then you wouldn't see me. Now you won't even talk to me."

She felt the distance but could not or would not accept it. She came over to the barstool where I perched, kissed me twice and retreated,

---

uncomfortable in the unwelcome. She sensed the barriers were up. And yet, she could not let it be. She sought reassurance. She was going away with someone else and I seemed not to care.

"Can't we get together somewhere before I leave?"

I told her I was committed.

Our parting had the echo of an epitaph. So what, I thought. There are other women. Kat seemed to want to get together. Maybe it was time for that. There was unfinished business with Sarah and I hadn't seen Sam for a while. She had left a message saying she had moved in to her first apartment "all my very own" and was thrilled at the prospect and possibilities it opened. But in truth, the last time I saw her I was put off. Her eyes had gone hungry. She spoke almost exclusively of singles parties, her parents, and being freed of their expectations.

"Hell, twenty-eight is not so old, is it?" she said. "It is not as if I were a tramp or sleeping around."

From the way her eyes wandered, I wondered. The men we passed in the halls of the Pentagon wondered as well. There was a license in their looks I had not seen before for any woman I was with, an invitation in her dress and walk, an answer in her eyes. Ten years of sexual maturity in an atmosphere of men will do that. Behind the bravado, there was a note of desperation.

"All I ever really wanted was someone to love and take care of me," she said.

I wondered who she was trying to convince.

Then there was Trish. The more difficult case. I wondered if there was anything but hurt there sometimes. Most would surely say she was the most attractive, but it came at such a high price. The price of such pursuit seems always at end a diminished sense of self and a loss of self-respect.

Trish lived in the external world of reactors. Her day was dependent on the number of heads she turned, the remarks made, and in relaying these remarks from one admirer to another for comment, comparison, and reaction. More than once a series of rebuffs had stimulated deep doubts, suicidal thoughts, and vengeful dreams.

This time is different, I told myself. So many things Dee said – things I might once have believed – seemed now calculated with specific intent. I still found her attractive, but I was not who I was. I had tired of posturing, poses, and lies – so many lies I wonder sometimes if she was congenitally incapable of truth. The pain that I felt in causing her pain had eased. The pain was of her choosing, a child's pain, ungratified.

I put it to rest, finished my drink, and was about to shut down when a text from Fine popped up with a video link. Broadbent had made the local news. John said the local TV crews were running extensive footage of him walking around his charred Chevy. Dick was flashing his box top, looking official.

———

The police were quoted as saying it was probably an accident. Most likely, he had parked a hot car over some dry leaves.

Chapter Twenty-Eight

Tuesday morning, I found Mrs. Clayton on the sidewalk before her house. Her face was wet with tears. A truck from animal control was double parked on the street.

"She killed Bruno," Clayton said, pointing to the right. "She has always hated him and now she's killed him."

While I watched, the animal control officer left his vehicle and disappeared inside her house. Clayton said Bruno was fine last night. She woke this morning to find him dead. She found several balls of hamburger in her yard. They were laced with something that looked like rat poison.

"Did you hear or see anything?" the officer asked when he returned.

There was nothing to see or hear. Clayton's yard was open and accessible. Anyone walking through the alley could have lobbed the hamburger over the fence. Turbiddy would be at the top of my list as well, but there were plenty of other possibilities. Half the block had complained about the racket Bruno made from time to time. Still, I felt for her and I felt for him. He was a beautiful animal and deserved better.

The officer knocked on Turbiddy's door but she was nowhere to be found. He parked his car in a space that opened up halfway down the block and began looking for someone to talk to in the adjoining townhouses. He was still working the neighborhood when I left.

All the usual annoyances were waiting for me at the office when I arrived. Today's burden was increased by the fact that the Omnibus Bill had passed the House late Monday night. I had hoped the amendment creating an Inspector General would ride through unnoticed, a small hitchhiker on a large train. Instead, it had been singled out by members looking to respond to the headlines. It hadn't taken long for lobbyists to connect the dots. The number of messages in my inbox had tripled. Kat and Tubin were among them.

"Wasn't that part of the package you drafted a couple of years ago?" Tubin said out of real or feigned confusion. With him, it could be hard to tell.

Kat was more direct.

"Congratulations," she said, "you made number one on the hit parade."

"How so?"

"You earned your very own task force. My boss is involved, which tells you something. He doesn't do anything he can delegate. They met twice last week. Now they are kicking it into high gear. They called an emergency meeting this morning just to figure out how to respond to you. They are talking about ads in the *Post*, *Times*, and *Roll Call*, spots on WTOP – a full-court press."

At 10:00, Rhonda Rosenfield, one of Stoessal's producers, called on my cell. Until I heard her voice, I had forgotten I had given her that number.

"I couldn't get through to Committee," she said. "Is there anything in this for me?"

"I'll see what I can come up with."

"Please. I could use a story right now. I'm being shut out of the rotation. Meanwhile, how about letting me have Max?"

It was the fifth or sixth time Rhonda had asked for Max's story. Others had as well. She was only the most persistent, but I could understand why. Stoessal would love it. It was his kind of story.

I told her I would see what Max had to say. "You never know," I said, "he might agree to do it, but don't count on it. He doesn't like talking about himself."

Half an hour later, Jay called.

"The Omnibus bill came over clean," he said, "but someone already has a hold on it."

"Who?"

"Dumb question. You know how it works."

Constantine was right. It was a dumb question. Whoever it was could have waited until the bill came up and filibustered but that tactic is generally reserved for those who want to make a show of opposition. Not only is that action public, it can also be shut down. More effective are the arcane rules rooted in Senatorial courtesy which allow members to anonymously delay any legislation they choose for any reason or no reason. Not infrequently, legislation favored by an overwhelming majority is derailed by a single anonymous dissenting voice. It's part of the club's rules. We were dead in the water until we could get the hold removed.

The only solution was to force him into the light. I made a list of people who might know or be able to find out and began working the phone. My third call showed color. Mike Atkins, Mancini's LA, said he had heard something about it. He couldn't come up with a name but he seemed to recall it was someone from Appropriations. He noted it because he thought it strange. Anyone from Appropriations would have had ample opportunity to wade into the budget reconciliation package.

...

Dick and John were visiting William Hill at the Statesville Correctional Center, two miles north of Joliet. I had asked them to take Merriman and Patterson along. It would extend their stories while providing some cover for the investigators. Only the truly stupid would try something with the cameras rolling.

Hill was in maximum security: level 1. At Statesville, visiting hours for maximum security are limited to two hours with a guest arrival no later than 1:45 PM. With any luck they would make the five o'clock out of Midway.

When Fine's team arrived they were ushered into an austere antechamber attached to the visitors' center. They met Hill in a grey room with a grey metal counter, separated by three inches of bulletproof glass, and supervised by two guards who could have played defense for the Bears. Hill wasn't required to cooperate with law enforcement agencies but he knew it would help when he came up for parole. The cameras provided an additional incentive. Even crooks want to be famous these days. Still, he was edgy.

"I was railroaded," he said. "I didn't do it."

"You copped a plea," John said.

"I had to, man. They had too much stuff on me. They were going to get me one way or another. And the public defender was worthless. It was life or death. Besides, with everything going down, I'm safer in than out.

"Why?"

"I can give you 50 million reasons," he said. "Fifty million is a lot. It will buy your death, my death, the cameraman's death. Anybody's death. So you can take it from there, you know. There's more to this that meets the eye."

230

"Do you feel safe here?" Sarah asked.

"Safer, maybe. Not safe. I am a worried man. I'm always worried. I am even worried in my cell, you know. Money talks. I got to sleep real light."

Chapter Twenty-Nine

At 4:10 PM, Allison came running into my office. She was trembling and breathless.

"I couldn't get through to you," she said. "Mark is on the phone. Michael is with him. They say they have to talk with you. They say something terrible has happened."

Mark was crying.

"Can you please come over," he said. "There is blood all over the place."

I had Allison call 911 as I flew out of the office. John's home was a dozen blocks away but I still beat the squad car from the First District by fifteen minutes. The boys were in the hallway, standing by the door, clinging to each other when I arrived.

"Mom's hurt," Michael said. "She's hurt real bad."

I found her on the second floor. It didn't take long to realize there wasn't much I could do for her. She had been killed OJ-style, someone big and strong holding her from behind and drawing a knife across her throat. She was lying face down in a pool of blood already darkening from exposure to the air and sun. She had been lying there for some time.

The one eye I could see saw nothing, staring vacantly in the general direction of the window. Blood covered the front of her pantsuit, the carpet beneath, and spattered the bedspread, nightstand, and wall. A kitchen knife with an ivory handle had been dropped on the floor by her side.

The boys were too close behind me to allow a thorough inspection but in the moment I had I gathered the impression she had put up a fight. The room was a shambles, enough so that it looked like it had been tossed either in the course of her struggle for life or after the fact by someone looking for something. A lamp by her bed had been knocked over and shattered. Pictures were scattered on the floor. Her jewelry box was open. I couldn't tell if anything was missing.

I herded the boys downstairs to wait for the cops to arrive. No good could come from their seeing what I had seen.

"It will be alright," I said, trying to comfort them, but it fell flat.

"No, it won't," Michael said.

It came out one word at a time.

"She's dead. I know she is."

The reality had already begun to set in. Things would never be the same. He dissolved in tears. I put my arms around the boys and held them close. There was nothing to say, no way to make it right.

The responding officers looked around and decided to wait for homicide. They didn't bother introducing themselves. They had already determined it was out of their jurisdiction. They didn't want to get involved. Still, they couldn't resist exchanging opinions.

"Whoever did this was either a real amateur or a real pro," one of them said. "Any of our boys would have thrown the silver, her jewelry, and all those fancy electronics into a pillow case and walked out the door like Santa Claus."

"Maybe that's what they had in mind," the other replied, "only they didn't expect her to be home. She surprised them; they got scared and ran."

The homicide boys and a mobile crime unit showed up 30 minutes later. They bagged evidence and dusted the place for fingerprints. Neighbors gathered outside, trying to guess what was going on. Whoever killed her would be covered with blood and carry her marks on their hands and face. Someone should have seen or heard something. Rather than ask, the patrolman shooed them away. There was no attempt to check names, see who was there, or ask what they might have seen. The animal control officer investigating Bruno's death had done a better job.

If you are going to take someone out in the states, Washington is the place to do it. On average, there is a homicide every other day in DC – 180 to 200 a year. Two thirds of them go unsolved. The homicide department sits on a backlog of more than 1500 cases accumulated over the last ten years. It's ironic since there are more police per capita in DC than any other city in the country.

The cops were in and out of Pam's bedroom for 45 minutes before one of them came looking for the boys.

"Brewster," he said. "Homicide. Who are you?"

He had sandy hair and the dead eyes of a man who had seen the loss of life too many times to care about one more.

"Alexander, friend of the family."

"You call this in."

"My office. The boys called me."

"Why?"

"Their father is out of town. He works with me."

"Where is he?"

It was predictable. Most homicides involve people who know each other. The closer your relationship the more likely you are to be the prime suspect.

"Chicago."

"Sure of that."

"Absolutely."

Brewster's face grew weary. He had hoped this one was going to be easy. He turned to the boys and asked for their story. They said they arrived home around 4:00 PM. The driver had picked them up from school as usual and dropped them off in front of the house. The door was open. They were surprised because their Mom had a rule about that. They thought at first she had seen them coming and unlocked the door. She did that sometimes. They called and when she didn't respond they went looking for her. Mark said he found her. Michael was not far behind. They saw the blood, got scared, and stopped, afraid to enter the room. They called the office hoping someone would help them find their father.

"What's going to happen to us?" Mark asked.

"I want you to come with me to the police station," Brewster said. "We'll find someone to stay with you until your Father comes."

Michael started to cry again. I pulled him close and told the officer I would stay with them. We waited in a beat up room at the First District's substation. I sent out for pizza but neither boy would eat. We talked a little but mostly I just held them until they fell asleep.

For an hour I watched the lens of the surveillance camera in the corner stare back. Finally, Brewster returned with another cop in tow. This one had a nametag that said he was Dwight Johnson, homicide detective and supervisor. He was big, trim, and in excellent physical condition. He wore his shoulder-length hair in dreadlocks.

"We've contacted your friend," Johnson said. "He is on his way from Chicago. I'll have a squad car pick him up at the airport. While we are waiting we'd like to ask you a couple of questions. Maybe you can help us understand the situation."

Johnson began by asking me to repeat what I had previously said. I did as he asked conscious the cameras were rolling. Then Johnson went fishing.

"How long have you known Mr. Fine," he said.

"About three years."

"How long have you known the deceased?"

"Less than a year. Sometime after they got married."

"Where were you this morning?"

"In my office."

"All day?"

"All day.

"The boys say your friend is their stepfather."

"She was married before. John adopted the boys last summer."

"Where's their biological father?"

"I have no idea."

"I hear it is quite a house. Where did the money come from?"

"Her. Her maiden name was Macklin, as in Macklin Magazines."

"Who gets the money now?"

"I have no idea. Probably the boys."

"We found drugs in the house – marijuana, meth, speed, ice. Do you know anything about that?"

"No."

"Does your friend use drugs?"

"I've seen him take Tylenol."

"Anything else?"

"Nope."

"Can you think of anyone with a reason to want Mrs. Fine dead – other than your friend?"

"I can't think of anyone who would want her dead."

Chapter Thirty

John resigned on the first day of October.

The boys were asleep on a sofa at the police station when he arrived. He looked like a train wreck, eyes red and unfocused, sleep walking in that detached way people get when the shock is so great it defies comprehension. They kept him at the station for two hours answering questions and filling out forms before we were able to take the kids home. John slept in my guest bedroom; the boys huddled on either side of him, seeking warmth and comfort.

John said he had been thinking all night. The boys had to be his priority. They would need counseling and support. Their house was sealed. They couldn't go back there if they wanted to and it was doubtful they would ever want to or feel comfortable there again. He would have to find another place to live. He was thinking of taking them home to Chicago where his family could help. There was no support here. He would have to settle Pam's estate. There was a seat on the Macklin Corporation's Board, assets to distribute, trust funds to execute, and a foundation to manage. Everything she did, he would now have to do. In addition, there was a criminal investigation in process. From the way they talked, he was their prime suspect, maybe their only suspect. He needed to be prepared to deal with that and he was expecting a custody battle from the boys' father. Their father was long out of the picture and had not demonstrated any significant interest in his kids but he was the kind of guy who would be interested in their trust funds.

John spoke with something approaching resignation. Life as he knew it had ended as well. Her life had subsumed his.

"Did you see her?" he asked.

"Briefly."

"What was it like?"

"Messy. It looked like whoever killed her was surprised to find her home. Someone coming with an intent to kill would have handled it differently."

I didn't go into specifics. Thankfully, John didn't ask. I was having enough trouble erasing the images from my mind without resurrecting them.

"That would make sense," John said. "Pam sent me a text message about ten saying she was going home. She wasn't feeling well."

"Save the text," I said.

Fine stopped and then nodded in comprehension.

"I'm sorry to leave you hanging," he said. "I know this is a tough time to bail but I don't think I have any choice."

I told him that was the last thing he should be worrying about and it was.

"There are some OSI files at home," John said.

"There is no way I can access them now. I'm not sure when they will let me back in or when I'll have the stomach to go back."

From the top of the stairs, Michael called - a single heartbreaking syllable full of doubt, fear, and pain – "Dad?"

"I'm here," John said, his eyes brimming with tears.

I tried to find something to say and came up empty. Fortunately, Trish found that moment to return with croissants and bagels from the Brasserie. Max was with her, still frisky from his walk. She set up breakfast while Max bounded up the stairs to entertain the boys. Somehow he knew they needed him. If that meant he had to allow himself to be held, hugged, and petted, so be it.

I went looking for something with a bite to pour in my coffee cup. I found a half empty bottle of Metaxa and made a mental note to visit Schneider's and restock the liquor cabinet. The way things were going, the house would be dry by the end of the week.

While they ate, I checked my mailbox. I found three items I hadn't picked up when we got home – a letter, an 8 x 10 manila envelope and a package, birthday wrapped. No postage. All hand-delivered.

"Monday was the worst day of my life," the note began. She had always loved Bermuda, she said, but now she hated being there. She wanted to leave as soon as she arrived, wanted to be with me not with someone else.

"I want to be with you somewhere I can have you all to myself. I don't want to share you with anyone," she said. "The only part of my life that's real now is when I'm with you. There are times when I don't want to do anything at all unless it's with you. I can't help wondering where you are and who you are with.

"Most people, five minutes after you say 'hello' you know - who/what they are, where they have been, what they think they've done, where they think they're going, and what they want from you. And 99% of the time, you don't want to know any of it."

"With you, I never know what to expect. When can we get together?"

She suggested a rather demanding program: Thursday, Friday night, the weekend, as far away Christmas. It made me weary. I would have to try to tell her again. Maybe she already knew but didn't want to admit knowing.

"He never writes, never calls," she said. "Hell, he doesn't care. He's got another honey. Maybe more. Maybe he's just decided it's not worth the trouble. Maybe he thinks it's too far gone to ever be what it could have been."

She could have been reading my mind.

The manila envelope contained twenty pages copied from her diary – three and four entries a day – some of it disconcerting, much quite charming.

___

242

"What you are about to read is the truth, the whole truth and nothing but the truth, so help me God," she said - an interesting choice of words for a beginning. Then, "What lies herein is a bit of my soul, quite fragile. Treat it accordingly."

Up front, there was a picture of us together with a note: Remember? There was a picture of Barbie wearing her beach outfit at the end with a large question mark. A gentle slam at my roommate.

She said she didn't want to die knowing no one ever knew what she was really like. What was she really like? I wondered.

She said she wanted to be professionally photographed. She had the pose all picked out. She saw herself reflected once, as she tried on a pair of pants in a department store. "Hmm, not bad," was her stated reaction, nude from the waist up, pants open and exposed. In another few years, she said, it will be too late and she'll have nothing to remember the way she was.

There has been such a short period of sweet time, she said. She was gangly, long limbed, and awkward as a child, painfully shy. Still, she did say she was a high school cheerleader, so it couldn't have been a complete loss. It was hard to imagine her as a complete loss – or painfully shy.

It was then that she lost her virginity – to the captain of the football team, of course. She wanted to wear his sweater. That's all there was to it. There was a suggestion she came out ahead. After all, she still had the sweater.

Like every beautiful woman I have ever known, she was inexplicably insecure. She was more than attractive and knew it – if anything, too well. And yet her comments about herself were all negative. On any other subject she spoke with confidence and authority.

She seemed sometimes to be so practiced, so deliberate and cold-blooded and sometimes so unsure, vulnerable, and afraid. Which was it? What was she really like?

"I chose the man I married because I knew he would take care of me and be easy to live with," she concluded. "But I know now that's not enough. There's got to be more. I went to a wedding last week. I had a perfect view of the bride's face when she said her vows and it was quite obvious that she thought the guy she had chosen is the only man in the world. For me, that was the only good part of the wedding. The next time I marry I'll do it right."

With a detached interest, I attempted an analysis of her handwriting. Her hand was large and angular with a slight forward inclination. There was diversity there and some extroversion. Several indications – trailing "i" dots and angularity – of enthusiasm. Definite indications she was more given to activity than reflection. Also, extensive evidence of a conflict between what the mind dictates and the emotions demand. A suggestion of difficulty making adjustments. Loops were tightly closed in the small letters - "o" and "e" - and baseline formations of "g" and "b" strokes – were almost filled with an ornate double stroke. Tops and bottoms of strokes were angular, unyielding, and exacting. Strangely, lower loops were minimal and controlled, another indication, perhaps, of conflict. There was no indication of overt sexuality, rather set, rigid, and deliberate emotions. Baselines were even, emotional zones minimal, middle zones large, terminal strokes short, blunt. Probably, the most accurate single characteristic.

The package contained an embroidered silk shirt from India. There was a note with it:

"As I see you. No ties or collars. Free!" And in parenthesis – "This shirt I handled so lovingly when I bought it the clerk commented on it. He said it must be for the love of your life."

"Again, I ask. When can I see you?"

Chapter Thirty-One

There was a small envelope on my desk when I arrived at the office Thursday morning. The stationery was pale blue – almost grey – and smelled of lavender. The handwriting was controlled, neat, and symmetrical. My name was on the outside. There were three lines inside.

"Every muscle in my body aches. Thanks! I had a wonderful time."

There were two stacked circles for a signature. The top circle had two dots for eyes, two half circles for ears, another dot for a nose.

The note explained the greeting I had received when I had checked in with the front office. Brent smiled. Allison turned away and wouldn't or couldn't look at me. Kat must have delivered it personally.

It made me even wearier than I was. It had been a long night.

I had been asked to stand in for Colgate at the opening session of the Health Policy Forum. It was a legislative conference like so many others organized by trade associations to lobby and show off for their members.

This one was hastily put together by the Coalition for Health Care, the name given to the group Kat had warned me about. It was a three-day conference. Half the Committee had been invited to speak. Undoubtedly, honorariums had been offered and campaign contributions would follow. By no accident, the contributions would come too late in the cycle to track before the election.

The opening session was a 'social event.' Members and key staff were invited to party with their constituents and their constituents' hired guns. I had been to enough of these events to have no appetite for another, but the Pennsylvania delegation was pressing hard. Somebody had to represent Colgate and I was nominated. It was Mary Jane's polite way of saying: "You got us in to this, you deal with it."

When I arrived, representatives of the groups sponsoring the conference were lined up behind the registration table monitoring arrivals. Several of them came to attention when I identified myself. Before any of them could approach, Kat was at my side.

She wore a black cocktail dress that fit her like a glove. A scarf, patterned in grey, black and fawn, was draped over her bare shoulders, accenting the paleness of her skin. She gave me a hug and took my arm. I had been claimed. She walked me away from the crowd to the elevator and pressed the button for the third floor.

"My boss called me into the office this afternoon," she explained. "I have been ordered to stick close to you tonight."

"Sorry about that."

"That's all right. I'll try and make the best of it."

We were in the National Building Museum, one of Washington's grand halls. Built after the civil war, the building was designed for a dual purpose – to house the newly created U. S. Pension Bureau and to provide an appropriate venue for Washington's premier social functions. Through the years one purpose atrophied, the other expanded.

The hall has seen more concerts, charity events and political fundraisers than any other facility in town. It has hosted an inaugural event for every President going back to Cleveland. Christmas in Washington is filmed there. Cirque du Soleil and Bono have entertained there. Reagan raised $80 million there in one night, setting the building record. The best the Democrats have been able to do is the $60 million Senator Kerry raised with the help of three past Presidents.

The exterior is modeled after the Palazzo Farnese, designed by Michelangelo. The interior, modeled after a church Michelangelo built in Rome during the sixteenth century, features colossal Corinthian columns, 75 feet high and 8 feet in diameter. The columns dominate a central hall the size of a football field.

From the walkway on the third floor, the crowd seemed tiny. A stage, draped in red, white and blue, was set on the east end between two of the four columns on that side. A matching banner had been hung from the ceiling as a backdrop, falling nearly four stories to the ground. Three bars had been set up around the perimeter. Waiters worked the room, passing shrimp on a stick, stuffed mushrooms, and miniature crab balls. Registrants who weren't entertaining guests, congregated around the bars, waiting for the program to begin.

"That's my boss down there," Kat said. "Actual size."

She pointed toward a cluster of people near the stage.

"He is the one on the left with the blonde hair and grey slacks. I'm supposed get whatever I can out of you and do whatever I have to do to get it. He said my job could depend on it."

Her boss stood next to a man who looked large even from a distance. Jabba The Hut in black.

"Who is that with him?" I asked.

"Henry Furth. He's the leader of the coalition."

The two men turned toward us. As they did, Kat took my hand. There was something in her eyes I hadn't seen before.

"Are they still looking at us?" she asked.

"Yes. They are trying to be sneaky about it but we've got their attention."

"Good."

She slipped her arms around me and pulled me close, fusing her body to mine. The embrace seemed to form a seal from head to toe. She held the connection, letting me feel her warmth and sense her promise, and then pressed her lips to mine in a long, lingering kiss. Though we had known each other for years, this was the first time either one of us had ever kissed anything other than a cheek. While I thought about that, she took my hand and led me back to the elevator.

"Where are we going?" I asked.

"To do what the man said. I'm going to stick as close to you tonight as I can."

When the elevator opened at ground level, she took my hand again and led me across the hall and out the door. A hundred eyes followed us.

Chapter Thirty-Two

We sat facing each other on the sofa in my townhouse, sharing a bottle of wine and then what was left of the brandy, an awareness of intimacy and remembrance building between us. We said little at first, the closeness of contact lingering and closing the distance between us and then began filling in the blanks we had stepped over in our previous public conversations.

The man she married had been her first real relationship. There had been a high school boyfriend and a few other 'friends" along the way, but no one that mattered. She met him during her second year at UVA. She was the serious one, the intense one, full of commitment and purpose and lack of direction, sure of a fate labeled Dean's list and Maiden aunt, too bright and too intense, too determined to escape the box that had contained her mother and show what she could do.

He was as big a man on campus as a small man can be, a part-time jock and class clown who kept his ambition in a thimble. Still, he fit in. He was accepted. And that was enough. So when he asked her out, she said yes, gratefully, and then again, gratefully, always convinced it was some unfathomable form of charity, wondering why he bothered. And she married him. Because it seemed the thing to do. Because he asked and she wasn't sure anyone else ever would.

There is an element of settling in many marriages –

an announcement of worth to the world. Part of the sadness of life is that like any another statement of worth, self-esteem can be inflated or depreciated. Sometimes that alone will end marriage. Look at Hollywood. It would be funny if it wasn't so sad. And sometimes all that is needed is an honest eye. A less heated, less restricted, more objective self-appraisal.

Six months into their marriage she realized she had nothing to say to him. She found herself stale mated to a chucklehead who spoke with his body because he had difficulty forming sentences, a man speechless now that he could no longer entertain her by sticking cigarettes in his ear.

By day, it was easier. There was work. They were apart. There was silence and distance and no need to face what she could not face, but by night as he watched the tube and she read, the silence was deafening. Living a lie, leaving the unthinkable unsaid, she lay goaded by suspicions of having bought dear and sold cheap, of having purchased first, not best. And with her growing discontent, came an embryonic awareness that there was more out there and a sense she deserved better.

Silently, she started saying the unsaid, thinking the unthinkable. Words of pride. Words of hurt. Words of dissolution. For five years, a marriage, two lives suspended by a thin thread of silence. Neither lovers nor partners in any full sense of the word. Never more than two roommates sharing time and space, surviving by inflicting their marriage on friends, filling their own emptiness with joy of others, spending as little time as possible together alone. And even with the social lubricant, still, nothing to say to one another. Only slight conversation, confined to incidental remarks and, increasingly, more and more broadly hinting in public at the privately unutterable. Complaints and painful comparisons. Picking and putdowns. And when the evening was over, others gone to beds of whispers and wonder, lapse into silence, walking softly over the soft spots, diverting once more the irretrievable words, again in silence, always in silence, until she wondered that the world could hold so much silence. She compared the picture of the life she thought she would have with the life she had and found it wasn't the way it was supposed to be. And couldn't be. And so she left, in the early morning after a quiet night while he sat at the breakfast table reading the Sunday comics.

Work had been her identity and refuge. Now she was being forced to consider the totality of her existence.

"This is my personal Fourth of July," she said, "Independence Day. They told me to think about my career and what was important to me. To be crass about it, they were telling me that if I wanted to keep my job I had to do what I was told - even if that meant betraying you. It was calculated and mean. I thought about it and I decided if I have to keep my job that way I don't want it. If I have to choose, I choose you."

After that we said the things that are said just to be said, filling the silence that haunted her with sounds that have meaning beyond words. We both knew we had crossed the line that had kept us apart. Then, the awareness of where we were and what we both knew would soon happen broke through thought and the need to say and hear.

For the second time, she closed the distance between us. She pulled me close again and whispered in my ear. I watched her grey eyes darken and deepen as she waited for my response.

"Have you no shame?" I said.

"Ask me in the morning."

"OK. I'll call you about eight."

"Uh, uh."

She took my hand for the third time and led me upstairs, looking for the master suite. She stopped beside my oversized bed and pulled her hair back, turning so I could work the zipper. As I did, I realized there was nothing under her dress but her fair skin, luminous against the dark fabric. It caught and held the light seeping into the room through the skylight.

She said her mouth was too large, her lower lip to full. She didn't care for her dimples. They made her feel like Shirley Temple, cute and adolescent. She said eyebrows should not come in segments, noses bend to a fifty-degree angle and flatten on the top. She said she was skinny enough, no matter how much she eats, to want to take the long way around the pound. She would look like this, that, or the other, be fuller here, thinner there, change seemingly everywhere. I saw the tip of her nose move as she spoke and told her she was nuts. She is lovely.

At first it didn't go well. Her breath bellowed with effort. Her movements, the waves and backwash of willing and wanting, of needing and needing too much, were forced and erratic – mind, body and soul divided. She was in too many places and nowhere enough, while I was too conscious of the need to deal with my own demons, chasing away the dark images that crowded the back of my mind. It had been a hellacious week.

We worked our way nearly there to fall away, then doubled back only to lose it again. She strained so hard at times I began to think she might break something, a little afraid it might be me. She was trying too hard, too tense, too aware she was in a strange place, too exposed, being intimate with a new partner for the first time in forever. I couldn't say that, of course, so I asked her if that was her huffing and puffing or a dying dinosaur and she began to laugh and somehow in the laughing it all worked itself out.

"Yes," she said finally. "Yes" and nothing but "Yes." And then she was lost and we were lost and I lost count. As our bodies sought release, once more she whispered, "Yes," in a dusty, distant, little-girl-lost voice – "Yes."

A little later, she said, "Happy Independence Day," rolled on top and began again.

Chapter Thirty-Three

Every day Congress is in session The Hill swarms with people from dozens of organizations looking for support for their company or cause. Each one is looking for their share – and perhaps a little more – of the Federal pie.

At 8:00 AM, on the 2nd of October, 100 leaders from the Conference on the Future of Health Care gathered in the Mansfield Room of the Senate side of the Capitol. With ceilings trimmed in gold, walls paneled in American black walnut, and a fireplace formed of Meadow White Vermont marble, Mansfield is one of the most elegant rooms on the Hill. It is a setting that suggests access, influence, and power.

Lynn Pennington was charged with focusing the group.

"On average," she said, "the staff you will meet see individuals or groups like you every 15 minutes. They are likely to be young, overwhelmed, and uninformed. At the end of the day, it is your job to make sure they remember who we are and why we are here."

"Here are our guidelines: First, do not be disappointed if you do not see your Senator or Representatives. That's not likely to happen. Second, limit the material you leave behind to the summary we have prepared for you. Anything more than that will dilute our message and probably wind up in the trash. Third, do not talk about campaign contributions, no matter how much you have given or plan to give. This is neither the place nor the time for that. Fourth, stay on message and be specific. We are here because we are concerned about government's intrusion into health care. We vigorously oppose S. 1249 and S. 1250 introduced by Senator Colgate. We also oppose the Dennison amendment to the Omnibus Reconciliation Act. Fifth, be brief. There are people lined up all day behind you who think their issue is every bit as important as yours.

"Congressional offices are small so we want you to break your people up into groups of no more than five. Do it by congressional delegation. Members are elected to represent their constituents. Pure and simple. If you are not their constituent, you are not relevant to them."

At 9:00 AM, the group was disbursed, energized and ready for battle. They were herded into elevators, dropped three floors to the subway and funneled out to the six office buildings where their colleagues waited, dividing to conquer. They trooped through the halls, clogging offices, overwhelming receptionists, and dominating staff schedules. Committees with legislative jurisdiction were singled out for special and repeated attention. Lobbyists from the sponsoring organizations escorted constituents with connections in these key places.

After the first wave, Colgate's office redirected the rest to Oversight and Investigations. I let Broadbent and Christoff handle it, telling them to listen politely and keep it in the hall until Kat showed up with a covey cut from the Pennsylvania delegation. She stood to the side and let them tell their story, watching as I tried to listen. I nodded in what I hoped were all the right places, hardly hearing what they were saying, while I looked at the somewhat demure professional beside me, trying to reconcile the woman I saw with my memory of the night before. Images of her sleek body cascaded through my mind. Once or twice I thought I saw her breath catch as, perhaps, her memory connected with mine. She followed as they filed out, thanking me for my time and giving me a sidewise hug. A subtle but deliberate bump of her hip came with it. Her hand came around my waist, lingering there long enough to put something in my pocket.

After she left, I found a small, pale blue piece of paper. One word was written on it: "Osborne."

I waited until they were gone to take the elevator up to the fourth floor.   People overflowed the reception area near Jay's office and spilled out into the hall. Viagra held court, telling everyone Mr. Constantine was meeting with the chairman and unavailable at the moment. She gave me a smile and a slight nod as I walked through the crowd into the back office. Jay had his feet up on the desk. He was smoking a cigar half his size.

"Are you compensating or trying to make a statement."

"Actually, I am amusing myself by considering the various ways I could put this out. I spent the morning in the Chairman's office listening to a parade of prostitutes tell him how difficult I was to get along with, how impossible I am to work with, how sexist I can be, and what an all around asshole I am."

"Not fun. Still, we both know you wouldn't be here five minutes if you weren't doing what he wants. You're the filter. You keep the scum out of his office and their hands out of the public purse."

"Granted. Still, I'd like to fire this thing up and tell them to stick it where the sun don't shine."

"Maybe this will cheer you up."

I handed him Kat's note.

"Sonofabitch," he said.

Jay was already in a foul mood. Kat's note gave him the outlet he needed. A member of Finance for years, Osborne was new to the Health Subcommittee. He was Paul Robertson's protégé. He had campaigned hard for the assignment, citing his personal interest and state experience, but Robertson's support tipped the balance. Robertson chaired Administration. He was a cockalorum, a small man with a small mind. It paid to keep him happy.

Jay picked up the phone and dialed Osborne's aide. He could have been meeting with constituents. He could have been with his boss. It didn't matter. Jay didn't let him get passed 'hello.'

"Listen, you sonofabitch," he said. "I know what you

are up to. If you are going to play games with me I'll cut your nuts off. Who the hell do you think you are? If you ever expect to get anything through this Committee again, you'd better back off. If the Omnibus package doesn't come up for a vote I am going to hold you personally responsible and you can take the rest of your life off."

Jay didn't wait for a response. The phone came down forcibly. As he leaned back, Viagra stuck her head in. She looked frazzled.

"Anything you want me to tell these people out here?"

"Yeah. Tell them I said, 'F--- you. Nasty letter to follow."

Jay fired up his cigar again. I watched him smoke until I couldn't stand the stench and then ducked out the back door. The line leading to Jay's office stretched half way down the hall.

Kat was right. It was a full court press. They stayed with it through the afternoon while members with reason to be sympathetic endorsed their efforts on the Floor. One of them was Carl Dunagan who took the Floor and passionately expressed his support for the medical establishment. He left out the fact that his wife, one of a half a dozen spouses registered as a lobbyist, was employed by the health-insurance industry. Dunagan was supported by Lamar Lewis who asked to be associated with his colleague's remarks and raised the fearful specter of socialized medicine.

I listened until I tired of hearing it. I put a muzzle on C-Span and left the picture on. I knew what they were saying, I just wanted to track who was saying it. I was still watching when Sarah called from Chicago. Until I heard what she had to say, it was a welcome interruption.

"They got Junior this morning," she said. "Two guys abducted him from one of his clinics and shoved him into a panel truck. A couple of hours later, he was dumped in the street. They sliced him up like a rump roast. He was rushed to the hospital in critical condition. He has stabilized now. Looks like he will survive."

"What's he saying?"

"Nothing. He told police he didn't want to talk about it. We have been trying to get to him – so far, without success. Witnesses say both men were wearing stocking masks. They walked into the clinic like they owned the place, found him in his office, and carried him out. One of them was huge. The receptionist said he threw Eugene over his shoulder like a sack of flour. We got that on tape.

"Yesterday, we got to a member of the Illinois payment section. I convinced him that confession was good for the soul. He admitted being paid to expedite payments for Star Financial. We had to shoot him in shadow, but it works. We've also got an interview with the past president of the Chicago Medical Society. He says he submitted a scathing report to the Governor's Task Force on behalf of the state's Medical Advisory Committee. The report was ignored. Afterwards, he was forced to resign. His life was threatened and his car firebombed. He had to leave town."

"You've been busy."

"We have, thanks to you. Whether we get Junior or not, we're going to go tonight."

I didn't have to ask if Colgate would get a mention. Sarah was a pro. She'd make the connection.

Lando, my contact at CBS, is a different animal. He arrived at 3:15 PM, following a lead from a source at the *Times*. He said a plea agreement was in the works for Dershowitz. Steinberg had tried to distance himself, but the possibility of plea agreement put him in jeopardy. Lando was trying to nail him down. He had been told Steinberg had personally intervened on Dershowitz' behalf at least three times. He was looking for corroboration.

I spent rest of the afternoon spoon-feeding him. Consistent with the way he generally operates, Lando didn't bother saying thanks. He is very much the sponge though calling him that might slander the sponge. He absorbs whatever he touches and releases very little. He treats his sources like toilet paper – to be used and thrown away.

Lando said he would run his story unconcerned by anything Steinberg or Dershowitz might say or do at this point. It will play in Des Moines, he said. People have already made up their minds. Denials will only make the story more believable.

After Lando left, Broadbent told me Allison had been trying to reach me. She had buzzed in several times.

"She's on five," Allison said, coming down hard on *she*. There was no need for any further explanation. "This is the third time she has called."

I picked up the line knowing who to expect.

"I have to see you," she said.

"I'm here."

"You know what I mean. I need to be with you. It's been so long."

True? Why did I doubt it? And why did I care?

"Whatever happened between the last time we were together and New York? What is it with you? You are so totally different."

She was confused. When she kissed me last I was so cold and unresponsive she thought it was over. She was desolate.

"You have to understand," she said. "You are constantly on my mind."

"I shouldn't be," I said and gave her pause.

"Maybe after all this time it's too late."

It was the first time I'd heard her consider that possibility.

"Maybe we waited too long," she said. "When I was a kid, I really wanted a bike. More than anything, I wanted that bike. It was pink and white, with streamers flowing from the handles. I pestered my parents for months. When I finally got it, I peddled it all over town. But it wasn't the same. Maybe it could never be the same. You know?"

"I know."

In the evening she called me at home. Worn out from shopping and ballet, she said. She was in a good mood. Her tone was far different, less desperate, almost relaxed.

"I may drop by your office tomorrow," she said. "If I can get up the nerve, I have something to tell you."

Chapter Thirty-Four

Colgate made the talk shows Friday morning. They booked him after Patterson's piece ran Thursday night and before CBS completed its evening update. An early release of *Times*' morning edition fueled interest.

As expected, Dershowitz had accepted a plea agreement – 10 to 15 years with restitution set at $3.8 million. In exchange, the U. S. Attorney had agreed not to press charges against other members of his immediate family. Given his age, Dershowitz was looking at life in prison.

At 6:30 AM, I picked up Colgate and drove him to NBC's studio on Nebraska Avenue. Colgate had the 7:15 slot on *Today*. After that we had to hustle downtown for CBS' *Early Show*.

The problem, Colgate told *Today*, was a complete lack of accountability. "Fraud, theft and waste are rampant," he said. "And it's not only in health care. It's everywhere. Billions are being wasted and no one seems to care."

"We know there is a lot of government waste," Curry said. "But how can you say it is everywhere?"

"Look at the numbers. Every year, we ask the GAO to audit all Federal expenditures. For the 11th year in a row, they haven't been able to do it. They can't even reconcile the government's accounts. There was more than $55 billion missing last year."

"Where did it go?"

"No one knows. That's the point," Colgate said, "and apparently no one cares."

Henry Smith's producer must have been monitoring Colgate's *Today Show* appearance and briefed him.

"Hasn't there always been corruption in government?" Smith asked. "What's changed?"

 "Two things," Colgate said. "The amount of money it takes to get elected and the amount of money on the table. The average Congressional race costs $1.5 million. That means members have to raise $15,000 a day – every day they are here. If you don't have it, like I do, you have to get it from somewhere. There are always people who will give it to you but they are always going to want something in return. It's turning politicians into prostitutes."

"So you are saying it's more pervasive now," Smith said.

"It's more than pervasive. It's endemic. Personal considerations and private concerns cloud every public decision. Even things that were once considered off limits."

"Like what?"

"Social Security. Social Security used to be

———

266

untouchable. It was the third rail. When Social Security was established, a trust fund was established to insure its stability. All the money people contribute for their retirement goes into this fund. Congress didn't know how to get at it until someone came up with the idea for a "unified" budget. Sounds simple, even reasonable, but what it did was allowed Congress to fold the trust fund in with everything else."

"So what you are saying is that they are using funds set aside for Social Security for other things."

"That's right. And now a lot of the people responsible are complaining Social Security is broke. It's like the lawyer's definition of chutzpah – the boy who kills his parents and then throws himself on the mercy of the court because he is an orphan."

"If it's that pervasive, what can we do about it?"

"In the dependence movement, they have a principal called 'the first problem.' The addict invariably has a host of other problems but you have to deal with his addiction before you can deal with anything else. The first problem here is Congress. We are not going to be able to deal with all the other problems our country faces until we deal with their addiction to easy money and lobbyists who deal in it."

"How do you do that?"

"We have to take a hard look at the way campaigns are financed. People have talked about public financing for years. Maybe it's time for that. Maybe there is a simpler solution. The Senate and the House could adopt a rule on their own prohibiting any member of Congress from accepting contributions from firms that lobby them. They have done that with other ethics rules. They could do that here. That way lobbyists could continue to argue their case but they would have to stop contributing to the jury."

Colgate had warmed to his task. By the time the interview concluded, he sounded more and more like a candidate fleshing out a campaign theme.

"Either way, it has to stop. I am a businessman and I can tell you no business could operate this way for long and survive," he said. "No individual could divert money from a trust fund without going to jail. We have to restore responsibility and accountability to government."

When we returned to The Hill, The Omnibus Reconciliation Act was on the floor. Colgate arrived in time to cast his vote but passage was never in doubt. More interesting were those in dissent – a total of thirteen. Osborne, the member who had placed a hold on the bill, was expected. Seven of the remaining twelve were vocal supporters of the medical establishment with long-standing ties to the AMA.

I was in the process of analyzing the rest of the vote, when Hugh called.

"Happy birthday," he said.

"You're six months early or six months late."

"I know but you are hard to buy for. I found something I think you will like. Are you free tonight?"

"I can be."

"Meet me at 7:30 at New York and Kendall. Take a cab and come alone. Wear a Senate uniform so we can recognize you. Have the driver drop you off at the corner, wait until he is gone, and then walk south on Kendall. When it's safe, we'll pick you up."

Dick was lost in one of the computer communities where people like him meet and mate. Christoff had not come in. That gave me pause. John's desk was empty, everything as he had left it.

As I was about to leave, Dee called. It was becoming a routine, like she was trying to catch me at the end of the day. Could I come out and play? A walk? Something to eat? Most anything. I declined.

"I know what's bothering you," she said. "It's my situation."

Situation, I thought, for pity sake. She talked about her marriage as if it were a bump in the road – something we had to go around – or a flat tire to be changed.

"I told you. Marrying him was a mistake. We're getting a divorce. What do you want me to say? Talk to me! How can I play the game when you never let me know the rules? What do you want? Tell me. I have to see you. There's something I have to tell you."

There was a surprising note of urgency in her voice.

Chapter Thirty-Five

Turbiddy must have been waiting. She came rushing out of her house as soon as I opened the front gate.

"Did you see anything?" she said.

"See what?"

"She killed my cat. I found her in your front yard this morning. The vet said somebody bashed her on the head and then slit her throat. It was mean and malicious. Did you see anything? Somebody must have seen something! She thinks I killed her dog but I didn't. She killed my cat to get even."

There was a shadow visible behind the shades in the windows to my left. Clayton was watching but I couldn't see her expression. I made a mental note to keep Max inside and out of harm's way. The two of them were so hateful it was hard to trust either one.

I called Yellow Cab before I went up to change. When I came out at 7:00 PM, the cab was waiting. The driver was young and Pakistani. His English was only slightly better than my Pakistani, but he came to attention when he heard the address.

"Northeast," he said. "You mean northwest?"

The address I gave him was in a part of town a suit would rarely visit after dark. The only public place within half mile is the nightclub known as the "Bucket of Blood." I didn't fit the profile of people who would party there. I wore a dark blue suit, a light blue, pinpoint oxford shirt, and a red power tie. My pants were cinched high enough to keep my underwear from showing. No wonder the cabbie felt I was heading in the wrong direction.

Kendell going north dies at New York. The corners on either side have been converted into parking lots utilized by the DC school system. An eight-foot chain wire fence capped with razor wire surrounds the lots and protects the school buses from the neighborhood until it is safe to release them for the morning run.

The cab driver pulleded over at the corner of New York and Kendell at 7:25 PM. There was still some traffic moving out of town on New York but Kendall was quiet. The cabbie looked around and then back at me. There were no pedestrians in sight.

"I wait?" he said.

I shook my head, handed him a ten, and told him to keep the change. I waited until the cab pull out into traffic before beginning to walk down Kendall.

New York Avenue is the primary point of access to Washington from the north and east. People by the tens of thousands fly through this area every day on their way in or out of town, passing and hardly seeing a collection of dated and dilapidated warehouses that front the Avenue on both sides of the street. They are even less aware of the neighborhoods tucked behind –

some of the roughest in DC.

A block in I found an elementary school surrounded by a wall and a fence. It looked like a fortress that had been under siege. Trash gathered along the base of the perimeter fence. Broken glass littered the grounds. The walls were covered with graffiti, most of it obscene. Several pairs of sneakers decorated the power lines, marking turf.

The few people I saw looked like they didn't want to be seen. As I walked the quiet street a surprising conversation with Bill Cosby came to mind. Cosby was talking about the way television had changed urban communities. Before TV, he said, the elders spent their evenings outside. They watched the streets and the children were safe. Those with evil intent operated inside where they were hidden from sight. Now, he said, law-abiding citizens gather indoors, glued to the tube or the computer, isolating themselves and their families, surrendering the street to those who thrive in darkness.

Three blocks in I became aware a car was following me. It was a block back, lights off, moving slowly. At the next corner, another just like it pulled out in front of me. The door opened. I could see a driver and a man in a dark suit in the back seat.

"Get in," the man in the back said, "and make it quick."

I got a glimpse of a third man as I got in and the door closed.

"Put this on."

The man in the back handed me what looked like a black bag. When I slipped it over my head, the car started to move again. I had no idea how long we drove, only an awareness of changing speeds and abrupt turns. Finally, I felt the car go down a ramp and heard a garage door open. A moment later we came to a stop. My door was opened from the outside.

"Follow me," someone said, taking hold of my arm and guiding me out.

I counted a dozen steps before we stopped.

"Coming up," my escort said.

For some reason, I had the image of a man talking into his sleeve and then the clear sense of being on an elevator. When it stopped, I heard the door open and a familiar voice.

"Welcome," Hugh said. "You can take that off now."

We were in a bright, well-lit room, carefully and expensively furnished. Jones stood before me. There were five other agents in sight, flanking a well-dressed, middle-aged man seated in an armchair. He didn't need an introduction. It was "The Snake."

"I understand you want to talk with me," he said.

Chapter Thirty-Six

Sam, "The Snake", Siciliano led a complicated life. He began his career as a small-time crook and pimp in Cleveland, moved to California, got involved in the porn industry, became an enforcer for Dragna, and worked his way up through the California crime family. Halfway up the ladder, he covered his bets and became a government informant.

Now, the cover had worn thin. When he heard a contract had been put out on him, he came in off the streets and joined the witness protection plan. He was the Bureau's most valuable asset. Every law enforcement agency in the country wanted to talk with him.

There are those on The Hill who prefer to believe the government's health programs have somehow escaped the interest of organized crime. These same people tend to believe that professional wrestling is on the level. Somewhere along the line in every investigation I led I found a link to the underworld. Almost as inevitably, sometime after that someone would try to pull a political lever and turn me off.

The crime connection is well established if not well advertised. In June of 1970, the Senate Select Committee on Crime asked Carlos Marcello, head of the New Orleans syndicate, what he was doing at the La Stella restaurant in New York in 1966, less than a year after Medicare was enacted.

"I went on a business trip," Marcello said.
"What was the nature of your business?" he was
asked.

"To try to get a loan on a nursing home."

Carlo Gambino, Santo Trafficante and eleven other
notorious racketeers were also found to be involved.
At about the same time, Mafia control of New Jersey
nursing homes was mentioned in tapes introduced in
evidence in the trial of Simone DeCalvacante.
During the next decade, Joseph Zerilli, the Detroit
boss, was found to be among the owners of a health
facility in Lake County, Michigan, and Frank
Fitzsimmons gave the go ahead for the creation of the
American Health Maintenance Organization. While
participating in Bob Hope's golf tournament in Palm
Spring, the Teamsters' President took time to meet
with three California mobsters. Alan Dorfman, was
hired as their "consultant" and asked to work out the
details.

Dorfman and his friends enrolled thousands of people
in the HMO and then did everything possible to limit
service. The *Los Angeles Times* would later find
AHMO turned a 3,000 percent profit. Pushed to
investigate the *Times*' claims, the State concluded
most of the money the plan took in was being taken
out for "administrative expenses" and profits. The
operation was shut down after it failed to pay more
than $2 million of its customers' bills.

In New York, investigators had tied Columbo,
Genovese, and Pagano to health rackets. Columbo

had always been particularly active, using strong-arm tactics, threats of arson and death to extort money from health centers. In return, the gangster offered insulation from the authorities and protection from competition, guaranteeing no other center would be allowed to open in a 20-block area.

To my knowledge, forty-five states had evidence of organized crime attempts to rip-off Medicare and Medicaid. All the major crime families were involved. The Snake was tied to two of these families and had an intimate knowledge of the rest.

It is said Siciliano earned his nickname while he was in the porn industry. There was no evidence of that in the neatly tailored suit he now wore, any more than there was any reason to believe this mild looking, elderly man had killed two dozen men and arranged the death of a number of others. He looked more like the owner of the local pizzeria than a hit man. His smile was amiable, his eyes opaque and unfocused behind thick, black-framed glasses. His body was so thin he almost appeared frail. Still, it didn't take a lot of muscle to pull the trigger on a .22 automatic.

Siciliano was looking at a laptop. Probably reading his press clips, I thought. He had that reputation. His living room looked like a suite at the Ritz inset in a warehouse façade, a room within a room. There was a bar, an oversized flat screen, diffuse lighting, a sofa, armchairs, a piano, and a Persian rug. All the comforts of home.

Siciliano put down the laptop and waited for my response to his question.

"I'm sure there are a lot of people who want to talk with you."

"Yeah," Siciliano said. "I'm a real popular guy."

"Do you know why I want to talk with you?"

"I know about Scarpace. I know about Ricca. I know certain people in Miami don't like you. I know you like to play games and sometimes when you play games people get hurt. I know you had a visit from Tiny."

"He speaks highly of you."

"I'm the one who named him. He is a prick – but a little one."

"Is that why he fingered you?"

"Colombo put $100,000 on my head. Tiny would love to be the one to collect. He would do it for free, you understand, but he would take the money anyway."

"It's nice to know there are some people out there who still enjoy their work."

Siciliano smiled.

"They said you were a wise ass. In the old days, you know who got whacked? People who were bought and didn't stay bought. People who betrayed the family. These people have no respect, no family, no loyalty. They'll whack anyone who stands in their way."

"Like you?"
He nodded.

"And you. Even him."

Siciliano gestured at Jones.

"Any of the old bosses would never allow that. It was part of the code. You never whack civilians. You never take out a badge. Other ways could be found. You made an arrangement. They would not interfere with us and we wouldn't interfere with them. You took care of the guy on the beat. You help him when he is starting out and he takes care of you later."

"Like Scarpace?"

"Scarpace, Dvorak. They are all the same. Dime a dozen."

"Dvorak?"

"The cop that worked Feinstein's case in Chicago. I hear he just made lieutenant."

Siciliano took off his glasses, pinched the bridge of his nose, and adjusted the frame. His eyes seemed to recede in his face.

"People make a big deal about organized crime," he said. "Organized crime is just big business. Just as often, big business is organized crime."

He replaced his glasses and looked at me.

"What's the difference?" he asked.

It was a rhetorical question. Siciliano continued before I could respond.

"The law? A punk from the projects gets locked up for stealing $1,000. It's a felony. Two to three years. Minimum. Three strikes and it's 25. Mandatory. The executive who steals millions walks away with a severance package and bonus. A kid doing drugs gets hard time. The celebrity doing drugs gets community service and a TV show. The bank that can't meet its commitments to its customers gets bailed out. The customer who can't meet his commitments to the bank gets flushed. You think that's an accident? Think about it. Who decides what's legal? Who writes the laws?"

He gave me a thin smile and lit a cigarette before he continued.

"The law is just a spider web. It only catches the little ones without the strength to get away. The bigger you are the easier it is to break through; the more connected you are the more you are protected."

He took one more puff and put the cigarette out. There were a half dozen just like it in the ashtray before him. Maybe he had read the warning label and decided it was time to quit.

"So, how do you build relationships? You find out what people need. You give them what they want. You know? You establish a connection."

I nodded. It was surreal. Was this a kindly uncle giving me a lesson on life or a mobster.
"It's an investment. The longer they are around, the bigger they get, the better your investment pays off. Who knows, the alderman could becomes a state senator or mayor or even governor. And so on. One hand washes the other. You help them. They help you."

"But you have to start early. You can make a deal with someone who is established but you can't build a relationship. If they are not in bed with you by then, they are not going to get in bed with you. You have to find another way. Sometimes they make it easy for you like Hoover. Sometimes someone else makes it easier for you like you did for Star."

"How did I do that?"

"You created a vacuum. You took out some of their competition. You weakened their organizations. You opened the door. You made it easy for Star to come in and take over.

"What about Hoover?"

"Hoover set himself up. He was a fruit loop. I used to see him at the track every once in a while with his lover boy, Clyde. They were careful, but there was no doubt what was going on. All the families knew. They had plenty of proof. Early on, Hoover was arrested in New Orleans. Who controlled the New

Orleans police? Marcello. He got word and copied the record. It got around. When Hoover started hanging out with Clyde at the Stork Club, Costello had two-way mirrors installed in the toilets and put microphones at the tables. He taped everything that happened in the place. Lansky nailed it. They used to go to the same watering holes in Florida – The Rivera, Doral, Mario's – sometimes at the same time. Lansky would be at one table Edgar and Clyde at another. Lansky got pictures of Hoover doing something with Clyde and made a deal."

"You get what you give."

"Right. Hoover used the FBI to collect blackmail information. We gave it back to him. As long as he was alive, the FBI was no threat to us."

"Now, it's a different ballgame."

"Now, anything goes," Siciliano said. "And health care is the pot of gold. Think about it. There's billions on the table. It's safer than dope, more profitable, and, less risky. It's up for grabs. In the middle of all this, along comes you."

"Lucky me," I said.

———

I thought for a moment and looked at Jones, wondering if this was what he had in mind.

"If I can pull a hearing together," I said, "would you testify?"

"Why not," Siciliano said. "I'm already a dead man. The testimony your friend wants me to give will put at least 30 guys away. Six of them bosses. I've got nothing to lose. The enemy of my enemy is my friend. Right now, you are probably the best friend I have."

Chapter Thirty-Seven

Jones walked me to the elevator.

"If you want him, you'll have to go fast. We can't keep him here long. He is costing the Bureau a fortune. We have five agents assigned to him 24/7. We have to keep moving him around and each safe house has to be customized. As you can tell, he likes to live well."

"We'll go as soon as I can clear Colgate's schedule," I said. "Thanks, by the way."

"No problem. You've been good to us, Nick, good to me. DipScam netted 50,000 phony professionals, including a lot of paper doctors. The Bureau's White Collar Division got beefed up after that. We would have never gotten there without your lead."

Jones looked back at Siciliano, feeling the need to comment on what he had said.

"The low point was when Kliendiest decided to discontinue surveillance of the mob leaders. It demoralized the Bureau. At least everyone I knew. We've turned it around since then and you've helped. You've given the Bureau a lot of positive press through the years. Hell, we even made Doonesbury."

He smiled.

"How is Max by the way?"

"To tell you the truth, I haven't seen much of him since Trish moved in."

"Smart dog."

"And he has the sheepskins to prove it."

They put the bag back over my head, ducked me into a car, and drove me around for a while before dropping me off behind the National Gallery of Art. Few places in Washington are as quiet as the Mall after dark on a Friday night. It took me twenty minutes to walk home. I didn't see anyone until I passed the Capitol where a cop stationed at the guard post on the south side of Russell gave me a puzzled look.

It was a quarter to twelve when I got home. Trish was still up. She was eating again. She had gone through whatever was in her kitchen and was working on what little there was in mine. Some cheese and crackers, chips, salsa, and soda were spread on the counter.

"What happened to Carson?"

"We broke up?"

"Why?"

"The chemistry was off. After the first rush, we had a hard time developing a real interest in each other."

She gave me a thin laugh.

"I think he was more interested in you than me?"

"What do you mean?"

"He always wanted to come over here. We never went to his place. He was always asking me about you. At first I thought he was jealous or trying to figure out our relationship but he was more interested in where you were and what you were doing than the boy-girl stuff. The last time he stayed over he came upstairs while I was in the shower. He said he was hungry and there was nothing in my fridge that appealed to him. I heard Max growling and found him at the foot of the stairs that go up to your bedroom. It was probably innocent enough. Max never liked him much anyway. But I had a funny feeling about it. I called him on it and he got defensive. We had an argument and I told him to leave. I don't think he'll be back."

"Regrets?"

"Not really. The package was nice and I enjoyed having him around but it was more something is better than nothing than anything else. I had a hard time persuading myself it was going somewhere."

The look on her face said it all. It was a look I had seen many times before: Why does it always end this way?

The pretty ones, especially the pretty ones who have grown up pretty, tend to live near the surface, without depth not because they have no depth but because they have no need for it. They have always been accepted, pursued, cherished, plundered, loved, bought and sold for being – just for being. And will continue to be, as long as the flesh endures. With that small thing given, whatever capacity locked inside that distracting, sweetly constructed body is lost. While it lasts, there is neither doubt nor regret nor concern that this is all you were meant to be, nor care, except for the ritual – the superficial self-appraisal. The wrinkly examination. A check for depreciation of assets. Pinch butt. Heft breast. Pull in the gut. And when things get desperate, see the man with the knife. Nip and tuck. Roll back the years. Buy a few more years. A few more good years...And when it is done, irrevocably, irretrievably done, wonder what remains.

It is such a waste – such a tremendous waste – I wanted to tell her. You are so painfully attractive, so obviously attractive; the rest is neither needed nor wanted. It is an unnecessary complication. An amusement park has neither intelligence nor warmth. It is there to ride. It shouldn't threaten or compete or make complicating human demands, involve the mind and, perhaps, even the soul. The world is full of pretty girls, Trish. They march interchangeably through the city from job to job, bed to bed, and marriage to marriage. One is as the other. Nothing more than a pleasant arrangement of features. When will you realize how much more than that you are? They undervalue you. Worse, you undervalue yourself.

All this I should have said, but I didn't. I am not sure why.

I went to bed late and had a restless night. The events of the last few weeks played on my mind. The DVD in the back of my head kept running images, shuffling scenes. They seemed to fit together, but I couldn't quite figure out how.

I was awakened by a low growl. Max had come upstairs to get me. He was at the foot of the bed, making the noise he likes to make when he is thinking about tearing into someone. It was his way of saying, "We've got company."

I followed him to the windows at the back of the house. A shadow moved down below along the fence carefully avoiding the light provided by the streetlamp in the alley behind the carriage house. Since the age of eight when I began understudying Ripkin, I have slept with a baseball bat by my bed. I picked it up and went downstairs. When I got to the kitchen, I flipped on the floodlights at the back of the house. The courtyard was bathed in light. I saw someone turn and run through the open door of the carriage house. He moved fast for a big man – faster than I would have thought possible. He filled the door and then he was gone.

Trish called the cops. Twenty minutes later, two blue suits arrived. They were the same pair I'd seen at John's less than a week before. While I recognized them, they didn't seem to recognize me. Their questions were predictable and perfunctory. Did you get a good look at them? Anything missing?

Why they said "them" was beyond me. I had only reported one intruder. I told them "no" and "no."

There were no signs of the intrusion below except for a five-gallon gasoline can and a couple of rags left under the deck at the back of the house. Inside the carriage house, they found the French doors to the alley had been forced open. The safety chain was dangling. There were black smudges along the doorframe and signs of a pry bar around the lock. The interior door had been opened from the inside.

They called the fingerprint brigade and went through the motions but I couldn't delude myself they would find something or, if they did, know what to do with it. In the morning, I called Colgate at home. Then I called Jones.

Chapter Thirty-Eight

There was another famine in the Sudan. Half a million people had died. Two million more were facing starvation. The perennial conflict in the Middle East had heated up, the market had dropped, the price of oil had doubled, but the lead story on Monday, the 6th of October was about a twenty-four year old girl who, it was said, had been shamelessly peddling her ass on The Hill.

StaffAss had been identified. *The Washington Times* broke the news with the lead: "Congressional Assets." The accompanying article read like and an editorial.

"The wicked woman that boasted of bedding six men at the same time and selling herself to others is Tiffany Sinclair, a legislative correspondent in the office of Senator Thomas Devlin (R-Ohio). A graduate from Georgetown University with a bachelor's degree in international relations, Ms. Sinclair, an aspiring journalist, started working on Capitol Hill as intern for Senator Hunter Johnson (D-CT) and joined Sen. Devlin's office as a staff assistant in February.

"Ms. Sinclair started her blog two months after joining Senator Devlin's staff. Her diary alleges two of the six people she sleeps with on a regular basis are also on Senator Devlin's staff. One of them is said to be her supervisor. She claims others paid her $400 to $500 an hour for her sexual services. According to

Ms. Sinclair, most of these people are high placed professionals on Capitol Hill. One of her clients is described as a married man who received a Presidential appointment. Efforts to identify this high-level federal employee have so far been unsuccessful.

"Ms. Sinclair could not be reached for comment. In a prepared statement, Sen. Devlin said Ms. Sinclair had been dismissed for using Senate resources and work time to post unsuitable and offensive material on the internet. Two other staff members have been suspended pending the outcome of an internal investigation."

StaffAss had been pulled down, but two other sites had captured it and were reprinting it verbatim. Within hours, the blog was being virally transmitted to millions. Nothing about Ms. Sinclair's writing suggested she might have found success as a journalist but the copy was so titillating it didn't matter. The fact that her paramours were not identified only added to the intrigue.

"Had a long lunch with JR," one entry said. "Says he'll go five next time if I let him use the back door. Why not? Maybe I should tell LM how handsomely I'm getting paid for what he gets for free. I could use a salary bump."

"Last night," the most recent entry reported, "I went to SD's house after dinner at the Hawk and Dove. A two-bedroom in Arlington. Needs work, but very cute. Had sex like animals. Took me around the world. Says he wants to use handcuffs next time. Intriguing but a little scary. If he knew that, it would probably turn him on."

We have become a nation of voyeurs and exhibitionists. Turn on the tube. All you see are reality shows, each one more outrageous than the last. Check the Internet – U-Tube, Twitter, Facebook, and all the rest. Few can resist the urge to share the intimate details of their lives or the temptation to live vicariously through the lives of others. Sinclair confirmed the obvious.

Broadbent, of course, loved it. He was glued to his screen when I arrived, taking notes. He had created an index and showed it to me with obvious pride. Maybe he thought I would be impressed by his detective skills.

He had identified nine players:

BD:	Intern in her office
LM:	Supervisor
JR:	Chief of Staff of a government agency
CM:	Old Boyfriend
SD:	New Boyfriend
DA:	BFF
LL:	Lobbyist
BA:	Lawyer
HF:	Sugar Daddy

I left Dick to his obsession and took Christoff with me to look for a secure hearing site. I couldn't help wishing Broadbent would show as much interest in the Committee's activities but there was nothing I could do about that.

The Snake would draw the press the way manure draws flies. His story had all the elements they love - blood, betrayal, greed, and corruption. The hearing would be a media circus and a security nightmare. The people who would like to see Siciliano dead wouldn't care where it happened. And they certainly wouldn't be intimidated by The Hill's Mickey Mouse police force.

The best option was in the Hart Senate Office Building. We went down the hall and through the corridor that has been jerry-rigged to connect Dirksen with Hart. When Dirksen was under construction, Senator Long made a fuss about the cost. He was probably right to do so. The Building took twice as long to complete as it should have and cost more than twice what was expected. Long's solution, which some would say was politically motivated, was simple and direct. He lopped off one end of the rectangle the building was designed to be and sealed the corridors being built, turning a square into an E – one corridor with three arms that did not connect.

Building Hart was the solution contrived more than thirty years later on a much grander scale and at a much greater cost, extending and completing the rectangle originally envisioned. But marrying the past and the present rarely works. The seams show. Traffic doesn't flow naturally. One building is neo-classical and the other contemporary. Corridors double back and are redundant. People get lost.

Tourists who think they are here find out they are there. It's confusing.

Still, Hart provides some benefits – some sorely needed others questionable. It houses half the Senate, three committees and several subcommittees. It also provides conference and meeting space; a state of the art hearing room, pre-wired and set for the modern media age; and a place to park a 51 foot Calder.

The Central Hearing Facility is on the second floor of Hart. Scotty McDew was waiting to let us in. A slender black man, Scotty has worked for the Superintendent for more than twenty years. Inside the office, he has a name but outside he will probably always be known as one of the boys sent by the Superintendent's Office to deal with minor concerns – lost keys, broken pipes, messes and spills.

The Central Hearing Facility is oversized, two stories high. The wall behind the dais is white and gray marble with a six-foot Senate seal centered halfway up. The other three walls are paneled in dark wood that contrast with the marble. Movable panels have been installed in the sidewalls so television cameras can operate without distracting the participants – a significant problem in other hearing rooms. There are two entrances, one public the other private. It is best known as the site of the Keating Five hearing, and Clinton's impeachment. It was also the site for the only coronation ever held on The Hill.

The crowning ceremony was for the Rev. Sun Myung Moon, ex-convict, multibillionaire owner of the

Washington Times and United Press International. Dressed in maroon robes and wearing a bejeweled crown placed on him by Congressman Davis, Rev. Moon declared himself the Second Coming and told a bipartisan audience that included 81 Congressmen – most of whom would deny being there – that he would save everyone on earth and that he had already saved the souls of Hitler and Stalin. He said they had been born again through him.

After walking the room and blocking out the staging elements of the hearing, I went looking for Capitol's Chief of Police. The Bureau would insist its people screen participants and control access, but The Hill's police would have to be advised and be involved on the perimeter – particularly at the doors where people without credentials are checked as they enter the office buildings.

The Capitol's cops are headquartered on D Street, a block north of Dirksen, next door to the Monocle. Marsden's office was on the fifth floor with a nice view of the Capitol. He looked like too many cops too long off the beat or jocks too long off the field – too much weight, too little hair. His greeting made it clear he had too little time to be bothered by me.

The Hill's police force was created in 1828 following an assault in the Rotunda on John Quincy Adams's son. Initially, the force was given the responsibility of providing security for the Capitol Building. Through the years, their role has expanded to a variety of other services similar to those provided by corporate security firms.

There have been repeated attempts to "professionalize" the 1,700-member force, but The Hill still swarms with paunchy professionals. Fifty-sixty. Big-bellied, bald, and bored. Retired E7, E8 and E9. Professional desk-bound sergeants, fresh from 20 years of shoveling papers, looking for a fresh pasture, a smooth ride, and another government paycheck. They spawn and multiply in traditional bureaucratic incest. Somebody is always looking for a slot for somebody's brother, nephew, or cousin. Lost in these, like a bloodline that didn't pan out, are the career cops, many of them college kids who stayed with it when college didn't work out.

I had a couple of this dying breed detailed to help with the Mills investigation. Friends from way back, they jumped at the chance, becoming the envy of the force and earning the ire of those they had to report to in the process. Who do these guys think they are anyway?

Marsden hadn't forgotten. He wondered what I was up to this time. He about had a coronary when I told him.

Afterwards, I celebrated by stopping next door to have a drink. Christoff went off, as was his want, to do something on his own, but Nick and John kept me company. One drink became two, and then dinner seemed like a good idea. It was well into the evening when I headed home.

Halfway there, my cell rang. The voice on the other end was distinctive.

"Do you know who this is?"

I said I did.

"Be careful," Siciliano said. "Last night was nothing. It is just beginning. Tell your boss to be careful too."

I couldn't imagine anyone would be that bold.

"Why?" I said, hoping for more specific information.

"I can't tell you why. I don't know what I know. What I can tell you is I know the way these guys think. If you cut off the head, what's the tail going to do?"

Chapter Thirty-Nine

The *Times* broke the story. The *Post* got the interview.

Tiffany Sinclair was on the cover of the Style section Tuesday morning. She was dark-eyed and dark-haired with a slightly exotic cast to her features. She gazed confidently at the camera, looking thoroughly professional in a dark jacket over a light colored blouse, a far cry from the way she was dressed at Pam's party. I couldn't help thinking that if I had entered Broadbent's pool I would have won.

Far from contrite, Sinclair was amused that her exploits had attracted so much attention.

"It amazes me that people have any interest at all in what I have done," she said. "It's so clichéd. It's like, 'There's a slutty girl on the Hill!' There's thousands of 'em. Like I said when I started my blog. I'm convinced The Hill is full of dealers and hos. I'm just paying the rent. Some of my friends do a lot better."

Steve Curtis had the interview.

"What do you mean?" he said.

"One of my friends got $25,000 for two days. That's more than I make a year. It's a different deal, but the same thing. Mine is in and out. No games. No pretense. No commitment. I may or may not enjoy it. Her's is more boy/girl stuff. They're buying the illusion of a relationship for themselves, showing off for their friends, or trying to impress business associates. She has to pretend to like it. Worse, she has to pretend to like them."

"Ego costs more than sex."

"Of course. If they had to choose, most men would rather have people think they are something than be whatever they want people to think they are."

"When did this start for you?"

"When I came to the Capitol Hill, I was in college and star-struck. I couldn't believe I was working with people I'd read about most of my life, people who ran the world. Then I learned the Senator I worked for was sleeping with a lobbyist and everybody knew it, his wife was on the payroll of another firm, the Chairman of the full Committee I covered had a boyfriend who ran a prostitution ring out of his townhouse, and on and on...It didn't take me long to realize they were just like every one else – particularly below the belt. I saw the way they behaved and said 'Why not.' It seemed like everyone I met was hitting on me anyway."

"Why the blog?"

"Again, why not? I'm not ashamed of what I'm doing. It's nothing compared to what they are doing.

At least, I'm honest about it. I spent eight hours a day shuffling papers, but that's not why I was there, that's not what I was being paid for, and everyone that mattered knew it. What I do on my own time is no different. I'm not trying to hurt anyone. Nobody is taking advantage of me and I'm not taking advantage of anyone else."

"It almost seems like you're bragging."

"Not at all. Maybe it's a generational thing. A lot of older people still believe it's all right for men to screw around but not a woman. The internet is how I communicate with my friends and how I make friends. I'm not trying to embarrass anyone. I'm not pretending to be something I'm not. Most of the people who seem so outraged have done things far worse. And they are judging me? Give me a break!!"

"Where do you go from here?"

"There is no such thing as bad press – is there? You tell me. It sure hasn't hurt Brittany or Paris. *Playboy* and *Penthouse* have already contacted me. They say they'll give me more than Parkinson got for spreading on the couch where she used to make it with the Chairman, twice what they gave Jenrette for wrapping herself around the pole on the portico where she used to get it on. *Hustler* has offered me a package deal. They want to do a 'tell all" built around the blog, illustrating it with pictures of me in some of the places I mention on The Hill. They'll go seven figures if I will name names – more if I implicate a

Member. I may cash in on that. It would be easy enough. And all of sudden when you would think no one would want to get near me, it seems everyone wants to hire me. I've got job offers here, in New York, and Hollywood. There's talk of a reality show. I'm going to take my time and sort it out. I have a friend who is a lawyer. He says he will help me."

"Is he one of the clients you mentioned in your blog?"

"He is a friend. That's all I will say."

Chapter Forty

After talking with Colgate, Snake's hearing had been set two days out – the day before the Omnibus Bill was scheduled for conference. I hoped to generate enough press to push it over the top and keep members from backing away.

I called Wilson and Skinner and asked if they would help set the stage for Siciliano. Both were quick to agree, but the Committee had already heard much of what they would say. While they could amplify previous testimony, speak to developments, and make a specific connection to the crime syndicates, I knew we needed something more. If nothing else, we needed to be able to demonstrate it was more than a New York/Chicago problem. Given The Snake's background, Ohio and California seemed to make the most sense. The fact that each represented a significant media market didn't hurt.

I called Pete Lazinzki, the U. S. Attorney in Ohio, first. A year earlier, Pete had arrested John Lester for kiting bills. Faced with prison, Lester, the millionaire owner of Atlas Laboratories, explained he had made a deal with the devil. To raise capital, he had borrowed $100,000 from a loan shark. He had more than that in receivables and was sure he would be able to repay his debt in 30 days. Inexplicably, payments on his claims were delayed. Meanwhile, interest mounted until he owed twice what he had borrowed.

Unable to pay and concerned for his safety, he was persuaded to seek the protection of "Tony Jack" Giacalone. Giacalone listened quietly to Lester's request and then said, "Come with me." Together they went to a pay phone at the back of the restaurant where they met and Tony Jack dialed a number.

"Put the lab thing on the back burner," he said when he had a response. "I'll take care of it. Tell the boys downtown to treat Atlas like family from now on."

With that Lester said, Giacalone declared himself a partner in the lab. The best estimate was that he took $700,000 from the laboratory in two years. Giacalone was sentenced to three years in prison. Lester went into witness protection.

Lazinzki was out. I left a lengthy message with his office and went looking for John David. David had been an investigator for the California State Department of Health for nineteen years. Before that he had worked in the Department of Alcoholic Beverage Control, the Bureau of Consumer Affairs, and the agency that licenses physicians.

He was the first hired to work up violations in the MediCal program and went on to develop the State's system for enforcing the Department's rules. Ten years later, he was promoted to Senior Special Investigator and was placed in charge of investigations in the Los Angeles, San Bernardino,

and San Diego regions with 10 staff members under his control. Three years after that, his staff was expanded to 50 and he was placed in charge of all of Southern California.

It took me two hours to find him. He was now a security guard for the May Company.

In the meantime, Lazinzki called and left word he would be happy to testify. He left a couple of times when he would be available. David had to wait until his break. He called back – collect – half an hour later.

"What happened?" I asked.

"Toward the end of last year we were told to send all our leads to the Bureau in Sacramento. We were getting literally hundreds of complaints but we couldn't investigate them. I met with my supervisors in the Department, Everett Charles and Bob Murphy, and discussed this with them. I told them as strongly as I could that our failure to go ahead was hurting the program and reducing morale.

"About the same time, the *Los Angeles Times* ran a story questioning the State's inaction. Right after that, I was given the go ahead. I thought I had gotten through but it only lasted a few days. When I raised the issue, they took the San Diego and San

Bernardino offices away from me. I was accused of being disloyal and made the scapegoat. They said investigating complaints was my responsibility. The backlog the *Times* had found – the cases Sacramento wouldn't let me investigate – were cited as evidence I wasn't doing my job. Murphy and Charles denied ever meeting with me or telling me to back off. I called them what they are and they let me go."

...

That evening I went to the Verizon Center. The Penguins were in town. I was a light blue shirt in the sea of red cheering for Ovechkin to mop the ice with Crosby.

A few minutes after I arrived, a big man came in and took the seat next to me. He was somewhere around 6'4", most of it legs. If his torso had kept up with their foundation, he probably would have been playing for the Wizards instead of watching the Capitals.

"Nick," he said, "nice to see you. How long has it been?"

"Too, long. Are you still working for the Pentagon?"

"Occasionally, but cyber crime has gotten to be such a big deal there is a lot of demand in the private sector. I can set my own hours, charge what I want, and pick and choose where and when I want to work."

He handed me a card. It said: Robert Moore,

Consultant. The address was on Arlington Boulevard

near the Pentagon.

"I hear you're back on The Hill."

I nodded.

"Why?"

"It seemed like the thing to do."

"As I recall, you said something similar when I asked you why you joined the Army. There aren't many professionals who would walk away from what they were doing the way you did."

"If I hadn't, we would never have met."

"I never did find out how you wound up with Counterintelligence."

"Neither did I. They may have seen something in the tests they give you or maybe they picked up something in my file. Who knows? I never could find a reason for half of what the Pentagon does."

"I can't quarrel with that. They are paying me more as a part-time consultant than they ever paid me while I was on staff."

I bought him a beer, got myself a coke, and some peanuts to share.

"By the way, thanks for the ticket," Bob said. "I don't get out as often as I should."

"Any problem getting in?"

"No. It was waiting at will call just as you said. The only challenge I had was getting past a couple of guys who were trying real hard to get into the game at the last minute. They wouldn't believe the girl when she said it was sold out. They were offering a lot of money for a ticket or a pair of tickets."

"What did they look like?"

"Mutt and Jeff. A couple of K Street suits."

After last night, it was not what I expected. Where's Rocco? I wondered as I watched Moore's mind work. It resembled the computers that are his life. I could see him process the information he had, fill in the blanks he didn't have, and knew when the pieces had fallen into place.

"Friends of yours?" he said.

"I would hesitate to call them friends."

"That would explain the rather elaborate lengths you've taken to plan our reunion."

"Let's just say it probably wouldn't be good for you to be seen with me right now."

Moore took a sip of beer. It seemed to help lubricate his processor.

"What can I do to help?"

"I don't know. Maybe answer a question for me. I have been trying to figure out if there is a way to disseminate a lot of information from a single source that can't be traced."

"Would the source be government?"

"Probably."

"So you would want recipients to know it came from a government source but not how it was sent and who sent it?"

"That's the general idea."

"Of course, this would not be for any unlawful purpose."

"Of course."

Another sip of beer.

"That's an interesting question. There are all kinds of worms and virus out there but most of them are tagged and fairly easy to trace. Most of them use a zombie computer or a proxy. Proxies are generally acquired by using a Trojan horse, which gets you to download a dangerous payload without knowing it. Sometimes a botnet is installed to coordinate the activities of a series of infected proxies. Theoretically, they can be programmed to do what ever you want – deleting files, transmitting information, spying on users, or gathering data –"

"Stop," I said. "You lost me at botnet."

Bob smiled.

"Let me think about it and I will get back to you."

I left at the end of the first period, taking advantage of the crowd's movement. It was a good game and I hated to leave, but I didn't want to push my luck after my conversation with The Snake. I dropped down to the parking level and walked out through the garage rather than leave the way I had come in. I walked away from the Capitol toward White House and then caught a cab back to The Hill.

About the same time, Colgate's car went off the side of the road on Route 41 in Southeastern

Pennsylvania. He was on his way home after a town meeting and a fundraising event in Lancaster. The driver was killed. I did not learn until later that night that Colgate was in critical condition.

Chapter Forty-One

Pennsylvania has the worst roads in the country. Forty percent are considered too narrow for safety. People are always running into the median or coming too close to the edge and drifting off the road. There are wild animals everywhere and enough potholes to keep the number of Corvettes and Mustangs to a minimum. Only the reckless and foolish drive fast in Pennsylvania.

Highway 41 is particularly bad. Sharp curves, limited sight distance, and narrow shoulders, make it a difficult drive under the best of circumstances. At night when visibility is diminished, it can be treacherous.

Mr. and Mrs. Harvey Donaldson, childhood sweethearts married half a century, were the first to arrive on the scene of the Colgate accident. They called it in at 9:46 PM.

At first they thought the car on fire at the bottom of the ravine would be the dark SUV that had passed them at great speed moments before, throwing a fright into them both, and causing Harvey to go off on a rant about drivers these days. Martha had just settled him down when they came upon the crash.

They were surprised to see a light colored Lexus on its side, one headlight broken, one still trying to penetrate the impenetrable dark, illuminating only the pouring rain. The car had gone off the road at the beginning of a hairpin turn fifteen miles out of Atglen, crashing through the guard rail with enough force to carry it 50 yards before smashing into the side of the mountain and then tumbling down to rest, wedged between two ancient pine trees.

What was left of the driver, Mack Johnson, had to pried and torched out of what was left of the mangled machine. He left behind a wife and two kids. Colgate had somehow been thrown free. He was found draped over a bush twenty feet from the car, clinging to life.

A Medivac unit from Lancaster General flew out and brought him back. He was rushed into surgery where surgeons, well aware of who he was, labored for six hours, trying to stop the massive bleeding and put him back together. At 4:33 AM on the 8th of October, a spokesperson for the hospital said Senator Colgate was in stable but critical condition. His wife and children were by his side.

At half past ten, Mary Jane called. She said Caroline Colgate wanted to talk with me and gave me a number. The message was delivered with more than a little resentment. There were others closer to the family, people who had been with Colgate much longer. Why was she reaching out to me?

Mrs. Colgate answered almost immediately. She was either waiting for the call or determined to keep the disturbance to a minimum.

"Thanks for calling," she said.

"Please," I said. "It's nothing. How is he?"

"Pretty banged up. God, it's hard to see him like this. He has bandages on every part of his body. Everything is broken and there is a lot of internal damage. Anyone else wouldn't be here. But he is tough. He has always been a fighter and he is holding his own."

"Anything I can do?"

"Pray, most of all, and then maybe help figure out what happened. All of our drivers are professionals. They are trained to provide security for corporate executives and their families. Mack was the best. He used to teach at Wharton. I've been sitting here all night trying to figure out how this happened. All I can think of is what Carl said in the morning before he left. He told me about your conversation and the hearing tomorrow. Do you think there could be a connection?"

"Honestly, I don't know. The same question has been on my mind."

"What would you do in my position?"

"Again, I don't know. But for what it's worth, don't let them dismiss this as an accident. They may want to do that because that's the easy way out. And don't leave it to the state police. Hire your own people. Get the best you can find and tell them to look for the worst. Otherwise, you'll never be sure what happened."

———

"What are you going to do?"

"I was looking for a fall back position when you called. My gut tells me there is a connection between what happened up there and what we are doing down here. If we miss this opportunity, they win. Siciliano will be gone. It will be hard to reel him back in and if we do, his testimony will be irrelevant. The moment will have passed."

"Is there anything I can do?"

"You've got more important things to worry about. You don't need this."

"Please. It may sound strange but I do. I need to do something. I can't just sit here and watch the man I love bleed and do nothing about it. If this wasn't an accident, we can't let them get away with it."

Colgate had more gifts than most men can imagine. I had never envied him any of it, but I envied him now. I was happy for him in the worst of circumstances, happy he had someone like her in his life. At the same time, I couldn't help feeling sad and sorry for myself as I contemplated my own solitary existence and the emptiness of my life. I wondered if anyone would really give a damn if something happened to me.

"Well, there's this," I said. "The best option we have at the moment is the chairman of the full committee, Pete Popper. He has been minimally involved with Oversight and Investigations since I got here but he might be persuaded to step in under the circumstances. The only other option would be to proceed with Mancini in the Chair. If we go that way, Sweet may come and assert his seniority. Given our history, I don't trust him enough to want to put our fate in his hands."

"What do you want me to do?"

"Call Popper. Ask for his help. The only access I have is through the staff director and we don't get along. As a matter of fact, he would love nothing more than to see us fail. I think Popper would have a hard time saying no to you. Ask him to step in and make sure the hearing proceeds as scheduled."

"Consider it done."

...

At 11:30, Kat called to express her concern. Was Colgate all right? Was I all right? When could we get together again?

Lunch was out the question, I told her. I had my hands full.

"Actually, I was wondering if you are free tonight."

"Tonight?"

"Say around 8:00. We can grab a bite to eat and catch up."

"It will have to be an early night. I have a hearing tomorrow."

"I know. I'll try to come a little earlier."

Tubin dropped in out of nowhere at 12:00. He said he was sorry about Colgate and asked if the hearing was still on. He said he had heard it would be explosive. That would explain his sudden appearance on The Hill. He asked for a copy of the press package. I gave him a sanitized advance and told him we were holding the general release until we heard from the minority.

I spent most the afternoon blocking out questions by myself. Christoff was missing in action. Broadbent was there but he wasn't. As usual, he was focused on other things. Colgate's death meant he was without a patron but he was either unaware of how that might affect him or unconcerned.

At 3:30, Christoff called.

"I'm sorry I couldn't call earlier," he said. "I've got a personal situation I have to deal with. I know the timing is not great but I have no choice."

It was the second time in less than a week I had heard that line. I couldn't imagine what Christoff was talking about.

"What's going on?"

"I expect to be arrested tomorrow. I got word from a friend that they are going to come looking for me.

They are going to charge me with diverting state funds for my personal use."

"What?"

"They are going to say I made up some dummy employees and put them on the payroll while I was the Governor's AA and had their salaries wired into accounts I control."

I was incredulous. It was the last thing I would have expected.

"Are you sure?

"I'm as certain as I can be. My friend is in the office that's bringing the charges. We used to work together. There's nothing anybody can do about it."

"Do you need a lawyer?"

"I can take care of that. I'm calling you because you need to know I did it. I'll deny ever saying that but you need to know I did."

It took a moment to process what Christoff was saying. Then the only thing I could think of was, "Why?"

"Because it was just so damn easy. You remember how we always joked about changing the laws so that only the smart guys can rip us off? After a while, I decided it wasn't funny. It's like the government is throwing away money and handing out blank checks. I just had some of those checks made out to me."

———

"If you're so smart, how did they catch you?"

"That's why I'm calling you. This wasn't random. It didn't pop up on a screen as part of some investigation. They knew where to look. What puzzles me is how. No one knew. I am the only one who could have told them where to look and I sure as hell didn't."

"Maybe you did without knowing it."

"That's what I have been thinking. I had some files at home. They were in one of the boxes near my office. The only one who had access to the condo was Olivia. Anyone else would have had to be buzzed in and then use a key or find some other way to open my door. So I am thinking, maybe it wasn't about the stamps. Maybe she let someone in, maybe she looked herself. Either way, it was done by someone looking for something specific, something they could use against me."

"How do you know that?"

"Because they could have found a lot more. Once they found what they found it was enough."

"Makes sense."

"That's the only way I can read it. The other thing you need to think about is John."

"What about him?"

"I never told him why I fired Olivia. She had access to his place as well mine. Maybe whoever broke into my place broke into his place too. Maybe she left the door open. Maybe she let them in. Either way they could have just walked in – only they didn't expect anyone to be there. Pam came home and surprised them and, knowing Pam, probably made a fuss. She could have heard them upstairs – maybe she thought they were kids ransacking the house looking for the drugs she always had around or something – pulled a butcher knife and tried to chase them out. Only they weren't kids. She fought them and they killed her."

Chapter Forty-Two

Furth was up early on the 9th of October. Things had gotten out of hand. The pressure to stop Oversight and Investigations had been intense. He had passed it on, adding topspin. But when you start things in motion, you don't always know where they'll stop. Things take on a life of their own. When you tell people to do whatever it takes, sometimes they do whatever they can. Judgment is lost. No one cares when one wiseguy pops another but when civilians begin to drop, people will take note – particularly when one of them is a United States Senator.

Macklin's death was unfortunate – a simple case of being in the wrong place at the wrong time. No one expected her to be home. No one would have expected her to react the way she did. He felt confident that had been contained. The maid had been paid off and shipped back to Columbia before the DC cops could get around to interviewing her. She was more than happy to take the money and run.

He had nothing to do with what happened in Chicago. That was Star's business. As for the Colgate matter, that was just plain stupid. He consoled himself with the knowledge that he could not be held responsible. He had told Beau that Saveco was getting out of hand. He could not control them or what they did with the information he provided.

Still, he knew there would be hell to pay. If Colgate survived, he would emerge a heroic figure with a motive and means to come after them. If he died, his family would not let the matter die with him. They would hire an army of investigators, turn over every stone, and keep on coming until they were satisfied.

What made it worse was that after all this, after all the resources he had invested and the time his agents had put into this assignment, he could still lose everything. Dershowitz was headed for jail. Total Health Care was dead in the water and Star was facing criminal investigations in two states. Three U. S. Attorneys were involved; the FBI was engaged; a charge of racketeering loomed on the horizon; and the media was eating it up.

If Star went down, he knew they would not go quietly, putting his business in jeopardy. The rest of his clients would also be under a cloud and under suspicion. Even if they escaped official scrutiny, they would be looking for different representation. He had made defeating the Inspector General amendment a priority. He had led the charge against it, used it to build a war chest, and distributed hundreds of thousands of dollars in their name for that purpose. They had believed him. He could not afford to fail. Alexander had to be stopped.

Furth spent the next two hours going through his Blackberry, computer, and hard files deleting and destroying anything that could connect him with Oversight and Investigations and what had happened. It would not insulate him from information provided by others but it would break the chain of evidence and make sure nothing in his office would support or connect him with the attack on Colgate or the effort to diffuse OSI's investigation and discredit the investigators.

Then he switched gears and began focusing forward. Like many who had never played the game, he was an avid sports fan. He had a skybox at the Verizon Center and season tickets for the Redskin. He knew that sometimes the best defense is a good offense.

...

Peter "Peanut" Popper was in his office when I arrived. It was 8:00 AM. I had seen Popper's schedule and knew he had been out until midnight the night before attending a series of functions. And I knew that was not unusual. Popper had kept nearly the same schedule every night Congress was in session for fifty years. He was three months shy of his 86th birthday and a couple of weeks away from the completion of his final term. Once one of the youngest members of Congress, he was now one of the oldest; but there was no quit or sign of fatigue in his eyes. They were a clear and piercing blue behind the thick lenses of his Magoo glasses.

In his college years at Georgia, a thoughtless and heartless belle turned down his invitation to go out saying that were it not for those eyes he would be the homeliest person on earth. It was one of the many scars he carried from his troubled and challenging youth as the son of a peanut farmer in rural Georgia, experiences that helped shape his social philosophy and gave him a deep sense of compassion for those on the margin of society. As a result, while most members staffed their offices with those who helped get them elected, filling in with the best and brightest, Popper went the other way. He filled in the blanks with misfits and lost souls. Somebody had to take care of them. He was glad he could.

Every office on The Hill has an ego wall – pictures of the member with seemingly everyone of distinction they have ever met as if to suggest greatness is contagious. All four of Popper's walls were covered floor to ceiling with photographs chronically his career. Pictures with presidents, foreign dignitaries and celebrities were everywhere. Over his dressing room, side-by-side, were two that seemed to say it all. One was an autographed photograph from Orville Wright. The other was a picture of the first moon landing. Both bore inscriptions of gratitude.

Popper wore a grey suit with a white shirt, and a state tie – blue peaches on a red background. He had the same tie in every conceivable color and combination. His driver and companion, George Conner stood nearby. George, an inch or two taller, twenty pounds lighter, and fifty years younger, was doing his best to look like Popper's twin. He wore the identical suit and tie and sported the same hairstyle, glasses and frames. The only difference was in the thickness of his lenses.

George had been with Popper for five years and his personal assistant for two, taking on that responsibility when Jim Buchanan, Popper's long-term companion, decided he was too old for the job and retired. Aside from everything else, Jim had developed night blindness. More than once members had commented on the quizzical site of Popper driving his driver home. Some wondered if either one of them was safe on the road.

When Jim left, George jumped at the opportunity and the proximity to power it presented. The fact that he was married and would have to leave his wife and move in with Popper was no deterrent. Truth be told, she was probably as happy to be rid of him. She was a mail-order bride from the Philippines. Their marriage had never been long on love. He moved out, she filed for divorce, and they both got on with their lives.

George took a seat on Popper's leather sofa while I gave the Chairman a quick overview of the hearing. I described the witnesses and what they would bring to the hearing, gave Popper a summary of each witness' statement and a copy of the opening statement I had prepared for Colgate – the statement Colgate would never deliver.

Popper reviewed the testimony quickly, glanced at the opening statement and handed it back.

"I'm pretty good with words myself," he said.

It was consistent with his reputation. When most members hire a team of speechwriters and legislative specialists, Popper did it all himself. No one told him what to say or how to say it. He was old school, the last of soaring eagle orators, used to charting his own course and asking staff to follow rather than give directions.

We were preparing to leave, when Rochelle Francis, Popper's Administrative Assistant, poked her head in. She said she was sorry to interrupt but Senator Lawson was waiting and wondering if he could have a quick word with the Chairman before he went down.

I waited with George in the reception area. Francis stayed with Popper. I saw the two former colleagues greet each other warmly before the door closed and tried not to worry about it too much. Popper was one of the few members who had less money than when he arrived in Congress. There wasn't much Lawson could offer him that he would want – other than his youth and a chance to do it all again. When Francis opened the door fifteen minutes later, Lawson was nowhere to be seen. He must have gone out the staff entrance.

At 8:50 AM, we left for the Hart Building, dropping down into the basement of Russell and walking through the underground passages that connect Russell with Dirksen and then Hart. A mob had gathered outside the Hart hearing room. Lobbyist and tourists attracted by the obvious sense that something was going on were waiting to get in.

Popper walked around the metal detector set up at the entrance to the hearing room. I walked through it, cutting into the line, hurriedly emptying my pockets into the plastic trays and passing through only to be greeted by an agent who patted me down.

Popper had already taken his seat by the time I made my way to the dais. Several members of the full committee – Sweet, Carrera, Jordan, Curtis, and Hynes – had exercised their prerogative and joined Oversight and Investigations for the hearing. The explanation came with the number of cameras I saw peering out of the portals in the walls. I took a quick count. There were at least four dozen. CNN looked like it was running a pool. Radio and print correspondents filled two press tables set on either side of the room.

Chairs placed along the wall behind the members overflowed with staff, including the Big Byrd, who had positioned himself directly behind Popper. Byrd glared at me when I took a seat next to the Chairman. It didn't take a mind reader to know what he was thinking.

"The purpose of the hearing it explore growing evidence of the criminal infiltration of the health care system," Popper said. "Previous investigations have tied Gallo, Genovese, and Columbo to health rackets in New York. Joe Bonnano had been linked to health care benefit plans in Arizona. The Dragna family has been connected to health care plans financed through the teamsters. Carlos Marcello is said to be involved in a number of health facilities in Louisiana. Today we will hear from three U. S. Attorneys and a former investigator from the State of California. Each one has valuable information that will contribute to our understanding of the magnitude of this problem.

"Finally, we will hear from a witness who can provide direct information about this matter. I will warn the gallery and the press in advance that this witness is under government protection. We take that responsibility seriously. Agents from the Federal Bureau of Investigation are here to insure his safety. We expect your full cooperation. Anyone causing a disturbance will be removed.

"Given the number of members present, the length and nature of this hearing, I will ask that the Committee forgo making opening statements so that we might proceed directly to the testimony. Written statements will be accepted for the record."

It was a better start than I could have expected. Deprived of an immediate press opportunity, two members backed away from the dais and worked their way out. One left his briefing package and name plate in place, suggesting he planned to return.

Wilson, Skinner, Lazinski, and David testified as expected. They appeared as a panel, reinforcing each other. Members responded by questioning them individually and collectively, looking for a sound bite that would express their concerns vividly enough to make the evening news. Several decried the government's apparent inability to protect the public and the integrity of health care programs.

Mario Carrera demurred. He quarreled with the focus of the hearing. He said there was no such thing as a Mafia.

———

"Organized crime as it is commonly portrayed is a myth," Carrera said. "There are always groups and gangs involved in illegal activity but to suggest these activities are controlled and coordinated by members of a Mafia or the Cosa Nostra is inaccurate. It is an unfair stereotype and a slur against people of Italian decent."

When The Snake was called, Carrera walked.

As the marshals prepared to escort Siciliano into the hearing room from the antechamber, Hartnett asked for a point of personal privilege. He said he was familiar with Mr. Siciliano's background. He had reviewed a summary of Mr. Siciliano's testimony and was concerned by what he saw.

"Mr. Siciliano is the government's principal witness in a number of important cases coming to trial," he said. "In most cases, the success of these prosecutions will depend almost entirely on his testimony. I am concerned that this inquiry and the publicity surrounding it might compromise these proceedings. I believe it would be prudent for the Committee take his testimony in executive session and so move."

The motion caught me by surprise. I was even more surprised when Popper accepted it without comment and asked for the 'ayes' and 'nays'. Still, I wasn't all that concerned. Asked to choose between press and principle most members will take press every time.

As I expected, the 'nays' seemed more numerous but to my surprise Popper called it the other way. I waited for a roll call vote for the record but there would be none and, later I would learn, no record.

Popper declared a half hour recess and ordered the room cleared. The press milled around in amazement, struggling to make sense of this unexpected event. They had sat through the opening acts only to be told there would be no finale.

After a few moments, comprehension set in, the press began to break down, and the gallery dispersed. By the time Siciliano was brought in, the room was empty. No cameras. No members. Only Popper, Mancini, and Sweet remained.

"Do you have a statement you would like to make?" Popper asked.

"Only this," Sam said. "It's too bad Senator Carrera isn't here."

"Why?"

"So I could ask him to say to me what he said to you."

I spent the next hour leading Siciliano through his testimony, trying to make what we had discussed privately a matter of public record. Siciliano was forthcoming and explicit and some cases brutally frank. It's a pity his testimony will never see the light of day.

Chapter Forty-Three

Late Thursday night, the conference committee came to an agreement on the Omnibus Reconciliation Act. The good news was that the bill included the amendment creating an Inspector General. The bad news was the Inspector General had been castrated.

It was business as usual. Nothing new.

Reconciliation is Congress' black hole. A lot of things go in that never come out. Others appear out of nowhere, driven by forces unseen. Under the cloak of darkness, conferees leverage their positions and power, inserting provisions and pet projects at the last minute, forcing the Senate and House to vote up or down on the bill as revised without having had time to read much less consider the changes made.

The House bill was 1,600 pages long, the Senate bill exceeded 1,800. For comparison, it only took 28 pages to create Social Security in 1935. The Federal Trade Agency was set up with 8 pages in 1914. Unlike the Omnibus Bill, they were drafted for one specific public purpose. Every page of the Reconciliation Act contained paragraphs and phrases worth millions if not billions to some specific interest – person, company, or industry.

Twenty-two hundred lobbyists worked the conference and provided input. A hundred and twenty of them were former members of congress. The vast majority of the rest – nearly two thirds – were former Congressional staff members.

With support from the White House, opponents deleted two key provisions from the Dennison Amendment. The first eliminated a requirement that the Inspector General report directly to Congress. The second stripped him of his independence, housing him within the Department he was being asked to investigate and requiring him to report to Secretary of that Department. It was the perfect political and bureaucratic solution, giving politicians an opportunity to say they did something when they did nothing, while creating another place for bureaucrats to duck and hide. They had turned a junkyard dog into a house cat.

Colgate never saw it. He never regained consciousness. He died as dawn approached. A spokesman for the state police said they had initiated a criminal investigation. Dark paint had been found on the side of Colgate's vehicle, creating a suspicion of foul play. They were looking for the dark SUV described by witnesses on the scene. *The Philadelphia Inquirer* reported a $100,000 reward had been posted by the Colgate family for information leading to the identification of this vehicle or any other vehicle that might have been involved.

The Omnibus Reconciliation Act was the first order of business Friday morning. It passed with only a handful of dissenting votes. Most of these complained they could not in good faith vote for the measure that contained so much pork. The senior Senator from Arizona noted the bill listed 541 earmarks worth about $9.9 billion. The Executive Order requiring disclosure of earmarks had been evaded with a simple amendment saying that order "shall not apply" to this legislation.

The Popper hearing was lost in all this. It played on page A10 of the *Post* with the headline: US Attorneys Charge Mob Infiltrating Health Care. Siciliano presence was acknowledged with a solitary line. He was believed to have presented corroborating evidence in a closed session.

No one seemed to care. There was more interest in the news that several of the men mentioned in Ms. Sinclair's blog had been identified. *The Times* reported one of them, Beauregard Amidore, was a partner in a downtown law firm headed by former Senator Larry Lawson. Another was said to be Henry Furth, a DC power broker and the owner of Jenkins Choice. Sources indicated both Furth and Amidore had engaged Ms. Sinclair for personal services and asked her to entertain their clients.

Authorities were close to identifying a third individual. A link posted on the internet had connected Ms. Sinclair's blog to another – SenateDick – and various U-Tube postings under the same name. Like Ms. Sinclair, the operator of this site was believed to a Senate employee.

I pulled up the site without needing to see what was there to confirm my suspicions. Like StaffAss, it was a chronicle of sexual adventures. It had been started some time after and clearly in admiration of Ms. Edward's site. There were frequent cross-references.

The most recent post showed a man and two women, their faces obscured. One of them, a pudgy woman, had a tramp stamp in the small of her back. There were two rows of Chinese characters parallel to her spine. Her position answered a lingering question: This side up. The other woman had an elegant pair of legs and a distinctive silver ankle bracelet.

I didn't bother looking at the rest. I went for a walk instead. Jim Roberts had sent a note saying he would like to see me. This seemed to be a good time to respond.

Jim was one of the Capitol Hill cops detailed to help with the Mills investigation. We had become friends when I was in law school and Roberts was pursuing a degree in dentistry at Howard University. Life and kids had intervened leaving him with too much seniority to throw away and nowhere else to go.

I had heard Jim had fallen into disfavor and assumed he was looking for help. I found him guarding cars in lot 12, the Siberia of The Hill. They had posted him as far away from the Capitol as possible and given him the most boring assignment they could find.

Jim was reading a book when I arrived. There was no one else around.

"Thanks for coming down," he said. "I have something to tell you and wanted to do it in person – partly because I don't know how to do it any other way. Do you know why I'm down here?"

"Not really."

"It took a while to get passed the grief they gave me for the work I did with you during the Mills investigation. They accused me of being a hotdog and showing up the department. God forbid someone should actually do something around here. I had to inch myself back into the building. And when I did, they gave me the night shift, but at least I was inside out of the weather and I could see people once in a while.

"Wednesday night, I was walking the halls, checking doors. It was around 10:00 PM. Everyone was gone. I found the door to Administration unlocked. That happens all the time. Generally, it's just some staffer who leaves in a hurry and forgets to lock up. I went in to make sure everything was all right and heard some noise. I flipped on the light and found the Chairman on the couch with a girl."

"So they shipped you out."

"And told me to keep my mouth shut if I wanted to stay with the force. You know how that works. Robinson has been known to cut off air conditioning to the offices of people who get on his bad side. You can imagine what he would do with this...Anyway, the reason I called you is that I recognized the girl. It took me a while to figure it out but finally it came to me. It was that woman you were seeing when you worked for Moss. After what happened last time, I thought you should know. Somebody said you were seeing her again."

The Dubliner was across the street. All of sudden a drink seemed like a good idea. I asked for Jamison straight up and drank until the work crowd came in and spoiled my solitude. Then I walked home.

There was a plain brown envelope in my mailbox. No return address. I opened it and found a memory stick and a note from Bob Moore.

"Sorry to hear about Colgate," he said. "I've been thinking about your hypothetical question. If I were going to do something like you described, I would use something like this."

I put the envelope aside and went looking for another drink. There was about a third of a bottle of Metaxa left. This seemed to be a good time to kill it along with whatever was left of my illusions.

I hadn't seen her since the Omnibus bill passed the Senate, hadn't heard from her in more than a week. After so much pursuit and persistence – nothing. This would explain that. Many of the things said or unsaid before, suddenly made sense. So many things, curious then, seemed obvious now, connected by specific intent.

"Life is a comedy to those who think," the philosopher said, "and a tragedy to those who feel." Caught in the middle, I wondered – Do I laugh or cry?

As she had so many times before, Dee called just as I was prepared to write her off.

"I was wondering if you would have the nerve to call again," I said.

"It's not nerve I lack," she said, "it's pride. I figured you would find out sooner or later. I wanted to tell you but you never gave me a chance."

After all that had happened, I was not surprised she knew I'd seen Jim.

"He also recognized who you were with – though he said he got a better look at you than him. I guess the Senator didn't put his best side forward. You've seen both sides. What do you think?"

"I think you are just trying to be rude and hurtful. And it's all right. I understand where it's coming from. What you need to understand is that this doesn't change anything. Everything I said was true."

"Everything?"

"Everything. I don't lie – except little white lies to people who don't matter."

"Just little white lies?" I couldn't resist asking.

"Yes, I would never lie to you."

Yet, another lie. She was as amoral as a cat.

"She's no different, you know."

"Who?"

"You know who. She just gave you a little to get what she wants. She's no better than I am."

"Now you are getting ugly."

Dee said something profane and slammed the phone down in my ear. I regretted my remark for all of 30 seconds before going back to my brandy.

Chapter Forty-Four

The transcript for Siciliano's hearing was waiting on my desk when I arrived Monday morning. Gene Cummings, the printer assigned to Oversight and Investigations by the Government Printing Office, had left a yellow sticky on top with a note.

"You're not going to like this," Cummings said, "but we still need it back by the end of the week."

Normally, it would be my job to edit the transcript and make sense of the questions, answers, and commentary. People don't speak in complete sentences or natural paragraphs. That's fine for average people but it is contrary to the image their representatives would like to project. Staff routinely goes through transcripts of Senate proceedings and look for an opportunity to "improve" the record.

This time, there wasn't much to improve. There was a blank page marked "classified" where the Snake's testimony should have been. Wilson's testimony and that of the other US Attorneys was printed as submitted and David's formal statement was intact, but much of the dialog had been removed. There was no point in trying to revise it. The hearing was being buried.

A party was in progress next door. Byrd was celebrating the passage of the IG bill, pouring champagne and orange juice, and trying his best to take credit for its success. He had represented Popper at the conference, he said, and helped work out the compromise that assured its passage. He was pleased to say his contributions were significant enough to be acknowledged by staff representatives from Appropriations, Administration, and the Vice President's Office.

Broadbent was in and out of the celebration, the last time bringing a mimosa with him. He sat down at his computer and opened his site. He said the publicity had brought so many inquiries he was having trouble keeping up. His wife was talking about divorce but it didn't seem to bother him much. There was no remorse, only a sense of greater opportunity.

The Committee on Administration had reviewed the Senate's committee structure in preparation for the next term and decided that the Permanent Subcommittee for Oversight and Investigations was redundant. Byrd interrupted his celebration long enough to deliver the news personally. He said Oversight and Investigations would be disbanded at the end of the year. I didn't have to wonder when or how that bargain was sealed.

In addition, Byrd said, Francis had tasked him with determining which files should be preserved for the Popper Library authorized by the Omnibus Bill. Twenty million dollars had been earmarked to preserve Popper's official papers and permanently memorialize his years of public service. Operating funds, starting at $2 million and growing to $5 million by the fifth year, were authorized to staff and run the facility.

Somehow, that made me the saddest. They had caught the old man by his posterity – the only place he was vulnerable. Apparently, Popper was planning on preserving his reputation and taking care of his staff through eternity.

I left the party in progress, took my laptop, and walked to the Starbucks at Union Station. You can question what makes a cup of coffee worth ten bucks and argue whether it's worth drinking but it's really not about the coffee anyway. The chairs are comfortable and the network is open.

I tried to find something I could drink while I was there but had to settle for water. It was too early for any of the liquid deserts they call lattes and chai. I found a table in the corner and settled back while I waited for the computer to come alive. When I was connected, I plugged in the memory stick Bob had provided and downloaded the program.

"Live like Christ," someone said, "and die like Samson." I loaded the files I had prepared as a contingency and pressed 'send.'

By the time I returned to the office, investigative reporters and watchdog groups around the country were receiving specific information from an unknown source at the Senate raising legal, ethical and moral questions. I didn't question the impact of what I had done. The genie was out of the bottle. Adversaries had been armed. Things would take their natural course.

I packed what few personal items I had in a small cardboard box, dropped the empty cognac bottle in the trash, and left the key on the desk. I didn't bother saying goodbye.

Chapter Forty-Five

Everything has already been said but since no one ever listens, we must always begin again. We keep making the same mistakes, learning the same lessons. We keep expecting things to make sense, men to be fair, heaven to be merciful, hoping to live happily ever after when we never lived happily before.

"Why are you here?" Doc English asked the class of first year of law students.

"Because I believed in justice," I said and my teacher laughed.

After forty years of practicing law, Doc knew better.

But, I said, if there is no justice, what about truth? Is it all rationalization, expediency and spin?

A dozen years later, I can still hear English's answer. What is truth, Alexander? You echo Pilate. Better to ask where is truth, for many truths there are, with truths in between. Truth bent by every hand seeking to grasp. Truth refracted by each eye trying to see until the one truth becomes many men's truths. It is a shadow in the night.

Yet, we are all wedded to our own version of reality and men will kill to prove their truth is true. We sell whatever serves; buy whatever suits, pursue whatever persuades. What matters is not the fact but the belief in the fact.

Congress adjourned at midnight, the 24th of October. Before they left town, the Senate passed S. 1249 and S. 1250, the last legislation introduced by the late Senator Colgate, and an amendment co-sponsored by Mancini and Sweet prohibiting factoring in federally funded programs. Caroline Colgate called the legislation a fitting tribute to her husband's memory.

It was ironic. The decoy flew. The AMA was quick to decry the legislation, claiming it created a legion of bounty hunters who would second guess medical decisions, disrupt the sanctity of the doctor patient relationships, and have a 'chilling affect' on the medical community.

Three days later, on the 27th of October, *The Capitol News* released a copy of an internal staff memorandum to the Chairman of Government Operations critical of Bill Byrd. It charged him with misuse of Committee funds, abusive and inappropriate behavior, and conflicts of interest. The story focused on Byrd's excessive travel and lavish lifestyle and his decision to hire his wife as Chief Clerk. Byrd resigned before he could be fired and accepted a position as a senior adviser to the Popper Center.

On the 29th of October, *Roll Call* reported the Chairman of Administration had engaged in an adulterous affair with a consultant on his staff. They said the affair had been discovered and was subsequently covered up by the Capitol Hill police. Marsden refused to comment. Robertson denied the affair, but his wife of thirty years was not persuaded.

She filed for divorce, asking for half the family's estate, including a significant amount of cash she said was stashed in a safety deposit box at the First Republic Bank in Houston. The source of this cash was said to be under investigation by the FBI and the Internal Revenue Service.

On Friday, the 31st of October, *The Washington Post* reported, "The FBI has searched the offices of former Senator Laurence Lawson, known to have a close relationship with Senator Lamar Lewis. A source close to the investigation indicates documents were found in Lawson's office connecting Senator Lewis with the scandal that has come to be known as MediGate. Lewis was said to have received $150,000 from HFC during the calendar year as well as other considerations, including the use of a yacht on Potomac where he lived rent-free."

ABC extended the story line with an investigative report broadcast on the eve of the election.

"The Congressional corruption scandal known as MediGate may soon also be known at the biggest sex scandal in Congressional history," Ross reported. "We already know cash, cars, and travel were exchanged for political favors. The FBI is now investigating whether hookers were used to sweeten the deal.

"ABC News has learned Senators Hartlett, Osborne, and Lewis shared a vacation cottage in Bermuda while on a golfing junket sponsored by the Coalition for Health Care, headed by Henry Furth, a lobbyist currently facing charges of corruption. Reliable sources indicate female companions were provided for the three Senators in exchange for political favors."

Stan Brant, a lawyer who specialized in defending public officials accused of corruption, minimized the matter.

"Everyone is all worked up into a lather right now," he was quoted as saying, "but in a couple of weeks everyone will forget about it and they'll go back to doing what they've always done. You're not going to get money out of politics and you're not going to get influence out of government."

He was probably right. If they did, he would have to find another line of work.

Citing ABC's report, a watchdog group called the Citizens for Responsibility and Ethics named Hartlett as one of the 10 most corrupt politicians in Washington. They said there was abundant and credible information Hartlett repeatedly used his office for personal gain and, specific evidence that he had an unethical if not illegal connection with HFC. Senate reports obtained by CRE indicated Hartlett had received $200,000 from HFC during the last reporting period.

"Hartlett is a disgrace to his State if not the Senate," CRE said. "He should do his constituents a favor and resign."

Unable to withstand the withering and unrelenting

pressure provided by the press, Welch, Steinberg and Espinoza, lost their bids for re-election. Steinberg and Espinoza lost to political unknowns. Welch was defeated by the enemy he had feared. Mark Everett, the new Governor of Illinois, promised to clean up the mess Welch had created.

Steinberg was intent on returning to work at his insurance firm until it was revealed the FBI had taped some of the conversations he had denied having. He copped a plea and joined Dershowitz in prison. Espinoza accepted a position with a New York law firm, Prendergast, Prendergast, and Collins. His first client was himself, fighting the indictment being sought by George Wilson.

In the weeks following the election, the cards continued to fall. Evan Jones admitted receiving kickbacks from Star Financial Management and agreed to cooperate with the US Attorney's Office in its on-going investigation. Merriman's reports indicated Jones was expected to implicate former Governor William Welch.

Henry Furth pled guilty to conspiracy involving the corruption of public officials, as well as, charges of fraud and tax evasion. As part of his plea agreement, he agreed to provide evidence against the politicians he had allegedly bribed. Furth's associates, Max Rudy and Jeff Tyson, were among those facing indictment for money laundering and accepting illegal contributions.

Mitchell and Pennington stayed clear. They formed their own firm, hoping to pick up the pieces of

Furth's practice. Beau Amidore and three former members of Ways and Means joined them, agreeing to serve 'of counsel.'

On the Friday following Thanksgiving, private investigators acting on a tip found the black Suburban they had been looking for abandoned in a parking garage near the Philadelphia train station. It had gone unnoticed pressed up against the wall in a dark corner on the fourth level. The passenger side of the vehicle had extensive damage. News reports indicated the owner of the car had reported it stolen the day after the incident on Highway 41.

The FBI analyzed paint found on the side of the SUV and matched it with the paint on Colgate's Lexus.

"The damage on the SUV was of such magnitude," Hugh Jones told the Gazette, "it must have struck the Lexus directly and at great speed."

At a press conference on the 1st day of December, Caroline Colgate presented a check for $100,000 to the parking attendant who provided the tip necessary to find the car and announced a $500,000 reward for information leading to the identification of the men witnesses placed in the vehicle immediately before the crime. She also said that after much consideration she had decided to accept the governor's nomination to fill the balance of her husband's unexpired term. Two days later, Frank Caprice, a security consultant employed by Saveco, was found dead in his Boca Raton apartment. A spokesman for the police department said his death was an apparent suicide.

346

Family members indicated he had been distraught and depressed for reasons unknown. His revolver was in his hand.

Chapter Forty-Six

"Funny," Kat said. "I've finally broken through. For years that's all I wanted. Now they are handing it to me and I'm not sure I want it anymore – Vice President for Governmental Affairs."

"A lot of things are like that," I said. "You want what you want until you get it."

It was the 10th of December. The new Congress was being organized. Kat was getting dressed, preparing to go home so she could prepare to go to work. She could have brought a change of clothes but we hadn't thought that far ahead or maybe she had and felt uncomfortable about it.

"I did what they asked me to do and got nowhere. They patted me on the head and said 'good girl.' When I didn't do what they wanted, I get rewarded."

"Maybe they think you did."

"What do you mean?"

"Perception is reality on The Hill. What you did or didn't do is less important than what they think you did."

"Whatever," she shrugged. "I still have to make a choice. I can go all noble and tell them where to put it or let them believe what they want to believe and take the position, the money and the perks. I feel like telling them what they can do with it. Still, I earned it. Maybe not the way they think, but I earned it. Maybe I should just keep my mouth shut and try it for a while. That would be reasonable wouldn't it?"

I said it would. When they ask a question like that it's not really a question anyway. Does this outfit make me look fat? Even if she looks like a tugboat in tights, there is only one answer. Her mind was made up. After she left, smiling and blowing a kiss over her shoulder as she went down the stairs on feet trying hard not to fly, I found myself wondering if she was ever really there.

It was early but not too early for a drink. I had replenished my bar several times since leaving The Hill. It seemed like time to break out the good stuff. I found the Glenfiddich and a glass and went looking for a chair, somewhere I could see the snow covering the patio. It was only a quarter of an inch deep but at least for the moment it provided an illusion of purity. I poured myself a drink and took a sip, savoring the elegant smooth taste with a hint of spice and a touch of oak, and uttered a single four-letter word.

I was feeling mellow and a little less sorry for myself by the time the mail arrived. In the midst of all the usual garbage, I found a letter addressed in a familiar hand. It was large and angular with a slight forward inclination.

"So now you know everything," she said. "You

thought I married after you left but I was married before you returned. I was always married, but it was always you I wanted. I couldn't believe it when you walked back in my life. All of a sudden, everything else wasn't real. I was married but I wasn't. Beau and I were never really a part of each other lives. He didn't care what I did as long as he got what he needed and I didn't care what he did as long as I got what I wanted. I never thought you were possible. Why did you have to leave? Couldn't you see we were meant to be together? Why didn't you come for me? You wasted so much time we could have been together. I have felt connected to you from the moment we met. Surely, you must have felt it. Maybe we can still be together. I don't know. It's up to you. If not in this life, maybe there is hope for us in the next."

I put the letter down and emptied the glass. Through the glass doors, I could see Trish exercising in the carriage house. After a rough spell, she was back in fighting shape, ready to try again. Max was at her feet. He was her dog now.

Trish had finished her workout and settled into the hot tub when the call came. I had been dividing my time between sipping my scotch, watching her steaming up the backyard, and watching the Clayton's puppy play. The pup seemed to find a soft rubber ball someone had left in the yard a source of immense pleasure. He was pouncing on it, tossing it, and chasing it around the yard. Like Bruno, he was coal black. His paws at six months were the size of a grown man's hand.

So as usual, when the phone rang it came as a bit an annoyance. I picked it up – more to eliminate the distraction than out of any interest in who might be calling.

"There you are," someone said.

The voice was familiar, but not one I could immediately place in my current state.

"You know, you really should get an answering machine," he said. "You are impossible to reach."

Finally, the voice registered. It was Mike Atkins.

"Hold on," he said. "The Senator wants to talk with you."

I filled my glass, took another sip of scotch, and tried to contain my excitement. I wondered when people would begin to realize that the fact they might want to talk with me didn't necessarily mean I would want to talk with them.

"Nick?"

"Yes, sir."

"How have you been?"

I couldn't believe anyone really wanted to know so I gave him the short answer.

"I'm fine, Senator."

It was mostly true.

Mancini paused long enough to make me reconsider my curt response and then proceeded to the point.

"I'll tell you why I'm calling," he said. "A doublewide is being moved into position in back of the Senate parking lot near the Monocle this afternoon. We are calling it OSI in Exile. Caroline Colgate is paying for it. They will put the sign up tomorrow. So far we have five members – the two of us, Paulson, Burdett, and Sweet."

"Sweet?"

"I know you have had problems with him but he wasn't bought. He was used and he knows it now. He also knows you could have made him pay and didn't. He's behind you 100%. In fact, he said the only way he'd sign on is if you come back. We've got five and we'll get more. The beauty of this is that we can pick them. We don't have to take anyone we don't want. We want you to run it for us, Nick. We made some progress but there is still a lot to do. You know that better than anyone. We'll give you a free hand and back you all the way."

"What about the money?"

"What did Nixon tell Halderman? OK, bad example, but good point. Money is the least of our worries. I think if she had to Caroline would bankroll the whole thing personally. She's that committed. She is the one who came up with this idea. Frankly, I think the only reason she took the appointment was to see this through. She's got a family to raise, a company, and a foundation to run but she agreed to do this. She's not just in, she's all in."

"Ad hoc?"

"That's right. Ad hoc. Think about it."

"I will."

Despite or maybe because of my condition, I had to laugh. Everyone knows the closest thing to immortality on The Hill is an ad hoc Congressional committee.

I put my drink down and sealed the bottle. I thought for a few moments and then picked up the phone.

Chapter Forty-Seven

On the 15th of December, Rocco was waiting outside baggage at Reagan National Airport. It felt good to be back in his blues. The insignia were a little off for DC but no one would notice. A cop is a cop.

His service revolver was strapped to his hip. A colt .45, custom-smithed with flash-suppression, walnut grip, oversized trigger, and a 3.5 inch barrel, it combined maximum firepower, maximum accuracy, and maximum speed. Joe had given it to him the first year he was on the force, noting the difficulty he had qualifying with a standard weapon. It was a strangely appropriate gift from a crook to a cop, acknowledging the importance of the tools of their trade.

Rocco hadn't carried it openly since that firefight in the Bronx. Ricca had asked him to sit on those wiseguys trying to muscle in on the family's business. When things turned ugly, he took them out, killing one outright before catching a bullet in the knee. He made sure the other one took a while to die.

Witnesses who weren't there swore they fired first, telling the story effectively enough to earn the mayor's citation for bravery. He received the award in the hospital during his rehabilitation. It was two months before he could walk without pain. His other wounds were superficial. Still, he took the out offered and retired with disability. Twenty years on the force was enough. There were too many rules

---

now, too many people looking over your shoulder, telling you to be nice to the scum of the earth.

People like Caprice, he thought. He had taken particular satisfaction out of killing him, using his own gun, forcing the barrel in the little weasel's mouth to make it look like a suicide, wiping down the grip with that dandy little handkerchief he always kept in his breast pocket, and then wrapping his bony little fingers around the butt of the gun.

Too many people could connect Caprice with the car they used. Any one of them could drop a dime on him, take the money, and run. Caprice was the only one who could put him in the driver's seat. Caprice was the only one who could put him in Chicago. Once the reward was posted, Rocco knew he had to go.

It hadn't been hard. Rocco still remembered the look of terror on his face when the Macklin woman surprised him and came after him with a knife. He probably would have run for the door if Rocco hadn't come up behind her. Truth be told, she put up more of a fight than he did.

He thought he was done with it and was working his way south when the call came. Rocco had planned on slipping across the border into Mexico and flying out of there. Once he got to the islands he knew he would be fine. He had enough stashed in the Caymans to be comfortable for some time. Who knows, at some point he might decide to return to the land of his father, find a house looking over the water, and a woman to take care of him. He still had family there. The idea had always appealed to him.

There was only one loose end – the woman, Olivia Garcia. She could put him in Fine's house and tie him in to Caprice and Saveco. When Rocco heard they were bringing her back, the first thing that occurred to him was that this would save him the trouble of looking for her. She would be a lot easier to find in Washington than Bolivia or wherever the hell she was from.

Amidore said she was returning voluntarily under a grant of immunity. There had been a story on the evening news. The reporter was that Patterson woman they chased around in Chicago, the one that was so close to Alexander. Amidore said Garcia had agreed to testify before a Senate panel and then assist the FBI and the U. S. Attorney investigating the scandal they were calling MediGate, like it was some big deal. It made him laugh.

Amidore's second call came two days later, shortly after he arrived in Washington. It confirmed Patterson's report. He said Alexander was going to pick the woman up at National Friday afternoon. She was coming in on direct flight out of Miami somewhere around four. Alexander would probably talk to her for a while and then stash her somewhere secure.

Neutralizing the woman was a necessity. Taking out the Greek would be a pleasure. He had proven hard to get at, but this time Rocco knew he would find a way. He had no plan, nor a need for a plan. Thinking just got in the way. He would follow his instincts as he always had and wait for opportunity to present itself.

Delta had the only direct flight out of Miami arriving around 4:00 PM. It was scheduled in at 4:15 PM. He arrived at 3:45 PM and parked the dark Ford he had rented where he could watch both Delta exits. His shield was on the dashboard where the security wannabees could see it. He gave them a hard look every time one of them thought to approach, keeping them at a distance.

At 4:32 PM, a black sedan pulled up at the first Delta exit. Almost immediately, Alexander came out with the woman. She wore a scarf over her head, sunglasses, and a tan coat. He had his arm on her arm, guiding her toward the sedan. She huddled close to him, either for warmth or protection. A porter followed them with her luggage.

Rocco tailed the sedan up the oldest highway in America, across the 14th Street Bridge, on to 295 and watched it take the C Street exit to the Senate. The traffic was all the other way. People were already escaping for the weekend.

The sedan pulled into the Senate parking lot on D Street and drove up to the trailer. It was right where Amidore said it would be, lodged in the back left corner of the lot. When he saw where the car was heading, Rocco made a right on First. He moved parallel until the sedan came to a stop and parked half way up the street in one of the spaces vacated by staffers heading out. The trailer was clearly in view. While he watched, the sedan turned around and faced east.

He saw Alexander get out on the passenger's side, open the trailer door, look inside and go back to the car. Alexander said something to the driver, opened the car door, and hustled the woman out of the car and into the trailer. As soon as they were inside, the car pulled around, facing north with its back to the trailer. It held that position, motor idling, until 5:30, and then pulled away. It went down D Street, back the way they came, probably toward the FBI field office on Third.

Rocco watched the parking lot empty for 45 minutes. Only a handful of cars remained. He considered his options while he waited. They had left the luggage in the car. It was probably only a matter of time before they came back for her. They would take her away and put her somewhere hard to reach. No one had come near the trailer. No one had come in or out. This might be his best opportunity to get to her and probably his only chance to get them both.

Alexander had come after him before. He would again. Rocco knew he would not be safe until the woman was gone and would not rest until Alexander had joined Caprice and Colgate. Nothing cute this time. No light the match and run. That was Caprice's chicken style, that and slicing someone up with his blade while someone else held him down – the sick, son-of-a-bitch. No killing poor dumb

---

animals to keep them quiet. This would be man to man. Up close and personal.

At a quarter to seven, Rocco left the car and made his way toward the parking lot, just another cop in the dark. He had waited until he couldn't stand it anymore. He knew time was running out. Traffic was light. The lot was nearly empty. There was some foot traffic around the Monocle but not much and that was at least 100 yards from the trailer. He released the snap on his holster as he approached the trailer, pulling his gun and as he went up the two steps to the door. The Colt was easy to carry and easy to conceal, fitting neatly in the palm of his oversized hand.

There was a curtain over the opaque glass set in the door. Light was visible but it was impossible to see inside. He heard something, but the conversation was indistinguishable. He turned the knob carefully, hoping to find it unlocked, but it would not budge. He was so close. The trailer was an oversized tin can. If he put his shoulder to the door, he could probably force it open.

Size and strength had always guided his life. Let Caprice play with knives, torturing Guthrie and trying to fake his suicide until he couldn't stand it any more and had to pick him up by the seat of his pants and throw him out the window. He probably should have thrown Caprice out with him. Macklin and Colgate were the same. You just did what you had to do. Hit 'em hard. Hit 'em and fast. One motion of the hand, a sharp knife over an exposed neck, one decisive move of the wheel at the right time, with enough speed and force to catch even an experienced driver off guard. Do it and get it over with. There might never be a better opportunity.

As he put his shoulder to the door, he heard the woman's voice.

"Who es it?"

It stopped him short. She must have heard or seen something.

"Police," he said.

The curtain parted briefly. He saw a shadow behind the glass. As soon as he heard the lock tumble, he bulled his way through, knocking the woman away, almost knocking her down – only it was the wrong woman. She was Hispanic and vaguely familiar, but younger and more attractive than the Garcia woman – even with the look of terror that filled her face.

Before he could make sense of it, he heard a growl to his right. A dog attacked and then something flashed from the left. Out of the corner of his eye, he recognized the aluminum bat that shattered his left knee, taking apart what had so carefully been put together years before.

Rocco fell to the floor in agony, struggling to get up on one knee and one arm, shaking off the dog, looking for a target and finding more than he expected – there was the woman in front of him,

Alexander to his right, a black police officer leveling his gun, and the would-be cowboy holding a Magnum with both hands to the left.

Rocco's gun wavered as he tried to pick a target. Before he could decide who to shoot or if he should shoot at all, he heard the shot that took him down. He felt a searing pain in his left shoulder, just below the collarbone.

...

Esperanza had followed Nick's instructions precisely. When Max signaled Rocco's arrival she went to the door, asked who it was in her mother's voice, and then unlocked it. She was backing away before Rocco rushed in. The policeman, Roberts, was next to her, his gun out and ready. Nick had his back to the wall next to the door. Broadbent pulled a revolver out of somewhere, aiming it loosely in her direction. It was a gun she had seen before in some of the old Clint Eastwood movies her brother liked to watch except Eastwood held it like he knew what to do with it. The one who asked her to call him Dick made her nervous with the way he was waving it around, like one of the boys on the streets where she grew up who always had to be told to zip it up.

As she went flying back, she saw the dog attack, Rocco react, and Nick bring the baseball bat down with a powerful backhand blow, turning quickly, pivoting on his hip and putting his shoulder into it. She heard the bone snap and Rocco scream. She couldn't move and didn't know how he could, but somehow Rocco struggled up, lunging toward her with his gun raised, until he saw the other guns on him. He turned to fire but by then it was too late.

...

Dick didn't know what to expect when Alexander told him he hoped to bait Rocco and bring him in, but he came prepared. The Model 29 had been fixed in his mind but beyond his reach most of his life. When Smith and Wesson created the anniversary edition, he was among the first in line at Eaton's gun shop in Fort Collins. It was nothing short of beautiful, blue steel, walnut grips. Perfect. Holding it always made him feel powerful. Shooting it made it that much sweeter. Jugs of ice splattered 20 feet in all directions, bottles exploded in a million pieces. If it would stop a bear at 30 feet, it would stop Rocco.

He had slipped it into his shoulder holster before heading out. Somehow it found his hand when the girl opened the door. He wasn't sure how. Everything was a blur. He remembered raising his weapon when Roberts raised his, but he had no recollection of firing. All he could recall was the terror he felt when Rocco burst in the room, the scream as he fell, and look in his eye as he struggled to his feet.

He heard two shots close together, almost as if the sound of one triggered the other. Rocco fell and then the sound of another shot filled the room. He realized later it was his but he had no memory of pulling the trigger. There was only a sick feeling in the pit of his stomach, the blood, and stench. His hands were shaking. He was shivering, yet strangely, he felt warm at the same time.

...

The trailer reeked with the smell of blood, urine, gunpowder and sweat. The floor was covered with blood. I saw Esperanza run for the bathroom and fought the urge to do the same.

Roberts had fired and Rocco fell. Then Broadbent fired. His first shot went through the trailer floor. The recoil almost knocked him down. He righted himself and then fired again, holding the gun with both hands and pumping a round into Rocco as he struggled to get off the ground.

Rocco might have survived the first shot. There was no way he could survive the second. The Magnum tore a hole in his chest the size of a half dollar.

I kicked Rocco's gun toward Roberts and walked around the body to take Broadbent's gun away. Dick was shaking and doing his best to contribute to the stench in the trailer. DC has some of the strictest gun laws in the country. I couldn't help thinking Dick would have a tough time trying to explain what he was doing carrying a concealed weapon let alone using one. There was no need to explain the smell.

"I told you I wanted him alive," I said.

I made no attempt to hide my aggravation, not that Broadbent noticed or cared.

The setup had worked. Sarah had baited the trap. Amidore had set the hook. But it was all for naught.

Rocco never mattered. He was just a tool - a tool they had used and a tool I had hoped to use to get to them. We would have to begin again. I picked up the phone and called it in.

Chapter Forty-Eight

At 7:30 PM, a cab dropped Katherine Catlett at the Monocle. There was a bite in the air. Winter was coming on. She wore a knee length camel hair vest over a silk, collared blouse and True Religion jeans. The blouse picked up the color of her eyes, the pants flattered her figure, the combination of textures making her feel soft and feminine, confidant and in control.

She couldn't help wondering why Alexander had asked her to meet him at the Monocle. It had always been their destination of choice for lunch – business meetings. Perhaps for that reason, they had always avoided it when going out for dinner. She had wanted to ask him about it earlier, but there hadn't been time.

He was preoccupied when he called. He said he had a lot to do if he was going to get to the airport in time to pick up the Garcia woman at 4:00. She was anxious to ask him about that as well. Her boss had been disturbed when she told him the news, enough to give her pause, but after Patterson's report she knew she had no choice.

If Nick was going to stir things up again, she would be expected to know about it. Everyone now knew how close they were. As Vice President of Governmental Affairs, she would have to help figure out what it meant for the association and what to do about it.

John Valanos greeted her at the door. His genial smile faded quickly.

Something was wrong.

"Is Nick here?"

She felt a knot forming in the pit of her stomach.

"Nick said to tell you he won't be able to join you tonight," John said. "He suggested you have dinner with that lady over there at the Magnuson table. He said the two of you have a great deal in common."

Dee looked up as Kat looked over.
In the distance, Kat heard a siren wailing low. It was a cruelly insistent sound, growing louder, coming closer. Soon it was joined by another, and, yet, another, until they formed a crying chorus. It was fiercely compelling. Inescapable.

Dee turned and followed the sound.

Kat turned away.

It was over.